THE CLOISTERED LADY

The Medieval Ladies Series
Book Two

Coirle Mooney

SAPERE
BOOKS

THE CLOISTERED LADY

Published by Sapere Books.

20 Windermere Drive, Leeds, England, LS17 7UZ,
United Kingdom

saperebooks.com

ISBN: 978-1-80055-583-9

For my wonderful parents, Brian and Noirin.

ACKNOWLEDGEMENTS

Huge thanks to my editor, Amy and the team at Sapere Books for their fantastic support and expertise. Thanks to my sensitive first readers, Nina and Susan. Thanks to my family and friends for being so supportive. Thanks to my readers. Thanks to Eleanor of Aquitaine (and the Plantagenets) for providing me with such rich material! Special thanks to darling Noel.

CHAPTER ONE

My eyes slit open onto the day, attempting to focus on unfamiliar objects. Rows of neat cots. Two figures in the distance whom I registered as strangers I could not trust. I was conscious of a mild pain in my head — or behind my eyes. Where was I? Remembering dawned on me then. Spit on me shockingly, like frozen rain. My heart and spirits clouded with darkness.

Queen Eleanor of Aquitaine had been taken. And I, Lady Joanna of Agen had escaped to a nunnery.

An oppressive sorrow accompanied the dawning truth. Tears sprang painfully from my sore, raw eyes — I had cried myself to sleep last night. Yesterday had been almost unbearable. French soldiers had stopped us as we fled the court of Poitiers and had arrested the queen by order of her estranged husband, King Henry II.

That brutal captain forcing Eleanor's head down. Abrasive weaponry bashing in our ears, intended to frighten us. Awful midday heat and the soldiers' stinking breath too close. Nauseating smells of turned milk and foul body odours. Cold fear causing the hairs on my arms to stand up. Were the soldiers laughing at us? At her?

I wished myself asleep again, to block out the pain. If only I could have crept back into my mother's womb for protection. But where was my aunt Alice? Fear and wakefulness pumped through me, but my limbs were so stiff, I couldn't move. Finding I was in a cot as narrow as a coffin, I cried out in fright. Two women in white rushed over.

Stiffly veiled, their shapes enfolded in crisp linen, they gazed at me, fearfully.

'Alice? Where is Alice?' My panicked voice sounded shamefully childish. I tried to free my arms, but finding them all caught up in the sheet, I thrashed them loose. The women flinched. Cast a look of dread between them.

Oh, God, let Alice not have been taken too!

'Where is Alice?' I said, my voice all hoarse.

Still, they didn't answer. Their pale smocks washed out their complexions. The sun was also illuminating their veils slightly from behind, making it hard for me to see their features. Their persistent silence was both maddening and spine-chilling. I threw my legs outside the sheets — a great relief, for I was burning up, but I shivered, despite myself.

'Where is my aunt, Lady Alice, if you please?' I repeated, drawing myself up. My muscles were only sore because of all the riding yesterday, I remembered with relief. We'd ridden all the way from the Loire to Paris and God knows where else over the previous days…

'Lady Alice is downstairs. Do not fear. She told us to keep watch for when you woke,' one of them whispered, conspiratorially.

'We missed all today's offices to watch over you,' whispered the other, as if I was to blame.

'Ah, so Alice is here, thank God,' I said, almost crying with relief. 'Please … take me to her.'

I went to rise, but the second speaker stepped closer and said, authoritatively, 'No, you must wait.'

I hesitated, studying them a moment. Now I knew Alice was safe, I relaxed a little. They were dressed identically in shapeless white smocks with wooden crucifixes hanging from their necks. Their heads were covered with a wimple and veil, making them look the same at a distance. Only up close could you tell the difference between them.

'I take it I'm safe here at Fontevrault?'

As if to applaud, the familiar chimes of the cast-iron bell rang out.

They nodded; the younger one who'd spoken first gave a faint smile.

'Queen Eleanor was taken.' I said it to myself, really. *Taken* wobbled and my eyes filled with tears. Ashamed of myself, I quickly brushed them off.

Be strong.

The young nun looked at me with pitying eyes. She wasn't pretty, her skin was ruddy, but she did seem kinder than her counterpart. Later, I'd know her as Francine — a farmer's daughter, great company and a skilled labourer at harvest time. The elder gave a hint of a frown. After that first day, I'd never set eyes on her again. Or perhaps I just never recognised her.

'Please,' she whispered, in a breathy, consumptive voice. 'Don't speak her name here.'

My heart started thumping, my head throbbed and my stomach was suddenly nauseous. Why should I not speak her name? It implied Eleanor had transgressed, when I knew she had not. I instantly disliked the elder nun. I'm sure she disliked me too, for my beauty — such strict, plain women usually do.

'I have a headache, get me some water … please,' I gasped. I was tired of them and wanted them to go away so I could find Alice.

When they'd gone, I lay back and closed my eyes. I repeated the queen's name like a mantra. Eleanor, Queen Eleanor of Aquitaine, Eleanor, Duchess of Poitou, Queen Eleanor of England.

My breath came fast and shallow, so I attempted to breathe more deeply, to calm myself.

I took in my surroundings — a long dormitory in a loft with beams overhead and wooden floors, lined both sides with cots, or narrow 'coffin beds'. I guessed it was afternoon from the way the light was shining relentlessly on the cots. I thought I'd counted twelve strokes of the bell — probably calling the nuns to Sext.

There were no shutters on the windows, nor trees to break the midday glare. Hard beds and uncompromising light, such austerity and lack of texture was surely designed to force the nuns to rise by the bell and pray from dawn till dusk. I wondered why anyone would choose such a life. It was baking hot and my night shift was sticking to me. Oh for a bath! I was certain I'd slept in this same dormitory before, when Eleanor first brought us here about five years ago. I was much lighter of heart back then. I thought of Heloise — the young nun I'd befriended and corresponded with ever since — how we used to laugh! My heart gladdened at the thought of seeing her again. But first, I needed to seek out Alice.

The nuns returned, one of them carrying an earthenware bowl and a linen serviette, the other, a woollen smock and veil for me to wear of an undyed, wheaten colour. After I'd quenched my thirst, I asked them for some rosewater to cool my puffy eyes. When they shook their heads, I sighed to make my displeasure known, but made do with dabbing some water on them instead. They stood by, watching me.

'I suffer from a headache,' I said, rubbing my temples. 'May I have some lavender or clove oil?'

'We have no such luxuries here,' the elder whispered.

'All right. You may leave, then,' I told them. 'I am going to rise.'

They hesitated, then stepped back only a pace. I found this farcical and almost laughed, as they were still there, watching me. Then I recalled how obedient the nuns were to orders and that they'd been given the job of keeping watch.

During all the time I spent at Fontevrault, their obedience would always confound me.

'It's *all right*,' I said, as if speaking to children. 'You've been most helpful. Lady Alice and I are most obliged, but now you are relieved of your duty.' I remembered my manners. 'Thank you for your care. You may go!'

The elder said, curtly, 'We've left your clothes over there,' then turned away, with the younger nun trotting off after her.

Finally!

As my feet touched the floorboards, I realised they'd brought no shoes. I pulled on the plain smock and tucked my hair into the requisite veil, pinning it as best I could without a looking glass. At least I didn't have to use any face paint here. I hated these shapeless smocks, but the veil made me feel invisible, or disguised, which was a novelty. Normally only married women were required to wear them, but they'd a different attitude here at Fontevrault. Conceal beauty at all times!

I flew down the stairwell to find Alice. My head was so full of noise and confusion, I needed her to provide me with some clarity. Some ugly, persistent thought kept probing at my brain, maddeningly. I needed her to help me work it out. I needed to know that what had happened to Eleanor yesterday was not the catastrophe it seemed.

That our lives had not changed forever.

Two more nuns stood sentinel at the entrance to the stairwell. They hushed my anxious enquiries, pressing their fingers to their lips in alarm and pointing to the abbess's apartment on the ground floor of this, the convent building. A seemingly endless line of nuns was snaking rapidly from the church and I stood aside to let them pass. I scanned them for

Heloise, but their heads were dutifully bent to their prayer books — to avoid distractions like me.

The sisters at the convent door were reluctant to admit me. They looked me up and down, taking in my youth and beauty, their eyes resting disapprovingly on my naked feet. My voice rose angrily as I insisted that I must see my aunt. They couldn't abide any noise or disturbances, so they were startled. One of them went to consult the abbess, while I continued to rant and rail.

'Please!' I shouted. 'Inform Lady Alice that her niece is outside *at once*!'

Happily, the abbess herself soon appeared, her bulky silhouette almost filling the doorway. She regarded me, critically.

I began to ask for Alice, but she hushed me.

'Silence, please,' she said, sternly. 'Silence must be observed in the cloisters at all times.'

I was on the verge of tears again. *Why were there no friends by to offer comfort?*

'Lady Joanna … follow me.'

'Yes, Holy Mother.'

I followed her down the hall, walking behind meekly, like some shrinking, narrow shadow. Her steps fell heavily and her body swayed from side to side as if under some pressure to disperse the weight it bore. She walked briskly enough — for an old lady — for I guessed she must be fifty. Unlike the nuns, the abbess had been a wife and even borne children, taking up vows only after her husband had died. She was therefore adept at running a large household — and Fontevrault was indeed a most substantial household.

I could understand why speaking was forbidden in the cloisters, but I found her imposed silence ridiculous when we were alone in her apartment. There was nobody by for us to disturb — apart from a couple of industrious ladies drawing up letters on writing tablets. They were composing their work by the pleasant light proffered by the generous-sized window.

I was sure it was her way of wielding power over me and it seemed petty. With a pang, I thought how Eleanor always encouraged me to speak freely and *she* was both a duchess and a queen! Still, Fontevrault had a different set of rules. I hoped my stay here would be short and we would soon return to court at Poitiers.

I somehow managed to follow the abbess obediently without asking any questions, or betraying the raging torment in my brain. I feared the excessive humours would somehow cause my head to explode. I needed to apply a cooling compress to draw the blood down. I was upset that she never thought to ask me how I was after yesterday's ordeal and the horrible idea occurred to me that she, like the old nun, would forbid me from speaking Eleanor's name. Intolerable.

My aunt Alice came to me at once, concern written plainly on her face. She looked as drawn and wretched as always, but her face was a welcome sight to my sore eyes. Her skin was as ashen as her smock and her mouth was set grimly. My voice choked instantly with unbidden tears. I attempted to swallow them, but some spilled over. In fact, the tears brought me some relief. The abbess looked away, as if the sight of such emotion, or the reason for it, was distasteful to her. But perhaps I was being unfair.

'Have you rested? Eaten? Had some milk to revive yourself?' Alice murmured, while at the same time managing to loosen and re-tie my veil rather expertly. 'My goodness, your feet are bare…'

'Yes, yes.' I stepped back, impatiently. *Such trivial concerns! I hadn't even thought of eating...*

She shrank away, remembering. At nineteen, I didn't wish — or need to be — mothered by my aunt.

'I suppose your muscles are aching, like mine,' she whispered. 'If I never ride again in this life, I'll not mind.'

'I'll have Ambrose make up a honey-suckle rub that should ease the stiffness,' the abbess offered.

'Oh, thank you!' I said. 'We had to wait up all night in the cold with those dreadful soldiers taunting us.'

The abbess cast her eyes nervously across to the lady scribes. 'There is no speaking in the convent, as a rule,' she said. 'Let us go somewhere more conducive to speech.'

'Lady Mary, Agnes,' she called to the scribes. 'Please leave them to dry in the inner chamber when you've finished, in case anyone enters while I'm out.'

So, *she* was allowed to speak!

They bowed their heads.

I was relieved — at last, a chance to talk and get some answers.

'Thank you,' I said. 'That would be most welcome.'

'Silence, please,' she said, unnecessarily.

I had a feeling she disliked me already. True, I thought her strict, but I was still prepared to like her and was hurt by the fact that she seemed to judge me poorly. Did my beauty unsettle her? I doubted it. She seemed too genuinely spiritual for such a vice as envy. I feared it was my *character* that unsettled her. Perhaps she'd managed to see right into my heart and discover the truth: I was not the unspoilt virgin I appeared to be... Maybe she'd even heard something of my past indiscretions. As a holy woman, she was supposed to forgive such sins of the flesh.

I studied Alice's face for signs of distress as we followed on the abbess's heels, but typically, I could see no emotion written there. True, she looked haggard and old — but didn't she always? She was forty, after all, and heavily lined with worry and age. I knew that under her wimple her hair was changing colour, like autumn leaves. I was grateful for her presence, though, as we walked together and felt instantly comforted. With Alice by, the world seemed more familiar, less dangerous. Her eyes met mine.

'It's going to be all right,' she mouthed.

Five years ago when we visited here, the nuns and monks worshipped in separate little chapels, while a proper stone church was being built. The church now stood complete, the new stone gleaming like an impressive, shining monument to God.

'Now the whole community can worship together,' the abbess remarked, proudly.

The church proved to be just as impressive on the inside. I was surprised — and pleased — to learn that men and women worshipped here together. This was surprisingly progressive — given the strictness of the place in general. In my mind it promoted much healthier relationships if men and women were allowed to mix. Even at court, the sexes were too often separated, with adverse — or even perverse — effects. There had been no need for prostitutes at Poitiers, where men and women cavorted more freely than at King Henry's castle at Chinon. They'd plied their trade there so frequently, he'd even employed a Master of the Whores! Not that there would be any sex at Fontevrault.

Two monks in cowled linen smocks were assisting the priest's unrobing after the holy office. A humble contrast to the priest's vestments, all flashing gold and crimson by the light of the stained glass window. The air was thick with fragrant smoke. Woody notes of myrrh and frankincense soothed my aching head.

The monks departed quickly on sight of the abbess, kissing her ring as they passed. Her ring's inscription read, *In Deus Noster, Quem Colimus. In God We Serve.* A reminder of the community's higher purpose.

We followed her to the altar where an enormous beeswax candle burnt constantly, a symbol of God's divine love, she said.

God's divine love. Sounded mysterious. Too abstract an idea for me to comprehend, but I liked it all the same. *Divine love.* I believed in love, especially the romantic kind.

'We make the moulds for the candles ourselves,' she said.

I bent to inspect it. The wax was impressed with a curious image of a heart, split and crowned with thorns. I smiled at the emblem, remembering how at Poitiers the emblems had all been naked, cheeky cupids with bow and arrow erect.

'And we have our own bees. We sell the honey, but the wax is for our chandler. We make almost everything ourselves, here at Fontevrault. Our brothers and sisters keep this flame burning all day and night. They are most dedicated.'

She lit a candle from the main flame and welded it expertly into a wooden holder (also crafted at Fontevrault). She led us down a dark stairwell to the crypt, underneath the church. This was the only part of the old chapel still remaining.

Like a blind pedlar, the abbess picked out the key by touch from the huge bunch at her waist.

'We'll not be disturbed here,' she said.

All was blackness inside.

The abbess tipped her candle to a bowl of oil, which instantly caught fire, spreading a low flame through an aqueduct running all around the wall. Alice and I both gasped in astonishment as the crypt lit up.

The walls were covered in gold leaf, which shimmered softly in the firelight. White marble effigies lay stretched on the floor — their subjects holding prayer books, or more personal objects to represent the sleepers within.

What really fascinated me, though, were the numerous jewelled caskets, either placed in wooden cabinets, or hanging from the ceiling. I recognised ivory carvings with priceless diamond finials. I had never before seen such abundant treasure and it was enchanting. I wondered what they must contain and dearly wanted to inspect one.

I had no chance to satisfy my curiosity, however, as the abbess asked us to sit. She pulled out a discreet table and low chairs, placing the candle in the centre, so our features glowed strangely.

'Now,' she addressed Alice. 'Tell me everything.'

'Queen Eleanor was taken!' I said.

'I am aware of that fact,' she said, curtly. 'How did it happen?'

'King Henry's men came upon us on the outskirts of Paris,' Alice explained. 'They found our party suspicious — we were all disguised as knights, but one of our party couldn't ride with legs astride — so they ordered us to dismount and remove our head gear. Eleanor saved us the humiliation by dismounting first herself and, naturally, they recognised her. They ordered her to be placed in silver irons till they'd informed King Henry of her capture. We kept vigil with her all night and in the morning, Henry sent word that she was to be taken prisoner and brought to his castle in Chinon.'

'But surely Henry cannot really make a prisoner of his own *wife*?' I said, incredulous.

'I assure you that he can and has,' said Alice, coolly.

'Is it true that all three princes were also captured en route to the French court?' the abbess wondered. 'And two of them had been staying at Eleanor's court prior to their flight, so of course they went to Paris at her bidding...'

'And she was hoping to join them there...' Alice finished.

'It is as bad as I feared,' said the abbess. 'Eleanor will be accused of treason.'

'Treason?' I exclaimed. 'Surely not!'

'I'm afraid you're right,' sighed Alice. 'Henry will see Eleanor's influence over their sons, and her encouragement of them to join forces with the French king against his wishes, as treason. If they were not of such a tender age, then they could be said to have acted on their own initiative, but the youngest, I believe, is not yet thirteen years.'

'I don't understand,' I said. 'Is this not just a family matter with the usual grievances? It's no secret that King Henry and the princes are always at odds because he refuses to hand any power over to them. Surely Eleanor's involvement will be read only as a mother's concern over the future of her sons?'

'Henry is King of England, Joanna,' Alice sighed. 'And the queen encouraged the princes to pledge allegiance to the King of France. Believe me, Henry will see her involvement in this as a public matter of State.'

'This is terrible, just *terrible*,' I said. 'I don't understand. Eleanor is Duchess of Aquitaine in her own right — apart from being Queen of England. Why were those common soldiers permitted to keep her in irons overnight? Surely *that* is treason? Henry should order them to be *hanged* for such an outrage!'

'It was Henry who ordered his men to treat her thus,' Alice replied. 'Henry must have known that she had fled to Paris with their sons, and that is why the gates of the city were swarming with his men.'

The confusion in my brain was getting worse, not better, as I'd hoped. 'They bound her hands when they took her away,' I recalled, my voice rising in misery. 'How could they bind her hands like that?'

It was unbearable to think of those coarse men roughly handling those fine, nervous hands with the slender fingers... I knew and loved every single ring on those fingers.

'Henry must have known that this was planned,' said Alice.

How did Alice know what Henry would have known? How did she know that Henry would treat Eleanor's involvement as treason? I had been in ignorance of any so-called treason, but then my mind had been on other things ... or rather, my body had been occupied with more sensual matters. *Jean. My love.*

'But, if Henry punishes her for treason... No, surely not!' *She could be sentenced to death.* I gasped in horror.

'No, it is most unlikely that Henry would execute the mother of his children,' Alice interjected, quickly.

'Yes, that *is* unlikely,' the abbess agreed.

My head hurt so badly I squeezed it between my hands. 'Oh no, no, no, this is just *awful*,' I groaned.

'Oh, Joanna, please be strong,' said Alice, forever practical. 'We don't know what Henry will do, or how he'll punish her, but we mustn't imagine the worst.'

In my worst imaginings, it would never have occurred to me that someone as powerful and wise as Eleanor could have been rendered powerless overnight — and by her own husband! There was no need to imagine the worst. The worst had already happened.

'It's so unfair!' I cried. 'She did nothing wrong! She only wished for better conditions for her sons and strove to further their ambitions as any mother would have done!'

'Lady Joanna, you must calm yourself,' said the abbess, sternly.

I tried to check my despair and breathe deeply. I did not wish to seem like a hysterical youth.

'Now, that's better. Please reflect upon this matter carefully,' she continued. 'A wife has a duty to be loyal to her husband, just as a subject has a duty to be loyal to their lord. We are all servants to God and have a duty to be loyal to Him. If we transgress in our earthly duty to our husband or our lord, we pay the price on earth. If we transgress in our spiritual duty, we pay the price in the next life. Our actions have consequences. Eleanor is my duchess too, but even she must pay the price of her transgressions. We can only pray that the price is not too costly. Pray that Henry will be merciful.'

Alice was eyeing me nervously, afraid careless words might fly from my mouth. And worry she might, for the abbess's words had inspired anger in me. *Transgression against her husband indeed! When everyone knew that Henry had been having an affair with Rosamund Clifford for years! Not to mention all his other whoring and illegitimate children...*

I turned to Alice. 'When are we to return to Poitiers?'

'Joanna,' she said, gently, 'we may *never* be able to return to the court at Poitiers... Poitiers is not safe anymore, but thankfully we are safe *here*, at Fontevrault.'

'Yes,' said the abbess. 'On her last visit, Eleanor thoughtfully made arrangements for you both to have refuge here, in case something like this happened.'

'She is always thinking of others!' I said, glad to champion my beloved Eleanor. It struck me how selfish it was to worry about not being able to return home to Poitiers, when Eleanor's life was possibly in danger. 'Then we must make our home here at Fontevrault,' I resolved. 'Until she is released.'

Alice shot me a grateful look.

'I'll show you to your apartment,' the abbess said, rising. 'Then I must leave you to oversee the preparations for our evening meal.'

I took a last, lingering look at the beautiful caskets, still longing to examine one more closely, but she hurried us on. I was always so drawn to beautiful things, and it would have been such a cheerful distraction under the dire circumstances.

'May I ask you something?' I ventured on our way up the stairwell. 'What is contained in those exquisite caskets?'

'Ah, yes,' the abbess said. 'They are reliquaries — though not of the usual kind. The caskets contain the embalmed hearts of the most esteemed bishops in France — mostly. At Fontevrault, we revere the sacred heart. The suffering heart.'

I caught my breath. I'd not been expecting such a reply — I'd heard of the practice of preserving organs before, but not like this. I recalled the emblem on the candle.

Real human hearts. A little sinister, but interesting.

'They're most prettily encased,' I said.

'They are. You may have noticed the perfume in the air?'

I had noted a pleasant fragrance, which I'd taken for incense.

'It is a combination of mint and frankincense — used in the embalming process — along with mercury, to preserve the organ. The heart is then wrapped in linen and placed in a precious casket, of silver and ivory, or pearl. We consider ourselves most fortunate to have had so many honourable hearts bestowed upon us here at Fontevrault.'

'The heart is the jewel of the body,' murmured Alice.

I glanced at her, but could read no emotion on her face. The discussion was giving me a queer, sad feeling.

I wondered about my own heart and where it would end up. I feared it was not such a pure heart and was therefore undeserving of perfume or preservation. It was a melancholy thought, so I dismissed it. What did it matter where my heart would end up, since I would not be alive to see it?

'It is a great honour to be buried at Fontevrault,' said Alice.

The abbess smiled at her warmly. 'We like to think so.'

She likes Alice better than me! I was surprised, for at Poitiers, my aunt had not been liked, whereas I had been a great favourite — especially with Queen Eleanor and the troubadours.

Outside, the bright sunshine was dazzling after the darkness of the crypt. The abbess walked us to a tower, where many chimneys were puffing out smoke.

'This tower is used as an extra kitchen,' she explained. 'For we have many mouths to feed here at Fontevrault. We have four separate housing dormitories now, as well as a number of private apartments, such as yours, for visiting noblewomen.' She stopped before a stairwell at the side of the tower. 'Please follow the stair all the way up — your apartment is at the top, above the kitchen. I must leave you now.'

I climbed up ahead of Alice, eager as I was to view our new apartment. I was unsure if I'd reached the top, for there were more stairs to climb, only they were blocked. Also, there was no door into the apartment to shut out the elements or, indeed, intruders. There were two small chambers — with only a bed and a chest in each, as well as a slit-like, glassless window with a seat for sewing or reading. It was bare, stifling and miserable. A cruel contrast to our former chambers at Poitiers. I wanted to cry.

At least I'll have my own room.

I halted when I saw it, or rather, when I saw *her*. There was a woman in one of the beds! I presumed it was a woman from the long, dark hair spilt out, though her face was turned away. She was really just a heap under the thin sheet. There was a stale odour in the air.

The abbess hadn't mentioned we'd be sharing the apartment with anyone.

I went to warn Alice. She was at the top of the stairs, holding her side and breathing hard. 'Is there no *door*?'

'There's someone *in* there,' I whispered, dramatically. 'A woman!'

Alice looked alarmed. 'Perhaps this is not the right place.' She gazed up. 'Perhaps there's a way to go up further?'

'There isn't, I checked. It is blocked.'

'I understood we were to have our own apartment,' she whispered, dismayed. 'The abbess never mentioned anyone...'

'Perhaps she's one of those *fallen* women they allow to stay at Fontevrault and the abbess was too embarrassed to say?' I suggested. 'Or, she may just be *hiding* here and the abbess has no clue of her existence...'

'Oh, I hope that's not the case.'

'Well, I suppose we'll both have to wait in this chamber for now,' I said. 'At least until she wakes. Why do you think she's asleep in the middle of the day? Perhaps she's sick? Perhaps she has leprosy,' I suggested, in part to amuse myself by frightening Alice. Where was her composure now?

'Joanna, please curb your wild imaginings. Of course the abbess would not have us share the apartment with someone infectious.'

I went to spy on the woman again, but could get no better sighting than of her hair, which was long and dark — so she could not be too old.

A young lady for me to befriend?

My only other friends were Heloise — who was a nun, and Jean — who was a man.

Ah, Jean! If only you were here to comfort me! How I'd love to fall into your arms now and cry my heart out...

The strange woman was the most interesting thing about the apartment. There was no glass in the window, nor rugs on the floor. I recalled our wonderful apartment in Poitiers, with its vaulted ceiling and costly fabrics, our looking glass and all our dainty trinkets ... my late mama's jewellery. I felt a terrible pang of loss, like a lance to the heart.

'I miss Poitiers,' I said.

'I miss it too,' Alice mumbled. We looked about our miserable surroundings, both of us bleak inside.

'Well, at least we are safe here. Remember that Eleanor may be in fear of her life...'

Alice was right.

Dear God, please keep her safe, above all else, even if we DO have to share this horrible apartment with a leper... Perhaps we could send for some of our nice things from Poitiers ... my new silk dress ... my porcelain comb ... my rose-crystal perfume bottle... All of Mama's jewellery and the few of her nice dresses that Alice might be prevailed upon to wear...

No, that was wrong.

No, dear God, just keep Eleanor safe, that is all I ask...

'We should air the sheets,' Alice suggested. 'In case ... they have been slept in.'

'In case they have fleas.' I sniffed. 'I can take them outside.' I was already craving a change of scene.

Below, the clatter and smells of the kitchen aroused my curiosity and drew me in. Soup was being prepared — with vegetables, but no spices. How plain! The cook was stirring the iron pot over the fire with one hand, whilst shoving hot loaves into baskets with the other — presumably to be carried to the dining hall. Two women dressed like me entered and plonked four heavy jugs of milk just beside me, without saying a word. I remembered Heloise mentioning that lay-women, not nuns, did the milking, as it was considered inappropriate for them to touch the great udders. I looked about for ale, but couldn't see any. They went out for another round and I took a few big gulps of milk from the jug. It was very warm — yuck! A boy in the shadows sniggered at the face I made, from behind a mound of turnip and carrot peels. I winked and made him blush. He bent down to tickle the ears of a beagle at his feet I hadn't even noticed.

My stomach growled with hunger and I boldly asked the cook for bread and cheese. The bread was much coarser than at Poitiers (and there was no cheese) but I ate it hungrily and washed it down with more milk. The kitchens in Poitiers and Chinon had been so noisy, with the cooks either shouting out orders, or disputing, or even just laughing (though that was rarer) but here it was all subdued. Apart from the clanging of the iron pots and earthenware jugs, like strange bells.

Outside, I looked for some place to air the sheets. If I came across a maid, I decided I'd ask her to do it. I walked towards the cloisters, in hopes of finding someone. The cloisters were leafy and familiar and I was drawn to the comfort they offered. Also, I longed to ask about the mysterious woman in the tower.

The cloisters were too busy, with nuns walking two-by-two, reading prayer books, mouthing silently. I didn't dare approach them. They seemed in a trance and did not notice me. It was an unusual feeling to go about unnoticed. At Poitiers I was used to being stared at, but then I was usually dressed in colourful silks. Also, I was so often singing and dancing at Poitiers, my heart much gayer than at present.

I decided to return to the tower and ask the cook about the sheets. She frowned, but at least she took them from me and said she'd send someone up with fresh ones. I began asking her about the woman, but she said she hadn't time for idle chatter — and neither had her staff.

Disheartened, I went outside again. Unable to face returning to the dark apartment, I cast my eyes towards the great oak forest surrounding the abbey. I longed for the woods of Poitiers that I knew so well and loved so dearly. My heart flipped like an egg onto its less sunny side. The great forest was unfamiliar and daunting by comparison, and I could not imagine exploring it alone. A pity, for without that favourite escape, I would feel most trapped. Such a miserable day this was!

The bell tolled for the afternoon office of Nore and I watched the nuns trailing from the cloisters towards the church. On the other side, the monks filed out of their house. Other figures clad in white trickled down to the church from where they had been labouring in the fields, or tending to the gardens. All in silence they came, like an eerie mime to the call of the bell.

The peals boy, whose name (I later learnt) was Arthur, rushed past with a pile of bread. I guessed supper would be soon, so I returned to the apartment.

'She *lives* here,' Alice whispered. 'Her things are in the chest. A wonder the abbess didn't mention it.'

''Scuse me, my ladies?'

We both jumped at the maid who had entered silently behind us with fresh linen.

'Shall I make up the bed?'

Her name was Claudine and — to my delight — she loved to chatter. Her face was covered in freckles and wisps of frizzy brown hair escaped from beneath her cap. She couldn't have been more than thirteen. She said she was a general maid for all the noblewomen like us. She smelt warmly of buttermilk and oatmeal.

'We didn't realise we'd be sharing the apartment,' I said. 'Could you tell us anything about the lady who's sleeping within?'

'Well, she's not much of a talker and she sleeps too much.' She frowned. 'I've heard that she was married... She doesn't eat much either, though the abbess insists she attends all the communal meals, like everyone else. A good thing, too, or I'd be trudging up and down these stairs with trays for no good reason...'

Ah, so the abbess does know of her existence!

'Is she ... sick?' I asked.

'Sick? I hadn't thought of it, my lady, but p'raps she is, now I think of it. That would explain the sleeping and the poor appetite, wouldn't it? Though if she *is* sick, I wonder why the medicine woman doesn't take her rounds up here? She goes round to all the sick folk, but she doesn't visit here, does she...'

'Has she been here long?'

'She was here when I arrived, wasn't she — two years ago I started, when I was twelve.'

'Did you say she was married?' I asked. 'But she came here alone?'

'Yes. she's alone now, but she was married, before, they say. The ladies do talk, you know, and it's hard not to listen, isn't it?'

'Ah, so…' *She must be one of those battered women that Fontevrault famously gives refuge to! Like Mama…*

I felt a great surge of compassion and protectiveness over the sleeping woman.

Alice was studying me. 'We'd better not make up any stories about her,' she said, 'before we know the truth. She could be here for any number of reasons.'

But my mind was already made up. I was certain that she'd come here to escape from a brutal husband. Although I'd only seen her hair, I felt she had a familiar aura about her. Like I'd known her in another life.

'There! All nice and fresh!' Claudine declared.

'Thank you, Claudine,' Alice said. 'You've been most helpful and informative.'

'Oh yes, thank you,' I agreed. 'I'm so glad you are to attend us! I apologise that we've nothing to offer you, but we left all our nice things behind at Poitiers.' I felt like crying when I said it.

Claudine looked awed. 'You came from *Poitiers*? From the famous court of Love? How wonderful!'

Alice shot me a warning look and I guessed I should change the subject, even though I longed to speak of Poitiers.

'Oh yes,' I said, 'but now we are here to stay at the abbey.'

'We shouldn't speak to everyone about what we've left behind,' warned Alice, after she'd gone. 'We don't know if we're safe … or if Henry has a warrant out for Eleanor's attending-ladies, also.'

I stared at Alice. I hadn't thought of that. *We could really be in danger.* Fear and uncertainty ran their icy fingers up my spine. How come she was so cool? All day, she'd seemed so unsurprised by everything that had passed.

'I have a dreadful headache,' I complained.

'It's because you have not eaten…'

'Shh, listen!'

The woman had begun to stir. We made a little noise to alert her to our presence, so she wouldn't be too alarmed on sight of us.

The supper bell chimed.

'Come, let's go down,' said Alice. 'We'll feel better after eating.'

It was strange and unpleasant not to change for dinner, as we had at Poitiers. I loved the feeling of silk or velvet brocade against my skin and the luxury of rubbing orange oil on my pulses. It made me feel — and smell — fresh as a flower. A little artful dusting of the eyes before the glass, some berry paste on the lips and cheeks… How dull to go about all day in smock and veil.

CHAPTER TWO

I could live without fine clothes — for a time — but I couldn't live without Jean. We had fallen in love at court and had given in to our passion for each other. We had almost been parted forever when I agreed to marry another, but that had not come to pass and now I was determined to be with him. I needed to get a letter to him at Chinon somehow.

As fortune would have it, Chinon was only a day's ride away. I was certain he'd come, once he knew where I was. Eleanor had also been taken to Chinon and I hoped that Jean would have some news of her. When I was at Poitiers and Jean was at King Henry's court at Chinon, we had corresponded almost daily, sending letters via the countless travellers, tradespeople, pedlars, musicians and merchants who went between the castles. Here at Fontevrault, it would be much more challenging. The abbess had spoken truthfully when she'd said they liked to make and do everything themselves at the abbey. I'd never seen a place so self-sufficient and with so little need of the outside world. Any visitor was greeted with ceremony by the abbess and kept under surveillance all the while, until their departure. I'd not anticipated such censorship, but I was determined to find a way around it. I started watching the comings and goings most attentively, in hopes of finding a solution.

Each morning I woke up desolate, my spirits clouded with anxiety, until I remembered Jean. Only then had I hope enough to rise. I'd pull the scratchy woollen smock over my head and tie my veil, impatiently. Eleanor's disappearance had caused me such confusion, I feared my head would burst. I needed to find her, or I'd go mad.

Anyone who travelled here came on horseback — not on foot — as the path to the closest town was long and rough, so I began hanging around the stables and conversing with the lay-sisters who groomed the horses. These women worked hard all day, mucking out the stalls and fetching hay and water. Sometimes, if a horse was foaling or sick, they'd stay up all night watching over it.

They told me that some noblewomen were given a pass to ride between the abbey and the surrounding castles, from time to time. Unfortunately, this would not apply to me. Later, perhaps, I could request a pass, but not under the present circumstances, as it was not deemed safe for us to return to Poitiers. Chinon, too, was out of the question, as King Henry himself was currently residing there.

We prayed that Henry would soon see sense and release Eleanor from the castle, but on the other hand, there was a danger he would do her some great harm or imprison her elsewhere. The uncertainty was chipping away at my brain, causing me great distress. I continued to suffer from daily headaches. The stables, with the cheerful women and the horses, at least offered some distraction from this constant state of trepidation.

I learnt that some of the noblewomen with passes sometimes went to Chinon and I decided to find one that I could trust with a letter. I'd need to hatch a plan, for they were all strangers — yet another disheartening fact. Having no connections made me feel insignificant and desperate, but also determined to make (useful) friends quickly.

The diet at Fontevrault was vegetarian and plain, but visiting nobles and the old or sick were, thankfully, allowed meat, fish and eggs. All meat consumed at the abbey had to be hunted on its own grounds, not brought in from other estates. Normally, hunting and fishing was the task of the monks, but I learnt that a group of noblewomen occasionally went hawking in those vast forests surrounding Fontevrault. I realised that this would be the best means of befriending them. Also, the abbess had made it clear that everyone at Fontevrault — noble or not — was expected to work and contribute to the community. What better way to contribute than by catching my own supper?

Happily, these expeditions occurred regularly in summer, so I'd not have to wait for long. The lay-sisters at the stables smiled now when they saw me coming, for I livened up their day with my chatter and songs. My heart ached for all I'd lost, but I lived in hope. I could tell they found my energy refreshing, for they'd been carefully subdued and taught to work in silence by the abbess. Cheerfully, they advised me that I'd not last for long at Fontevrault unless I grew more patient — and more silent. I advised them, in turn, to grow more vocal, lest they lose their voices! In truth, I meant what I said, for I did not understand the point of all this silence. I suspected it was the means by which the abbess kept control, and this ignited some fire of rebellion in my belly. When I recalled the constant noise, the music and laughter at Poitiers and the joy that it evoked, I was convinced that the abbess was wrong.

One dazzling summer's morning, already sticky with heat at dawn, a group of ladies met in the courtyard and I helped bring out the mares — including my own, spirited Smokey. I'd not slept the entire night in anticipation, but my blood was coursing with vitality. By the end of today, I hoped to have found an ally — some noblewoman with the right connections.

We were dressed in our usual wool smocks — impractical, except for the daggers hanging from our belts. Our hair was tucked behind veils instead of into feathered caps. I missed the leather camouflage I used to wear at Poitiers — tough and tight as toad skin. Men and women alike had gone out thus attired, prepared, combative.

Here, by contrast, the abbess saw us off with a prayer and a basket of fruit. I'd left Alice asleep in our gloomy chamber — she never had enjoyed the sport at Poitiers. Eleanor had taught me everything about hawking and I'd never missed her more. How well she'd taught me when I came to court as a girl of fourteen — to dress, to hawk ... to kill.

I resisted the impulse to ride up front, for as a newcomer, this would be perceived as bold. I found myself in the curious position of trailing behind — exceptional hawker though I was — with an intimate perspective of the mares and ladies' backsides. The indignity only spurred on my desire to befriend the other ladies quickly, to win their respect and admiration. I watched the group up front closely — without appearing to — for the most powerful always led the hunt. It was strange for me the be the observer and not the observed, for I had been accustomed to riding alongside Eleanor.

We all sat side saddle — not astride — except for one. She was a superior rider on a very tall, deep brown stallion. It was unusual for a woman to ride a stallion, so I deduced she was a woman of independent means. Experienced, though not yet old. Riding alongside her was a pretty girl with a few golden curls springing from her veil and apple-red cheeks which changed shade often, charmingly. I smiled at her, but she ignored me. This hostility did not put me off, for I was used to women disliking me at first sight.

The horses descended with awkward slowness through the density of trees, but you could tell they knew the route by heart. Bits of our smocks got pulled by brambles, so we left behind a woollen trail. This, as well as the plodding slowness of the horses, offended my well-honed hawking instincts. I grew impatient and felt an anger rising. Surely they knew better than to leave a trail!

I would have to speak with the abbess about more suitable clothing.

Also, the ladies were talking so loudly, they'd surely alert the prey. For once, I wished the abbess was here to impose her silence. I noted with irritation how all pursuits at Fontevrault were opposed to pleasure — even hawking. With great difficulty, I suppressed my desire to take command, reminding myself that my first purpose was to make friends. To contact Jean. To learn of Eleanor. To ease the imbalanced humours in my brain. It was enough to have endured the loss of my mama as a girl, without having to suffer the loss of Eleanor too. And of Jean. I would find them. All would be as it was before.

With that thought, I started to enjoy the trail through the thick oak forest. Sparkling light filtered through the foliage and I breathed the fresh air gratefully. I'd always felt so at home in the forest, it was as if I was part-bird.

I decided that the forest was not a safe place for me to return alone. The forests of Fontevrault were vaster than those of Poitiers. Trees more ancient and dense. No one could trust a place of such history. Who knew what lurked in those depths? A lone rider would soon be lost, fall prey to cruel nature — or man — their body undiscovered.

Vexation nibbled at my nerves — was I to have no freedom in this life?

I recalled my present task with renewed focus. It was imperative I found a way of contacting Jean at Chinon. I didn't think I could suffer being imprisoned here for much longer. Chastity was treated as a special jewel to be locked in a casket at the abbey, but my body was aching for Jean. Afterwards, I could pray to God for forgiveness! Hopefully in the little chapel at Poitiers…

Around midday, we stopped in a glade for lunch. To my surprise, the lady who appeared to be the leader called me over. I sat with her and the pretty, tansy-haired girl. We removed our veils, letting our hair loose. I still had a slight headache. We'd only the abbey's coarse, wheat bread and water instead of wine — not what I'd call a feast. Still, we'd a block of goat's cheese and fruit. The basket of fruit was passed around. I picked a pear and took out my knife to peel it.

'That's curious,' the leader said. 'Don't you eat the skin?'

'The skin's the best part,' said the tansy-haired girl.

Were they judging how I ate my fruit? I wouldn't let my annoyance show. 'You're probably right,' I conceded. 'But it was customary at Poitiers to remove the skins. In fact, we were quite spoilt there — having our fruit peeled and cut up for us like children.' A slight boast I couldn't resist.

The rest of the group had gone quiet. I could tell they were straining to listen. The mention of Poitiers stirred their interest. Probably, they'd heard a rumour we'd come from there.

'Gracious,' said the leader, 'I wondered where you'd learnt to ride so well. You were at the court of Poitiers before, the seat of all refined tastes of the South?'

Her remark appealed to my vanity and I allowed myself to relax. She seemed an elegant person. Still, Alice's voice cautioned almost immediately in my head, warning not to disclose too much. Years at court had taught me not to trust anyone at first.

'Indeed,' I replied carefully. 'We were fortunate enough to reside there for some years, but I believe the abbey has much to offer, also…'

She let out a great laugh. 'Come, come, be candid, Lady Joanna,' she said. 'I don't believe that one as young and beautiful as *you* would happily swap the boundless pleasures of such a court for the austerity of the abbey.'

Again, my vanity was appeased. I was amazed — and thrilled — that she knew my name. I thought I'd gone about entirely unnoticed. I found myself blushing under her cool gaze. It was indeed an awkward moment, for all the others were watching me.

'My goodness, it's hot today.' She dipped a peach in water and held it to my forehead. It felt marvellous. I closed my eyes and sighed as she pressed it against my hot forehead, my cheeks.

Eleanor's voice had been quietly commanding, but this lady's was quite loud. Now I saw her up close, she looked vigorously healthy, with strong white teeth. I was conscious of my own teeth, which I'd only been able to clean with water and no charcoal since arriving here. She had an intelligent, or shrewd, look in her pale eyes and struck me as someone powerful. Fortunately, she changed the subject from Poitiers.

She took a bite of the peach, then offered it to me, but I was reluctant.

'Come.' She smiled. 'At Fontevrault, we do not waste the skin. Taste it.'

The way she said it reminded me of the way Eleanor used to speak, with innuendo.

After lunch, she invited me to ride up front with her, so we could speak together. I didn't confide in her about Jean, for it was too soon, but I was convinced I'd found my ally. I sensed that some of the other ladies were afraid of her and thought, proudly, how well I could hold my own in exalted company. I hinted that I was finding the transition from court to abbey life difficult and that I could do with a friend. I did have Heloise, but she was much more serious and pious, now that she was older.

We returned to the abbey with only a couple of old woodcocks after a full day's hunt. The poor birds had practically given themselves up. Eleanor wouldn't have tolerated such a poor kill — even from a novice. Had this hunt been conducted properly, our sacks would be bursting with partridge and our horses' sides would be running red with rabbits' blood as they dangled legs first from our saddlebags.

At Poitiers, I'd have been undressed by Eleanor's maid Amaria and lowered into a hot bath — the water tinting pink with blood from the kill. Water jugs would have been blended with rosemary to wash the mud from my hair. Then, I'd have rested before a roaring fire, wrapped in a crisp linen towel, while my hair was combed and braided.

After, I'd have stepped into a cool silk dress in preparation for the evening banquet where we'd get to enjoy the spoils of the hunt. I would have been petted and praised by Eleanor and admired by all the men. My skin would have been radiant and my heart bursting with pride.

The bell rang for Nore. Soon it would ring for supper.

I grew cross when I realised I'd nothing to look forward to all evening — only more bread and prayers. I consoled myself with the thought that I would speak with the abbess about the sub-standard hunting conditions and suggest making improvements.

At least I'd met a potentially useful friend. Someone who could unite me with Jean. On parting, she'd told me her name was Sarah. I hinted that I'd like us to be friends. We would be well suited, I believed, for she was elegant like me.

Wearily, I climbed the steps to our miserable apartment and found Alice in her usual spot under the slit-like window, employed with her needlework. Only even that was different here, I observed, bitterly. The bright scarlet and gold silk spools we'd used at Poitiers had been replaced with 'more natural' linen thread. *Tell me this*, I'd said to Alice, *are there not brightly coloured flowers aplenty in nature? How then, is washed-out, pale thread more natural?* Was it necessary to suck all colour — as well as pleasure — out of life, at the abbey?

Alice rubbed her eyes. Her sight was failing and nothing could be done to save it. The poor lighting in our apartment would not help.

'You look clean, Joanna,' she said, blinking and peering. 'I thought you went hawking today?'

I should be covered in dirt and blood. I groaned. 'Oh, Alice, it was the worst…' I began, but she placed her fingers to her lips, warning me the woman was within.

Silent and sedentary, she was easy to forget. She was kneeling in the inner chamber, praying. All she did was pray and sleep, it seemed. Her skin was olive, her hair was jet-black and she had mesmerizing eyes with gold flecks that made you want to stare into them as into a goldfish pond. Like the eyes of a wild animal. I longed to speak with her, but to my tremendous disappointment, the abbess had informed us that she'd taken a vow of silence. Presumably, there was nothing wrong with her hearing, though.

I therefore whispered my complaint to Alice, who kept her eyes cast downward on her needlework. It was only when I mentioned speaking to the abbess that she looked up and set her work aside.

'Joanna, please, *listen*. Our position here… Our position in this *world* is precarious at the moment. We must be careful not to draw any attention to ourselves. Please try to fit in with life here and don't upset the abbess with complaints.'

She pursed her lips then, the same way I did when I meant to close a subject. I couldn't help finding any resemblances between us unsavoury.

She never let me speak my mind. She'd no idea what torture today had been, after the hunting skills I'd learnt from Eleanor at Poitiers. To be told to keep my skills, my knowledge, to myself? Alice always denied me a voice — just like the abbess. Looking at her now, taking up her tedious needlework, it seemed there was something impossibly nun-like about Alice. Also, something unwholesome or bloodless. Her lack of appetite made her unnaturally thin and her skin was so pale, she looked green. She was a joyless, sexless old maid. The loss of Eleanor and my mama swelled inside me, like a powerful wave.

'You don't *understand*,' I said, almost crying with frustration.

Just then, the woman inside coughed, drawing our attention.

Alice looked at me darkly, warning me to stop. Without another word, I left, with Alice calling after. She'd worry I'd not come back in time for dinner. Well, it served her right — let *her* explain my absence to the abbess.

I wandered disconsolately towards the abbey's old walled orchard. We weren't supposed to pick the fruit, but to hell with that, after the day I'd had. The grounds were deserted anyway, as everyone was either at Nore, or preparing the evening meal.

Three resident goats, named Debbie, Lily and Daisy came ambling my way, pulling at the bushes and roots. They had a reputation for being destructive.

I passed the beehives and the physic garden, with its flowering lavender, ceanothus and clover borders full of humming bees. I wove my way through the ancient olive grove, the olives sharp and black as jet.

I entered the orchard through the hollow archway containing a deep sapphire sky. I knew the orchard well, having come here frequently with Heloise in the past. I passed under the shaggy pear trees, admiring the golden fruit. I picked some figs and almonds, stopping for a moment to admire the sunlit leaves. When I came to the apple grove, I picked a coral apple and sat beneath a tree to enjoy it. The sun was low and played warmly on my face, and I pulled off my annoying veil — setting my curls and my spirits free.

A voice from out of nowhere made me jump. I looked up to find a monk standing before me.

'You stole that apple,' he said.

My whole body tensed and I quickly covered my head. 'What do you want?' I asked, defensively. 'Why are you not at Nore?'

'I saw you steal that apple,' he repeated.

'So, you are a spy,' I said.

'Not a spy ... a gardener.'

'Are you going to tell the abbess on me?'

'That depends,' he said. 'Do you promise never to steal from the orchard again?'

'Look,' I said, 'I've had a horrible day and I just sat here for a moment's peace...'

He shrugged. 'Your day does not concern me,' he said. 'What concerns me is that you stole the fruit. What if everyone decided to disobey the rules and steal the fruit? We'd soon have bare trees and no preserve for winter, when it's needed. We do not act on selfish whims at Fontevrault. We must first consider the good of the community.'

In God We Serve. The abbess's cumbersome ring. I was fed up with the good of the community. It struck me as farcical that I was being told off by a monk, for picking an apple.

I took a big, deliberate bite. 'Delicious.'

He was standing a little distance off, but I could see he was young and nice-looking, with large, pea-coloured eyes. He wore the linen smock of the monks and his shaved head was tawny. He was wearing clumsy-looking gloves.

'You are a monk?'

'I am a brother.'

Was this the same as a monk? I supposed my virtue was safe, so I stepped up closer. 'Please don't report me to the abbess,' I said, sweetly. 'I promise not to steal the fruit again.'

'All right,' he said.

'Thank you.' I was pleased to be speaking to a man, even if it was only a brother. 'I'm Lady Joanna.' I extended my hand for him to kiss, but he ignored it.

'Lady Joanna.' He stepped back. 'Please do not steal my fruit again.'

He marched off without so much as a bow or a goodbye. I felt slighted, on one hand, but on the other hand there was an undeniable authenticity about him that I'd never encountered in the men at court. I quelled any budding feelings of admiration with the thought that he was just a brother, following orders.

I gazed longingly towards the forest, wishing it was safe for me to go there. I badly needed a long walk, or a ride, to ease my troubled mind and restless spirit. At this rate, I would not last long at Fontevrault.

I had no choice but to return indoors. I had to be patient and remember my plan to get a letter to Jean. He would rescue me.

Alice and the silent, olive-skinned woman were sitting together under the window engrossed in needlework. I watched them unobserved from the doorway. She was deftly assisting Alice, cutting the loose threads. I'd never caught such a good look at her face. She was a much younger woman than Alice, but tired-looking, with dark circles under her eyes. When I entered, she glanced up, nervously.

'It's just me,' I said gently. She'd already jumped up. I wished she'd stay!

'So, you decided to return. Where were you?' asked Alice, coldly.

The woman slipped back to her own chamber.

'Nowhere.'

'You missed dinner, Joanna,' Alice said, angrily. 'I *told* you we must not draw attention to ourselves. I was forced to tell an untruth — that you weren't feeling well.'

'It wasn't a lie, Alice. I *am* feeling unwell. I hate it here!'

'That is not the same!'

I knew it was pointless to argue. She never understood. 'Look, I have figs! What difference does it make whether or not I attend dinner? I couldn't face more bread and prayers!'

'What if everyone decided to skip meals and do as they pleased? There would be no order.'

My goodness, Alice was parroting just what the brother had said. My thoughts stayed with the brother as Alice continued lecturing.

'Are you listening, Joanna?'

'Yes,' I lied.

Alice mistook my lack of retort for acquiescence. 'Yes, Joanna, that's right. We're part of the Order of Fontevrault now, so we must abide by the rules they set out for us.'

'I'll do my best, Alice.'

She glanced at me sharply to make sure I wasn't being smart. Of course, I didn't agree with her — or the brother — for that matter, but I wished to change the subject. I was really curious to learn more about the woman.

'Did you speak with her?' I whispered. 'Did she tell you her name?'

'No. She does not speak, as you know.'

'But she came to sit with you?'

'She observed that I had some difficulty seeing the fine threads. She seems very competent at needlework.'

'Did you attempt to speak with her?' I asked, impatiently.

'No, I did not. She has undertaken a vow of silence, as you know. I only pointed out where she could help. She didn't need much guidance — unlike you, Joanna. I wish you'd take more of an interest. It might occupy your mind, you know, and help you with your ... your restlessness.'

'Oh, Alice, you should at least have *tried* to discover her name! It's farcical living with someone whose name we don't even know. You are certain she didn't speak at all?'

'No, but she pointed and smiled, a little.'

'Aren't you even curious?' I asked, incredulous at her lack of interest.

'No, I am not. She is none of our business, though she does have a good eye for needlework.'

'Don't be silly, Alice — she lives with us, of course she's our business! Tomorrow I'll ask her to walk,' I decided. Her vow of silence couldn't last forever. I would tempt her to converse.

Lying in bed, my rumbling stomach was punishment enough for missing supper. My thoughts scanned over the events of the day, flitting between the various encounters and conversations, from Lady Sarah to Alice to the brother. I was flattered that Lady Sarah had known my name — unlike the brother. He was a curious fellow, but who could blame him, being brought up at Fontevrault? How annoying Alice was, always so fearful and rule-abiding.

I prayed to God that Eleanor might soon be allowed to return to Poitiers — and us with her. I prayed I would be reunited with Jean. I prayed that our beautiful things might be restored to us. I finally drifted off just after the bell sounded for Matins. How odd to think the nuns were rising when I was just going to sleep.

CHAPTER THREE

I woke up ravenous before the breakfast bell and decided never to skip dinner again. I devoured the bread and milk I'd turned my nose up at the day before. I remembered with relief that as today was Friday, there'd be fish. The dining hall was as long as a cathedral and held all three houses of Fontevrault together. There was a fourth house for lepers, apparently, but they dined elsewhere — thank heavens. Though I was curious to see one (at a good distance).

Each person had a designated seat, so the abbess could survey the hall to check if anyone was missing. Mealtimes were strictly observed, as was the communal washing of hands before and after the meal. The abbess sat at the head the Order of Fontevrault nuns' table and made a ritual of pouring water from a copper pitcher over each nun's hands before sitting. I remembered, sorrowfully, how Eleanor used to sit at her right hand side and was always the first to receive the honour of having her hands washed by the abbess.

On those occasions, us ladies had seen little of Eleanor, who'd spent all her time either praying, or in company with the abbess. I suddenly felt ashamed of my secret dislike of the abbess — especially when I recalled how much Eleanor had esteemed her. In a calmer mood than yesterday, I decided not to confront the abbess over the hunt. I would broach the subject with Lady Sarah instead. This would also be a good means of furthering our acquaintance. This decision — and the promise of fish for supper — lifted my spirits so much, I remained absolutely silent for the meal and bowed respectfully to the abbess on our way out. Poor Alice smiled at me gratefully. She probably thought I had heeded her advice.

The dark woman turned down my invitation to walk with a shake of her head. I tried not to take it personally. I hoped I'd find a way to communicate with her eventually.

After breakfast, Alice and I joined the nuns who always walked in twos and threes around the cloister. How rigidly their days were structured! We too mumbled our rosary. Afterwards, we sat on a bench to meditate, enjoying the shade and gentle rustling of wind through the leaves.

'You were respectful to the abbess this morning,' Alice whispered. 'I am glad.'

It was her way of thanking me, but she couldn't have been more wrong. I was merely plotting a way to make my existence more tolerable until I could escape. Poor Alice, I didn't intend to deceive her, but it was impossible to be straight with her. I couldn't tell her about my plan to write to Jean. She'd only get angry and make me abandon it. Then I really would go mad.

'I did not *choose* this life, Alice,' I sighed, giving her a little glimpse of truth.

She peered at me. 'Maybe not. But I suppose all of our choices and actions have led us to this place.'

An interesting notion. Perhaps she was right. Our sworn fealty to Eleanor had led us here.

I spotted Lady Sarah then, walking with the pretty girl. 'Excuse me, Alice,' I said. 'I see someone I know. I promise not to skip meals again.'

I approached Lady Sarah, shyly, and whispered that I'd like a word.

She nodded.

The pretty girl — all smiles a moment ago — blinked at me coldly.

'Gertrude, I shall see you at supper,' Sarah whispered.

I was pleased she'd sent her off.

We walked in silence across the park to the forest's edge. My nerves were strangely jittery and I feared I would be awkward and tongue-tied, when I'd rather be eloquent. We stopped when we reached the outer band of trees and removed our veils. We spread them under us and sat with our backs to two adjoining trunks.

'Now we shan't be disturbed, I hope,' Sarah said.

The change of temperature from the midday sun to the shade of the tree suddenly made me shiver.

'Come closer, pretty one, I'll warm you!' Sarah said, drawing me to her.

I was uncomfortable with the proximity, but didn't dare object. Her embrace was firm. Close up, her eyes were stony-grey, like blackbirds' eggs.

'What's on your mind?' she murmured.

My brain was addled. Her affectionate tone and manner suggested we were either best friends or blood relatives, yet I barely knew her. 'I ... I just wanted to say that I enjoyed meeting you yesterday,' I stammered. 'However, I was a little disappointed in the hawking exercise overall, as we didn't have much success. I think it's ridiculous to send us out in our everyday clothes, with no camouflage and with hardly any sustenance... I wanted to speak to the abbess about it, but my aunt wouldn't allow it, so I thought I'd discuss it with you...'

'Ah, yes, my dear, I see your point,' she sighed. 'I'm afraid there is little we can do about it. The abbess is against all violence, you know.'

'But that makes no sense!' I said, passionately. 'She sanctions the hunt, but hopes we'll not make a kill?'

Sarah smiled. 'She hopes we'll not be *too* successful in our endeavours.'

'Surely we could appeal to her better judgement?' I suggested. 'Surely we could at least request more suitable clothing, for practical reasons?'

I searched for agreement, but she shook her head.

'I'm afraid not, my dear,' she said, maddeningly resigned. 'Believe me, if I thought she'd change her mind, I'd be the first to approach her... All of the community must be identically dressed, you see, to be recognisable at all times. I imagine all this austerity must be intolerable to you, after the lavishness of Poitiers. Tell me, did you have beautiful gowns? You must have had lots of admirers...'

It seemed a sudden change of subject, and I dearly wanted her to realise I was not just coming from a privileged, spoilt perspective. 'Yes, I had beautiful gowns, but...'

'My poor girl,' she murmured, affectionately. 'I bet they were cut to reveal your shape and show off your creamy skin. Your beautiful hair.' She stroked it.

I was most uncomfortable now. I felt like a rabbit clutched in a falcon's talons. Tears of shame sprang to my eyes.

She rocked me like a baby in her arms. 'There, there, don't cry, there now, you're safe with me. Whatever is troubling you?'

It was my present predicament that troubled me, but I didn't dare tell her that. Embarrassed and flustered, I blurted out a confession about Jean. 'It's just that I miss my friend, Jean, terribly,' I said, carefully pulling away.

Her pale eyes narrowed. 'A romantic attachment at court?'

'He's a musician from Chinon. We used to keep Christmas there, with the Royal family.' I regretted the words as soon as I'd spoken. I'd given away too much intelligence.

She'd a cunning look in her eyes now. I was out of my depth and knew I must escape before I foolishly revealed more secrets. I stood up quickly.

'Please forgive me,' I said. My voice sounded small and weak. 'My aunt says that I am prone to being overcome by powerful feelings that I've not yet learnt to manage. I am just a foolish girl. I must go now, or my aunt will worry.'

'Run along, dear girl, by all means! We would not want your aunt to worry.' Sarah laughed, but her eyes were hard as pebbles.

I ran as fast as I could back to the abbey. A dark shadow slid across my path and I shivered uncontrollably. I realised I'd been foolish and vain to believe that Lady Sarah found in me a kindred spirit. She was a powerful person and only thought to use me to her advantage.

Blinded by tears, I almost fell into a dangerously placed hole in the ground I'd never noticed before. I fell on my arm, cutting my hand. I swore loudly, to the shock of a passing superfluity of nuns.

I clenched my chattering teeth and somehow, I managed to reach the tower kitchen. For once, I welcomed the homely smell of soup, the cave-like warmth and echoey silence. I went straight to the stove. My frazzled state attracted attention and aroused concern. I found myself surrounded by the cook, Claudine and two kitchen women. The beagle — Coo — sniffed and licked my hand.

'Lady Joanna, are you all right?' the cook asked.

'Yes. I ... had a shock,' I said. 'I'm cold. I think I need a bath.'

'You're bleeding, aren't you?' Claudine exclaimed.

'I fell... I was running so fast that I didn't see that hole in the ground, just at the back of the cloisters.'

'That'd be where the bell was cast,' said the cook. 'You should mind where you tread.'

To my relief, no more questions were asked and lovely Claudine came to my assistance.

It was the first bath I'd had since Poitiers. The cook gruffly suggested cleaning out a large earthenware vessel normally used for kneading dough. We carried it up the stairs together and Claudine heroically made a few trips with jugs of boiled water, while I undressed. She merrily produced a piece of soap she said she'd been saving, which I tried to refuse, but she insisted. I promised to repay her whenever I could. She lathered my back so lovingly that I was moved to grateful tears. Alice was still out — but the dark woman was asleep within. Grateful for the distraction of Claudine's good-humoured chatter while I bathed, I began to relax and cheer up. Soon I was clean, dry and wrapped in a crisp linen towel, my spirits and health restored.

'Your hair is the colour of autumn leaves,' Claudine declared, admiringly. 'I wish my hair would not frizz up so! I have some ribbons that would look just divine on you, they would. Let me just run and get them.'

For someone who had so little, she was a remarkably generous soul. I hoped I'd have the means to repay her kindness sometime soon.

When Alice returned, she looked different. When I paused to consider why, I realised her eyes were all lit up with — could it be — joy?

'Oh, Joanna!'

'Alice... What is it?' I said. 'Oh, have you heard something about Eleanor?'

Her step as she approached was lighter too. She looked so odd with that queer smile on her face.

'I had a letter from Princess Marie! The abbess read it out to me.'

I wished I'd been there to hear it. No wonder Alice looked happy. She idolised the queen's daughter, Marie, just as I worshipped Eleanor.

'Oh, Alice, that *is* wonderful! Is she safe? Does she have intelligence of Eleanor?'

'She's safe and happy to be reunited with her children, but she says she misses our court terribly and is having trouble adjusting to the change. Of Eleanor's fate, I'm afraid, she is as ignorant as ourselves, but she plans to travel to Chinon soon and will visit here en route.'

'Marie is going to visit us here en route to Chinon?' I repeated, not believing my ears.

'Yes, isn't it wonderful? She hopes to be here by Sunday.'

I was so excited, I spoke without caution. 'Alice, do you think she would carry a letter from me to Jean? He has no idea of my whereabouts…'

'Ah, yes, you still think of Jean… Well, yes, we can surely ask her.' I knew Alice had never approved of my attachment to Jean. A musician without wealth — he was not the sort of man she had in mind for me.

'But, the abbess… She won't allow it,' I said.

'No,' Alice agreed. 'The abbess mustn't be told. She would not approve of your corresponding with a man like Jean and would be shocked to learn of your history with him. Still, there's no harm in him knowing your whereabouts.'

Alice never suspected that I planned to summon Jean to Fontevrault. That I was contemplating escaping with him… 'Thank you, Alice!'

As I hugged her, I felt well and whole again. The morning's unpleasant encounter with Lady Sarah had already faded —

nothing really bad had happened, anyway. She'd cleverly extracted some information from me, that was all. I felt foolish now for overreacting and running off.

That evening after dinner, I went to find my friend Heloise. She'd lost the pinkness and plumpness of her youth and had become a thin, sallow woman. She prayed as fervently as the rest of the nuns, but had retained her delightful capacity for unexpected bouts of joyous laughter.

We strolled together in the orchard, which was far enough away from the convent to have a conversation without risk of reprimand. I didn't dare tell her about my recent episode with the gardener, for I sensed she'd disapprove of my unlawful taking of fruit. Nor could I disclose the cravings of my body — and mind — for Jean, lest she think I was depraved. The nuns were taught that chastity and obedience were the root of all good, whilst indulgence in earthly desires was the root of all evil. Talk of sex was taboo.

I knew that Heloise's beliefs revolved around the idea of earthly denial leading to spiritual reward, so I shielded her from the knowledge of my various appetites. I did, however, confide in her about my grief over Eleanor and the loss of my community at Poitiers.

'Eleanor's daughter, Princess Marie, has heard nothing of her whereabouts since she was taken,' I said. 'Princess Marie is coming here this Sunday on her way to Chinon, where she hopes to meet the king and have some news of her mother.'

'Do you think King Henry will let Marie see her mother?' Heloise asked.

'I don't know,' I worried. 'Marie is not his daughter, you know, but the eldest-born of Eleanor's first husband, King Louis of France and Henry's enemy. Marie may be risking her life by going to Chinon. I hope he has not harmed Eleanor. I'm so afraid for her, Heloise.'

'Shush, Joanna, don't even think it. He'll not harm his own wife, surely. He's not a monster, is he?'

I considered this as the evening sun turned the leaves golden. I picked a leaf, stroking it while Heloise studied me. 'He has the foulest temper I've ever witnessed,' I concluded. 'And he *is* capable of murder,' I added, darkly.

We both shivered, remembering poor Thomas Beckett, but neither of us dared speak his name. Heloise began mumbling prayers.

'Thank you,' I said, simply.

'Don't thank me,' she said after a while. 'I think of all the suffering you've had to endure, Joanna, compared to me. Your troubled life seems so unfair compared to my contemplative one. I'm sorry that all I can offer you is my prayers.'

Her generous words warmed my heart. We may have had different views, but she was truly a good friend. Walking back in silence to the cloisters, I considered what she'd said. I'd not swap my adventurous life — hardships and all — for Heloise's quiet one for all the world. *She* pitied *me*, but little did she realise that I actually pitied her, with her sheltered existence.

It struck me then that Eleanor probably felt the same — despite her present predicament. As long as her life was spared, she would regret nothing. I joined Heloise in prayer.

Dear God, please let Henry be merciful.

CHAPTER FOUR

On Sunday, Alice and I woke before dawn in anticipation of Princess Marie's visit. Quivering with excitement, we decided to rise and take a walk before breakfast.

We lit a pair of candles and descended. The ovens in the kitchens had just been lit and the aroma of wood perfumed the fresh morning breeze. By first light, a sticky heat would already have pervaded the air.

'I hope the day is not too hot for riding,' worried Alice. The heat had intensified over the summer, like a burning furnace.

'Oh, it would be terrible if she didn't come!' I agreed, touching the letter in my pocket. In it, I begged Jean to come under some pretence of bringing news from Chinon.

As we reached the cloisters, the bell rang out for Lauds. Soon the nuns were filing out from their dormitories, each holding a candle to create a trail of flickering light. They were chanting psalms in soft unison and the charming image and sweet voices filled my heart with peace. Watching them, holding my own candle, I felt a sense of unity with them. It was the first time I had experienced anything like it. I looked up to the heavens at the stars and felt at one with everything. I reached for Alice's hand. She flinched at the unexpected touch, but then grasped mine greedily in return.

'How beautiful,' she whispered.

The smell of freshly baked bread came wafting through the air and my hunger rose. Under my veil, my hair had been braided in pretty ribbons by Claudine and this small vanity — as well as Marie's visit — made me temporarily content. I knew that even an ugly smock couldn't hide my beauty, but I felt more like myself when I could bathe and wear nice things.

After breakfast, Alice and I separated to embark on our daily duties. The abbess had advised us that time would pass more happily if we were dutifully employed. She constantly reminded us that nobles were not exempt from contributing to the community. Alice, therefore, spent the best part of her day helping some sisters who embroidered vestments and linen shrouds in the church. My own skills of hawking, dancing and singing were more suited to court than to the abbey, so I continued to spend my time in the stables. That meant that I would be well placed to spot Marie's arrival.

'Call me at once, Joanna, when you see her party!' Alice urged.

The lay-sisters in the stables were so excited about the princess's visit they forgot their rule of silence. They were amazed when I told them we were friends, and I caught them regarding me suspiciously — as though I might be lying. If only they realised how close I'd been to the queen! Then they would really be impressed. As an exception, I'd taken off my veil to show off my ribbons, and they all stood around admiring me.

'My, your hair is the rarest colour!' one of them declared. 'It shines just like copper. Wasn't Eleanor of Aquitaine's hair a similar colour?'

Why the past tense? 'Our hair is the same colour,' I said. 'She used to remark on it and once, when I admired a nightgown she was wearing, she had a matching one made up for me, as it matched our hair so well.'

'My word, is that the truth? Your eyes are as clear as hers too, I'll warrant. And you have such a shapely and elegant form… A shame you are cooped up here, a young lady as fine as you…'

Secretly, I agreed with them, but Alice's voice came to mind, warning me of my vanity. Still, I was certain I deserved more from life than to be hidden away in a convent for the rest of my days.

I won't be here for much longer, I thought, fingering the letter with excitement.

'You are all fine women, too,' I said. 'And I hope that none of you are here against your wishes?'

'Oh, but we have lived the best part of our lives,' said one, 'and have found our peace here. But you are still so young.'

I sang to pass the time and they scolded me for wrecking the silence, but they did so fondly, with a twinkle in their eyes.

I was just carrying a pail of water from the kitchen back to the stables, when I heard the first sound of horses' hooves in the distance. I knew it was the princess by the distinctive crimson and gold flags of her entourage. I set down the pail and ran as fast as I could to find Alice.

The nuns who worked with Alice looked up, startled at my noisy entrance, my exclamations.

'What on earth is going on?' one demanded, crossly.

'Forgive my niece,' Alice explained. 'She is young and excitable and she forgets the rules, sometimes. Princess Marie has arrived, that is all.' She laid down her work, carefully. 'I shall finish this later.'

'Do hurry, Alice.'

'Oh, let me fix my veil,' she said, flustered, once we were outside. Her hands were shaking uncontrollably, so I helped her with it. I was surprised at her strong emotion and the fact that two bright red spots had appeared on her withered cheeks.

'You are just as excitable as I!' I laughed. 'You *do* look better with some colour in your cheeks, Alice.'

She rolled her eyes. 'I'm sure I look a fright,' she said. 'But it hardly matters. What a glorious day! What a rare joy to see Marie again!'

The joyous princess. Marie's nickname at Poitiers.

It suddenly struck me that Alice didn't look as strange or seem so out-of-place here as she had at court. At least here everyone wore the same homespun smock and veil and many of the nuns were desperately plain, the lay-sisters pock-marked. Her quiet manners fit in perfectly with rest of the community. *I* was more out of place here than she was.

'I believe you are happier here, Alice,' I observed.

'Happier? Oh! Perhaps, yes, perhaps I am more content. I have missed Marie, though. I can't believe she's here,' Alice said, tears in her eyes. Like me, she must have been thinking of Eleanor and all we'd endured.

Back at the stables, the party had dismounted and Marie was being greeted by the abbess. As soon as she saw us, she ran to us, throwing her arms around us, to the amazement of all the onlookers. *Now see if they believed me!* Crying, we hugged her back, with gladness and relief, but also sorrow, for the sight of Marie brought Eleanor and our court of love acutely, painfully to mind. It felt like returning to the tomb of a loved one and finding it drenched in sunlight, detracting from the darker truth within. I reeled a little dizzily after the embrace.

The abbess turned away, either out of discretion or discomfort. She quietly commanded the sisters to return to work and, presently, advised us to retire to our apartment where we could talk.

Marie had gained weight and her colourful gown made her a startling vision at the abbey. Her sallow skin had darkened in the sun and she glowed with health. She tucked our arms in hers and asked us to lead the way. We'd never really been friends at Poitiers, but I was glad to see her now.

She was familiar with Fontevrault from her youth, so our gloomy apartment didn't shock her. 'At least you have a place to yourselves,' she said. 'I was afraid you'd be housed in a dormitory. The abbess invited me to stay in her apartment, but I asked to be housed with you,' she said pointedly to Alice.

She settled into a chair — kindly carried up by Claudine — and it seemed like old times. I let myself imagine that we were all just visiting from Poitiers and would be returning soon with Eleanor. I gazed with longing and envy at Marie's rich silk dress and fashionable headdress. How hungry I was for such beautiful things! I also envied her grand estate and the powerful, rich husband who supplied her with every luxury.

I wanted that.

We warned her about the lady who shared our apartment, so she wouldn't be surprised when she returned.

Marie was at once curious, especially when we told her about the vow of silence.

'I'll have to sleep with her tonight,' I declared. 'So, perhaps I'll manage to squeeze a word out of her.'

Alice and Marie exchanged looks.

'Or perhaps not,' I laughed. 'But at least I can try! There's something very mysterious about her,' I added, 'but also very natural…'

'You make her sound most fascinating, Joanna,' smiled Marie, her dark eyes twinkling.

'I'm afraid Joanna's overactive imagination has conjured up some fantastical tales about her already,' said Alice, warmly.

'Well, I hope she does not disappoint,' laughed Marie. 'I used to spend such lonely times here as a child. How I dreaded it! I did come to appreciate it as I grew older, though. There's something about Fontevrault that gets to you. Mother always loved it here, of course. It gave her a sense of peace that nowhere else could give. It touched her in a spiritual way. I must admit, I love returning here now too.'

I listened with interest. I sensed that the feeling I'd had this morning was the same that Marie was describing. Suddenly, it felt sad and wrong to be here without Eleanor. To be in her special place, when she was imprisoned. Loss hit me hard, winded me like a blow to the stomach.

'I hate being here without her,' I sighed.

Marie and Alice nodded sadly. We suddenly seemed a pathetic, helpless group of women, powerless to defend our queen. What effect would Marie's appeal have on Henry at Chinon? Probably none whatsoever.

That brutal captain forcing her head down ... laughing. Sour stink on his breath. Us ladies just standing helplessly by, watching.

'I hope Henry will at least be merciful enough to let me see her,' sighed Marie. 'I've brought some things to ease her hardship a little — just some clothes and jewels. She's lived in luxury her whole life — she'll not survive without some comfort, especially once winter sets in.'

'That is true,' I agreed. I thought about her beautiful clothes. The importance of her bathing and beauty rituals, her oils and scented candles.

'That reminds me,' said Marie. 'I brought some things for you, too. Perhaps you could ask the maid to bring them up, Joanna? I know you arrived here with nothing, that terrible day. I apologise for taking so long to come, but it took some time to persuade my husband to let me travel.'

'You are gift enough for us, Marie,' said Alice. 'You should not have burdened yourself unnecessarily on our behalf.'

'Surely the Count would wish for you to go to your mother's assistance?' I said.

'Under normal circumstances, perhaps,' Marie sighed. 'But these are not normal circumstances. Which reminds me — I'm afraid I must warn you not to return to Poitiers, upon your lives. Henry's soldiers were sent to dismantle the court...'

I gasped in shock. Alice stiffened.

Dismantle our court? Pull it apart like a child's wooden toy?

'Oh, no!' I cried. 'Eleanor will be heartbroken.'

A wave of grief crashed over me. I'd been hoping to return there, soon. To return to the wood and the hawks, to the singing and dancing of the banqueting halls. My home!

The bell rang for Nore.

'Yes... It's true. I'm so sorry. All of Eleanor's attending-ladies are being shipped back to his court in Salem, England, where he says he'll deal with them. They may be tried for treason.'

'My God!' Alice exclaimed, making a sign of the cross. 'Then we were most fortunate to have escaped on time. We are most fortunate to be here.'

We were silenced then by the return of the dark woman. After we'd introduced Marie, she — predictably — disappeared within.

The dinner bell sounded and we went to join the rest of the community in the dining hall. Marie sat in Eleanor's place, on the abbess's right-hand side, and her colourful presence livened up the nuns' table considerably.

After dinner, Alice and I were sitting in the cloisters, when Lady Sarah sidled over.

Ever since our awkward encounter, I found myself tensing around her. This evening, she was all sweetness and smiles, but her manners could turn suddenly, like a cloud passing over the sun.

'You must be *so* happy to see a friend from your old court,' she whispered, flashing her white teeth. 'I can only imagine what a *relief* it must be to hear that all is well. I hope she brings welcome news? Of your duchess and court?'

She lingered for a reply.

'Yes,' I murmured.

'So, all is well with your duchess? You can expect to return to court?'

My word, but she was bold! 'Hopefully...' I lied.

'Truly?' Her stony-cold eyes narrowed. 'Ah, that *is* good! One hears such awful rumours, but I'm glad they are not true! We heard the king was holding the queen prisoner somewhere. That her ladies were up for treason. You, of all people, would be anxious to dispel such a lie — if it were a lie. One *hates* being kept in the dark, especially when there are so few noblewomen here. We must stick together. Support one another.'

As she left, she ran her hand along my arm, sending a chill up my spine.

'My goodness, what a distinguished-looking lady,' Alice whispered. 'So tall and ... striking. You were right not to tell her anything, Joanna. We still don't know who to trust.'

So true — I deeply regretted mentioning Jean to Sarah.

We sat up with Marie until the midnight bell, when I took myself to bed in the other chamber, leaving her and Alice alone.

The dark woman had retired much earlier and was curled up, tidily, on one side — though her coal-black hair spilled across the pillows. We'd explained the sleeping arrangements to her earlier, but I was still afraid of waking her. Her shallow breathing suggested she might still be awake, though.

'I apologise,' I whispered, slipping in beside her, 'if I disturb you. My aunt tells me I am a restless sleeper, especially when it's hot like this. I may thrash about in my sleep — though I shall try not to.'

I hadn't expected a reply, so a little bolt ran through me when she touched my arm. I caught my breath. Something fragile was within reach, like a little bird. I sensed I should not speak, but lay there, tense and wondering. Just as I was finally falling off, some thought pushed me back to wakefulness. My ears tuned in afresh to the faintest sound of staccato breathing, and I realised she was crying.

My heart flushed with sympathy for this gentle, tortured soul who — for some reason — was punishing herself with silence.

CHAPTER FIVE

At breakfast next morning, Marie again sat at the abbess's right-hand side. I noted that Alice's eyes were creased with tiredness, her manner distracted. She looked over often at Marie. I supposed they'd stayed up late, fretting over Eleanor. Alice's were not the only eyes turning frequently towards the princess, in her brilliant, lapis silk dress.

That afternoon, Marie would ride on to Chinon, carrying my letter to Jean. I was certain he'd come to me at once.

Alice and I walked in the cloisters and prayed, before returning again to our apartment. In our absence, Claudine had carried up Marie's gifts and laid them out on our bed.

'How *lovely*!' I cried, dashing over to them.

'Oh, *yes*, aren't they?' Claudine said, gleefully. 'I couldn't wait for you to return. I took such pleasure even in laying them out and they are all yours, for keeps. And from a princess, too, aren't they?'

'Oh, yes, Claudine! And you shall have your pick, for you have been so generous with your things.'

'Oh, no, Joanna, I couldn't. Mine are just silly ribbons and things that can be picked up for a trifle, but these are really costly gifts.'

'Why shouldn't you take your pick?' I insisted. She fell uncharacteristically silent then, moved, I believe, and awed.

There were silk dresses for me, made exactly to my measurements. They would fit me like a second skin. I buried my face in them, almost crying with joy. I ran my fingers over a precious, ivory comb. What a joy it would be to run its fine teeth through my hair! There were four embroidered night shifts — two apiece — and two velvet cloaks, one black (for Alice) and one emerald green. There was a variety of crystal vials and bottles containing different oils and perfumes, among them my beloved orange oil. Marie had had a black, crepe silk made up for Alice, who could never be persuaded to wear any other colour. Also, she'd included some costly poetry books with musical notations and delicate illustrations, as well as a herbal mix for general use. There were pointed, leather shoes and silk undergarments, as delicate and finely spun as cobwebs. She'd clearly spared no expense.

It was hard to get Claudine to accept anything, but I finally persuaded her to take some bottles of perfume, a comb and some silk undergarments with a matching nightdress. She strongly objected to the last, but I insisted, telling her to save it, if she wished, for her wedding night.

'Who would have me, with my face covered in freckles?' she said, mournfully. The mention of her wedding did the trick, though. I happily watched her stow the undergarments carefully away, like a squirrel with winter nuts.

'Alice, look!' I held up the black crepe dress. The stiff skirt made a swooshing sound I'd been familiar with since youth. Just then, we heard Marie's voice as she greeted Claudine on the stairs. I flew out to thank her for the gifts.

She waved my praise away.

'I was just showing this dress to Alice,' I said, excitedly. 'It was so clever of you, Marie, to remember she only wears black. And it is just her style, with this stiff skirt. Isn't that so, Alice?'

I held the dress up to her. Alice barely reacted, which I thought rude.

'Oh, Marie,' I said, embarrassed for my aunt. 'I thank you from the bottom of my heart! From both our hearts!' I glared at Alice.

I really meant it, for the nice things had brought great solace to my soul. It gave me great pleasure to think of Jean running his hands over the undergarments…

Marie smiled. 'I brought some woollens and caps for winter, too, but I asked Claudine to store them away. I hope that sometime you'll be allowed travel passes — but not until it's safe. I'll come again as soon as I can.' She pressed Alice's hand, but Alice's face was turned away. I believe she wanted to hide the fact she was crying. I thought her manners odd today.

I held the prettiest pearl silk dress against me, with ivory ribbons adorning the bust and sleeve. It was the latest fashion, where the lining was a darker hue than the sheathing, as light as gossamer over it.

'I'm going to try this on at once,' I said. I carried it into the inner chamber, where the dark woman lay in bed. 'Hello,' I said, softly. 'The princess brought us such beautiful gifts. I'm just going to try on this dress to show them.'

She looked up, casting her eyes over it, and I held the silk out for her to touch.

'Look! Isn't it *lovely*? Please do feel it, it's the finest silk.'

She nodded with a hint of a smile, but didn't touch.

'Is not the colour delicate?' I tried, but she'd looked away, or perhaps even closed her eyes.

By the time I'd dressed up, she'd turned to the wall, so I skipped out to show — and be admired by — the others. I halted, finding Alice and Marie in a tight embrace, their arms wrapped around each other. Their whispering sounded both urgent and sorrowful, and I suddenly felt embarrassed to be interrupting. I wavered between returning within, or declaring my presence. Happily, Marie spotted me and achieved a weak smile.

'Joanna.'

They looked pained as they pulled apart, their faces bathed in tears. I'd never seen Alice looking like that.

'Is everything all right?' I asked. 'Has there been news of Eleanor?'

'No. Nothing like that, Joanna,' Marie said, quickly. 'We are just sorry to be parted.'

'Ah, yes, I understand,' I said. Though I didn't, really. Marie would return soon, surely, with or without news of Eleanor.

'What do you think?' I twirled for them.

'Joanna,' Marie said. 'You look wonderful. You were always so beautiful. I wish that things could have been different for you... For us all.'

Her words were like a flood to quench my joy. She was full of regret and I understood why she would miss our life at court, but I did not wish to be pitied. I did not see myself as an object of pity, for I still had the twin advantages of beauty and youth on my side.

'You will give my letter to Jean?' I implored, again. 'You won't forget?'

'Joanna!' Alice snapped. 'Marie has already given her word. She is about to leave on a perilous mission and all you can think about is yourself.'

Her words stung me deeply. She was badly out of sorts and was taking it out on me. As if I didn't have enough troubles of my own.

I managed to steady my quivering lip. I mustn't cry like a scolded child. 'I am *not* only thinking of myself,' I said. 'You should have seen how Claudine's face lit up when I shared some of Marie's gifts with her. Not that you would care or even notice such a thing, Alice. At least I showed *gratitude* for these gifts,' I said, my voice choked with angry disappointment. '*You* didn't even acknowledge them. If I were Marie, I would consider you very rude.'

'I *am* grateful to Marie,' Alice said, slowly. 'She understands that, don't you?'

'I do,' said Marie quietly.

'But don't you see, Joanna? It's so thoughtless of you to prance about and be happy over such trivial things at a time like this.'

A little comfort was all I asked for... To ease our daily hardship. What harm was there in that?

How frivolous she thinks me. How wrong she is! What greater suffering is there than a heart in love? She knows nothing of my heart...

When I regarded Alice more closely, I noted how wretched she looked and my anger abated a little. *She suffers too...*

'Please, my dears,' said Marie, 'do not argue on my behalf. We are all overwrought just now. Perhaps a little lightness would do us all some good. It *does* bring me pleasure, Joanna, to see you looking so beautiful!' She came to inspect the silk. 'It fits perfectly,' she said. 'I must congratulate Ida, my dressmaker. Of course, none could ask for a better mannequin. The pearl suits you very well... I thought it might!'

'It is one of the nicest I've owned,' I said. 'Come, Alice, must you always be so gloomy? Why don't you let Marie see you in your new gown?'

'Please, Joanna,' Alice said, curtly. 'I'll do nothing of the sort. It would be absurd when Marie is about to depart.'

Her cold reprimand was like a splash of icy water when I needed warmth. *To hell with her.*

CHAPTER SIX

Three weeks had passed since Marie's departure and still no word from Jean. I calculated that she'd have arrived at Chinon the day after leaving us and had almost expected Jean to arrive within the week. With so few diversions at Fontevrault, I spent more and more time wondering over the mysterious woman in our apartment.

Marie's gifts had brought some real solace to my soul, for now I could dress myself finely after I bathed. I regretted that I could not display my beautiful clothes and fretted over my wasted talents, but I was certain that Jean would come soon to set me free.

Alice and I had not been on friendly terms since Marie's departure, so I continued to sleep in the inner chamber. It was as though a dark cloud was constantly hovering about her head. She'd grown so wan and irritable, it was best to avoid her. I hoped either Jean or Marie would come soon and put an end to our misery. I'd imagined us returning to Poitiers, but it seemed that was no longer possible. I hoped that Jean would come up with an alternative plan, at least until Eleanor was released and we could rejoin her.

I found the dark lady's muffled crying by night both baffling and distressing. How I wished I might help her! She seemed to me half-animal, and helpless animals in pain cause the greatest heartache. I began to learn her peculiar habits — how she would lie completely still with her eyes closed, without being asleep. How she often seemed to wince in pain.

One hot, sleepless night, I was restlessly fingering the embroidery on my nightshift, when she began talking in her sleep. Every muscle in my being tensed with stillness and listening — it was the first time I'd even heard her voice!

'Oh, Albert, forgive me. They forced it on me... My heart was always yours. It is yours still, for all eternity, even if you wish to dash it to the ground. Oh, forgive me!'

She was agitated — as most dreamers are — but she also sounded heartbroken.

She kept repeating the name 'Albert' and 'Forgive me!'

I was both intrigued and worried at her obvious distress. I felt the urge to wake her and put an end to it.

I almost went for Alice, but pride prevented me. I was grown up enough to handle this myself.

I peered at her face, but her features were obscured by darkness. She continued to toss about and I laid a hand on her — to ease her nightmare. She fell silent then, to my relief.

As the days went on, I wished she'd sleep-talk again, so I might learn something of her. During the day, I kept trying to get her to speak by talking about myself. It was a relief to talk about Poitiers to someone. I told her about my hawking adventures and the close bond I'd had with Eleanor. I told her about my first suitor, Bertran de Born, being vicious towards me when I refused his hand and I hinted that I was in love with someone else. These confidences were a valuable release for me, and I grew accustomed to (and grateful for) her silent companionship. I wanted to help lift her out of her profound melancholy, so I attempted to cheer her up with good humour and song, as I did with the women in the stables. It was no good, I perceived — she was too lost in despair. I noted again — with much envy — that she was more drawn to Alice. She'd sit with her in the evenings and help her sew. Otherwise, she didn't have any employment and was solitary — apart from the obligatory mealtimes.

It was puzzling that the abbess allowed her to idle away her time while everyone else had to find employment. I guessed she must either be very wealthy or very sick to merit such treatment. Yet, she didn't have the usual superior airs of a rich noblewoman. I hoped she was not sick, but feared it might be so, for she often seemed to wince in pain. I'd offered to assist her once or twice, but she'd recoiled fearfully from my touch.

Claudine and I whispered about her while I bathed.

'I find her quite beautiful,' I said.

'Yes, in an odd way,' she agreed, 'but not nearly as beautiful as you, Joanna.'

Compliments were rare at Fontevrault, so I lapped them up like a kitten supping milk. Claudine was a treasure trove of compliments, and I loved her for both that and for the fact she tended to gossip.

'She's older,' I said, charitably.

'Yes, I suppose she is a great deal older, isn't she?' said Claudine. 'It's hard to guess her age, isn't it? She walks quite slowly up the stairs anyway — not like you, Joanna. Your figure is so lithe, you do stand out here among all the nuns and old folks.'

I thought about the woman's form — which was slender, even in a smock. 'Does she ever bathe, Claudine?'

Even Alice bathed once a month, but I couldn't imagine the dark woman bathing.

'Ah, there's a good question,' Claudine said, gleefully. 'I offered to bathe her — as I bathe you — in the comfort of your apartment, but she seemed appalled by the suggestion. You should've seen her face, Joanna; it was quite contorted with horror, as though I were a gargoyle offering to get into the bath with her!'

I chuckled at the image, but I wondered if she'd been violated and if *that* could be the source of her horror. After the prince Henry had attempted to molest me at court, I'd not allowed anyone to touch me for some time afterward. The feeling had only fully subsided, in fact, when Jean had touched me with love.

Jean! Why did he not come? What could be taking him so long? It was no more than a day or two's ride between here and Chinon. I couldn't even discuss it with Alice, for she'd think me abominably self-centred to worry over my lover when Marie and Eleanor were in danger. I *was* worried over them, but I did not see the point in dwelling on something over which I'd no control. I prayed for them constantly, but nowadays I couldn't pray with the necessary purity of heart as my thoughts would always turn to Jean. Jean not only inspired impure thoughts, but jealousy was creeping in, too. This vile emotion rose forcefully from the pit of my stomach and was powerful enough to blacken out my love. It also wreaked havoc in my brain, churning up a mix of ugly thoughts which threatened to destroy my peace of mind.

What if he had found someone else? Jean was a handsome young musician, so plenty of girls would desire him.

I knew my image was implanted in his breast forever, but I worried that it might be fading. This fear sprang from the unpleasant truth that *I* could not recall *his* features clearly. Time and distance was creating a rift between us. My new environment challenged my sense of identity. My talents, even my beauty, were not appreciated as they had been at court. I'd need to develop other skills if I were to stay at Fontevrault.

But that was not my plan.

I felt like a different person from the girl who'd boldly made love to Jean at Christmas in Chinon and in the woods of Poitiers in summertime. What would he make of me now?

One evening, Claudine and I chatted as she braided my hair.

'Have you ever kissed a boy, Claudine?'

'I have,' she surprised me by saying. 'But only when playing Hot Cockles with the village boys, so I don't know if it really counts as kissing.'

'A kiss is still a kiss,' I said.

She was pleased. 'I liked it very much with one boy,' she confessed. 'Have you ever played Hot Cockles?'

'No, I don't think such a game would be allowed at court. But,' I confided, 'I've kissed boys too and liked it! What's this game, then, that you play in your village?'

'Oh, it's just a silly game where we chase each other round and smack each other's bottoms, and if a boy catches both your hands in his before you smack him, you have to kiss him.'

'It sounds good fun.'

'You know,' she said, 'when I first came to Fontevrault, some of the maids played it *here* with some delivery boys and the abbess walked right in on them. It was here in the tower, up higher. There is a chamber at the very top where they used to play it. When the abbess discovered them, she dismissed them and had the stairwell blocked.'

We were laughing so hard at the idea of the abbess walking in on such a scene that we didn't notice Alice appearing in the doorway.

She said to get dressed quickly, as the abbess wished to see us. I normally dressed for bed after bathing, so this was an inconvenience. Grumbling, I pulled on my day smock. We quickly pinned on our veils and went — with some trepidation

— to the convent. The nuns were just returning from Compline and we stood aside to let them pass. I was worried it would be bad news from Chinon, or else that Jean had written and the abbess had intercepted his letter and demanded an explanation. Either way, I was afraid and sensed that Alice was similarly fearful. Despite my dislike of the abbess's rules, I sought her good opinion and would feel ashamed if she were to learn about Jean.

To our relief, she greeted us with a warm smile and invited us into her apartment. So, my illicit affair had not been discovered! I breathed easily again.

I hadn't been back in this apartment since that awful first day when I'd come here seeking Alice. I'd hardly looked around me then, but now I allowed myself to relax and take it in. We'd stayed here once, when we'd stopped secretly on our way to Paris with Eleanor. This was where visiting royalty — including Eleanor — were housed on short visits and it was royally furnished, with oriental carpets and lanterns and intricately carved furniture. There were marble writing tablets on stands dotted about under the windows and rows of richly illustrated, costly manuscripts I'd have dearly loved to inspect, even if they were only the lives of saints. The abbess's plain clothes and practical manners were at odds with these surroundings. I caught a quick glimpse of another chamber adorned with rich hangings and ornaments, but a lady was chanting psalms within, so she closed the heavy partitions to give privacy, either to us or her.

Pity, I'd have liked to sneak a peek at the beautiful things.

The abbess sat us at a well-seasoned oak board she clearly used for her daily administrations, judging by the piles of scrolls, ink stains and remnants of spilled wax. This chamber was plainer than the others, but a stained glass window tinted everything a pleasant ochre. She prepared a jug of barley water and poured it out in clay cups. I cringed when I remembered how at Poitiers, the least important visitor would be offered sweetened boiled mint in laurel motif crystal. The abbess's drink was not only humble in appearance, either; the stuff was so horrible it seemed like a punishment, rather than a refreshment. I put the cup aside, ignoring Alice's frown.

I was curious to learn why we had been summoned here this evening.

'I've been meaning to invite you in for some time now,' the abbess said, apologetically, 'but there is always something to be done. Please tell me, how are you both settling in here at Fontevrault?'

'Very well, thank you, Holy Mother,' Alice said at once. 'Our apartment is comfortable and we are well occupied throughout the day. The meals provide sufficient nourishment — I never enjoyed meat much, so I do not miss it.'

The speech annoyed me, as I very much missed meat and didn't understand why I should have to go without.

'Ah, that is good news,' the abbess said. 'And you, Joanna?'

I hesitated. They peered at me. 'The same,' I lied, knowing it was the only acceptable answer.

'You are employed in vestment work in the sacristy, I believe?' the abbess said to Alice. 'Do you find this work satisfactory?'

'Oh, yes,' said Alice. 'Though my sight is not as it once was.'

'Your sight is failing? You should have told me. I'll send for water from St Cuthbert's well.'

'Thank you, Holy Mother.'

I doubted that would help.

'Lady Joanna, what do you do? I've seen you, I think, in the stables?'

I sing and try the make the lay-sisters laugh by parodying how strict you are. 'Ah ... I do little tasks, Holy Mother, such as fetching water for the horses, turning the hay.'

'Ah, yes, good. Even these small, helpful tasks are acts of God, are they not?'

'Yes, Holy Mother.' I felt a wretched liar. *Can she see right through to my wicked heart?*

'Are you settling in to the community?' Her eyes were still fixed on me.

'Yes, I believe I'm settling in well,' I lied again.

I felt Alice exhale with relief.

Is it a mortal sin to lie to an abbess? If anything, I was distinctly unsettled, but I had accepted my current environment as a necessary — though temporary — arrangement.

'One small matter I neglected to mention before,' the abbess said, 'my fault entirely, but not too late to rectify. Princess Marie generously bestowed some gifts on you en route to Chinon, may the good Lord protect her. In past times, the abbess would have confiscated such items and sold them for food. I, however, am willing to let you keep them, on the condition that you share them with the sisters here at Fontevrault.'

She paused, checking we understood. I wondered if she was joking, but quickly saw she was not.

'But many of the items are clothes,' I explained. 'Made up to our specific measurements. Holy mother.'

'Yes, we must share the clothing, too,' she said.

The idea of sharing clothes that had been made especially repulsed me. I was shocked she would demand it. It seemed as bad as theft! 'Surely... You do not mean...' I began.

'Yes, Joanna.' She sighed. 'You see, I have travelled all over in my life, before entering the abbey, and I have seen much poverty. A lady brought up in court has no idea that in many houses, the women may have one dress to share between them all, if they are lucky enough to have any clothes at all.'

I can't believe she's going to take this one small pleasure away from me as well. I felt vexed enough to scream.

'Yes, of course, Holy Mother,' Alice said, hastily. 'As you wish. I only regret that we were unaware of this custom of sharing. It seems selfish now, hoarding the things for ourselves.'

'No, no, you were not to know,' she said. 'It was my oversight. No harm done that cannot be undone.'

My new dresses. The pearl one I wore in the evenings… The sage silk with the crimson hem I'd put away for Jean. It was too much. 'But surely it is not hygienic,' I declared. 'That's how disease spreads.'

'Joanna,' the abbess spoke slowly, as if to a child. 'Are you aware that we house lepers here, at Fontevrault? If we were worried about disease, we'd turn these poor souls out. Would you have us turn them out?'

A trick question. 'No … no, of course not, Holy Mother.'

'Ask yourself this. What use are silk dresses to you here at Fontevrault? Silk garments can be cut up into kerchiefs to sooth fever, or into scarves to ward off winter chills. Think how many scarves could be made from a single dress. Think how many of your sisters could be comforted. Well, it's your choice,' she said. 'I shall not force you to give up anything you don't want to. I care so little for worldly things, myself, I suppose I imagine the same of everyone else. *I'll* not be wearing any of your silks, Joanna!

'I know this philosophy must be strange for you, after growing up at court, but in Fontevrault we fully embrace the communal life. You may cut up a silk dress for your sisters today; tomorrow, you may be in need of such a gift yourself. Remember how happy you were to receive the gifts in the first place? It might surprise you to learn that the pleasure in giving can be greater than that of receiving. This philosophy fosters equality amongst all the houses of Fontevrault, for in God's eyes, we are all equal.'

She thinks I'm spoilt and careless. 'I am aware of the joy of giving,' I said, stiffly. 'Holy Mother.'

'Good, then you understand!' she said.

'She just wants us to give up our nice things!' I later complained to Alice.

'Not at all,' said Alice, maddeningly. 'I quite agree with her. I shall happily relinquish my share to anyone who wants it — or needs it.'

'That's because you don't *care* for nice things, Alice! Therefore, it's not the same sacrifice for you as it is for me!'

'Don't cry over it, Joanna. It's not worth it,' she said.

'I'm *not* crying!' I said. 'I'm *vexed*! I could swear the abbess tries to turn any chance of happiness into suffering!'

We arrived at our apartment just in time to catch a fleeting glimpse of the woman retreating within.

I immediately went and dragged the silk dresses from the chest, practically choking with anger. I tore off my woollen smock, grabbed the sage and red silk I'd been saving for Jean and stepped into it.

'What are you doing?' Alice asked. 'It's almost time for bed. Why are you dressing up?'

'By God's teeth,' I swore, 'if I'm about to give away my things, I'll get some wear out of them first!'

I saw her suppress a smile — the first I'd seen for some time.

'Well, as long as you're back before dark,' she cautioned. 'I suppose the abbess *is* a little hard on you. I believe she's testing you and trying to teach you.'

'I do not seek her guidance!'

Throwing a veil carelessly over my shoulders, I ran towards the orchard. I ducked through the gnarled olive trees with reckless disregard for my fine dress. I felt almost like myself again.

I entered the orchard through the archway filled with twilight.

Why did Jean not come? I was beginning to doubt his love.

His long, brown hair, his worn, flamboyant jerkin, disappearing round the corner with some maid.

Why couldn't I just see his face, his dark, beseeching eyes?

Turn around, Jean!

A sudden noise startled me, and I spun around to find brother gardener in my path.

We stared at each other, like two startled animals.

'It's *you*,' I said, finally.

'It's you,' he echoed. 'Have you come to steal more fruit?'

'No, I tested the peaches, but they're overripe,' I teased.

He didn't smile. 'Why are you walking here alone?' he asked, suspiciously. 'It's almost dark.'

'Why are *you* walking here alone?' I replied. 'Am I not to have any freedom at all? May I not even walk in peace in the walled orchard of an abbey?'

I was ready for an argument, but he just shrugged.

'You are free to walk where you wish, Lady,' he said.

'It's Joanna,' I said.

'Pardon?'

'You may call me Joanna.'

'Lady. It is my job to oversee the orchard. It's unusual to find a woman walking alone in the evening, but if you are not afraid, I believe it's safe enough.'

He pushed past me. So rude!

'I'm not afraid!' I called after him.

I craved male attention and, as he was young and quite attractive — despite the shorn pate — I stalled him.

'I would appreciate your company, if you'd care to walk with me a little?' I ventured, coyly, certain the prospect would thrill him. I'd subtly slipped off the veil covering my bosom. I knew the crevice between my breasts was irresistible to men.

He paused, so I skipped up alongside him. Despite my efforts, he barely looked at me.

'Lady,' he said, firmly, 'if you are not afraid to walk alone here, then you don't need my protection. As for company, I do not desire it. Good evening.'

I stared after him in amazement.

Well! I couldn't believe it! Never had I been so dismissed by a man! The challenge was appealing.

I arrived back, subdued, to our apartment and peeled off the dress. It occurred to me briefly that not everyone was struck by my beauty. I thought how the dark woman was too tired-looking to be beautiful, but still had some mysterious quality that made her so. She seemed to exude some kind of purity of heart. Brother gardener himself had a similar quality, I realised.

I knew I was in possession of physical beauty, but what of this other quality? I wasn't sure. At court, only my appearance had been celebrated, but perhaps, like my other talents, this was not valued at Fontevrault.

The heart is the greatest treasure. The image of the hearts in their jewelled caskets suddenly came to mind. *Of what stuff was my heart made?* If I stayed at Fontevrault, would the substance of my heart be revealed to me? I would be so curious, but also frightened to learn the truth.

However, as I was not planning to stay here long, it was hardly relevant. I remembered the abbess's request with renewed frustration and annoyance. I'd not stay in a place that forced me to give up what few pleasures I had.

For the good of the community. Was *I* not one of the community?

CHAPTER SEVEN

Alice and I were, thankfully, on speaking terms again when we went to the abbess's apartment at the end of the week to deposit our things. She invited us in, and I prayed she'd not produce the drink she had offered us previously. She received our offerings (my sacrifice) with only a curt nod, which enraged me.

She asked us to follow her through to her office and, after closing the partitions, produced a letter with a royal seal. My heart leapt on sight of it. It must be news from Chinon! Alice went still, her eyes fixed rigidly on it.

She looks so fearful. Oh God, please let it not be bad news of Eleanor!

'I think we'd better go somewhere more private,' said the abbess, grimly. 'Follow me.'

We followed her bulky form through the hall — nodding briefly to the ladies at the writing tablets — to her bedchamber. I glanced about with some interest. Her bed was huge and had just been neatly made by our Claudine. Behind it was elaborate panelling with religious scenes. First, she lit a candle, then, to our astonishment, she pushed one of the panels open to reveal a secret passageway.

'Follow me.'

So this explains how the abbess manages to be everywhere at once and to seemingly appear out of nowhere.

'Eleanor had this passageway built,' she explained, 'in case an urgent escape was needed.'

'Where does it lead?' I asked.

'Through the stables to the chapel crypt — now under the new church,' she replied. 'As you know, the abbey's most priceless objects are kept there, so in case of a raid, this passageway is invaluable.'

We followed her through the long tunnel until we emerged inside the crypt. She set the low flame of the aqueduct alight, and we blinked and gazed again in wonder at the gold-leaf walls and the countless jewelled caskets containing the hearts.

'Come. Sit.' She took out the letter. 'This arrived a few days ago. It's from Prince Richard.'

'Oh,' Alice and I said in unison.

Bold, red-headed Richard with a spear expertly in hand. Light of Eleanor's life. Sun of sons.

'He has been staying at the Paris court with King Louis all the while.'

'Well, at least he is safer there than at Poitiers,' I said.

'He is under the mistaken impression that his mother is staying here at Fontevrault,' the abbess said, shaking her head. 'He doesn't seem to know that she was taken. Clearly, Henry is being most secretive about her whereabouts.'

'Well, then we must inform him of the truth!' I said.

'That was my first thought,' said the abbess, doubtfully. 'The trouble is, how can we inform him without putting ourselves in danger? Also, we do not know for certain Eleanor's whereabouts, only that Henry has taken her somewhere.'

'There has been no word from Marie?' asked Alice, timidly.

'I'm afraid not.'

'We *must* get word to Richard that Eleanor was taken,' I insisted.

'Indeed,' said the abbess. 'But, how? If Henry's men intercept the letter — and his men are everywhere — he'll know that some of her ladies came here to Fontevrault and he could send his men to have you arrested. He obviously intends to keep Eleanor's whereabouts a secret, even from her sons.'

'Especially from her sons,' said Alice, gloomily.

'This is what I was afraid of,' continued the abbess. 'If Henry discovers that we are communicating with Richard, he'll certainly have you arrested. Can we agree that we'd better be patient and wait for news from Princess Marie?'

'Oh, but if Eleanor's life is at risk and we don't inform Richard, that surely *is* treason ... against our duchess!' I objected, passionately. 'If Richard knew that she was taken, he'd go at once to rescue her.'

'No, Joanna,' said Alice, firmly. 'In Henry's eyes, Richard is just a rebellious seventeen-year-old boy. He'd have Richard arrested as soon as he set foot outside the protection of Louis's court. And he'd have us arrested as soon as he learnt that we'd informed him of Eleanor's whereabouts.'

'Yes,' said the abbess. 'We'd better leave things as they are. Richard is powerless to help Eleanor, so what good could come of putting all our lives at risk?'

'No good at all,' said Alice, to my dismay.

'But, surely we have to do *something*,' I argued. 'We can't just wait and do nothing to help Eleanor?'

'We are powerless against Henry's forces, Joanna,' said Alice. 'Even Richard is powerless.'

'Then we are agreed,' said the abbess, rising briskly. 'I shall burn Richard's letter and you must promise not to breathe a word of it to anyone.'

I fell uncharacteristically mute. *It was all so hopeless.* I was not courageous enough to argue further, nor had I any worthwhile suggestions. We were abandoning Eleanor to save ourselves, and my stomach felt sick with shame.

A few minutes later, we were outside the church in broad daylight. Alice and I walked in dazed silence back to our apartment. The light outside was dazzling after the dark chamber, and I felt disorientated and greatly out of sorts. Alice seemed similarly downcast. Our situation was truly hopeless.

'How could you agree to just let Eleanor rot in prison?' I said, angrily.

'We had no choice.'

'What if it was Princess Marie?' I said, suddenly. 'Would you just wait around doing nothing if Henry imprisoned Marie?'

Alice looked stunned and offended. It took her a moment to compose herself enough to reply. 'Why do you say that?' Her voice was shaking.

'I don't know,' I said. 'We've abandoned Eleanor, Alice, after all she did for us!'

I was crying. She sighed heavily.

'I too am sick at heart,' she admitted, 'but we have no choice. It is out of our hands, Joanna. All we can do is pray.'

She said she was weary and needed to lie down.

I was too out of humour to face the women in the stables yet. I knew I needed some physical release to relieve my agitation, so I decided to go to the forest. Impulsively, I grabbed my hunting knife and concealed it underneath my robe. I felt like making a kill.

It was the season when the trees were laden with nuts and berries and the evening skies were full of burning sun, darkening early to a vivid bruise colour. I'd noted some pleasantly plump pheasants, drunk on overripe grapes, wandering at the edge of the forest and thought what easy prey they'd make.

Alice and I had both lost weight since our arrival, and I'd already determined to hunt for meat before the arrival of winter. Today seemed a good day to start. I'd have the cook throw it in a pot with some herbs. I was confident she could be bribed with a share of the spoils. The forest game was free for all, so I wasn't breaking any rules, as far as I knew. I'd been so terribly good and restrained, I felt I deserved a reward. What better reward than a nice plump pheasant for dinner? My mouth watered at the thought. I'd keep out of danger by not wandering far into the forest. With good fortune, I'd be back before I was missed. The bell had just rung for Terce, so most of the community would be occupied for the next hour or so.

Brother gardener was at the beehives and I saluted him as I passed, but either he didn't see me or ignored me. He was busy gently applying the copper smoker to a hive, so I deemed it best to avoid going any closer, for fear of being stung. I've always marvelled at the dedication and bravery of beekeepers. I made a mental note to beg a few jars of honey from him.

I went through the olive grove and then veered off the path, towards the forest. I soon arrived at the thin, outer band of trees, where Lady Sarah and I had had our awkward rendezvous. Sometimes she and some other ladies walked here after dinner. At this time of day, however, I was confident that everyone was either at prayer, or in dutiful employment.

I ventured deeper, but kept the abbey in sight. Moving lightly, I listened for signs of wildlife. Coming to a splayed oak, I swung up a couple of lower branches and nestled into the thick, golden foliage. I knew from experience that if I waited long enough, something would come my way. I kept a watchful eye out, whilst quietly sharpening my knife. I loved the subtle craftsmanship of my knife — gilt handled, with a fat, tapered steel blade — most precious of gifts from Eleanor.

Sometime later, my ears tuned nervously into the sound of footsteps. Alarmed, I climbed lithely up a few more branches, to be better concealed. Two women in smocks and veils came gradually into view — but too far off for me to see their features. They stopped at exactly the same time, as though they had a task to complete. I thought it odd they didn't speak. I wondered if they'd also come to hunt, in which case I might reveal myself presently.

One of the women went to a tree and — to my surprise — lifted her smock right over her head so her back was bared. She bent, with her arms round the tree, and stayed motionless in this pose. Meanwhile, the other woman had taken out what looked like a leather strap with a thin piece of willow attached and begun flexing it against the ground. With shock, I saw the woman administer the first lash on the other woman's back. The poor woman didn't scream, but merely flinched and shook with sobs. The beater was heavy, and after five lashes she paused for breath.

'More! Please, more!' cried the abused, to my amazement.

I'd never witnessed such violence between two women before. I guessed it must be the meting out of a punishment, but what on earth could she have done to deserve it? My anger was stirred and my hand clutched my knife with intent. I was poised and ready to jump to her defence if the lashings continued.

'That's enough for today,' said a voice I recognised. My God, the abuser was the abbess!

I was stunned. Pinpricks of horror broke across my scalp. All this time I'd assumed that she was good. All this time, I'd been worried about what she thought of me.

They passed right underneath me then, and I got a good look at their faces. It was indeed the abbess, and the other was the dark woman who lived with us. I was doubly outraged, for I knew her to be the gentlest, meekest of souls. I didn't cry out in protest, but remained frozen to the spot with shock and fear. Afterwards, I was ashamed of my cowardice and my blood boiled with anger. Incensed, I decided to confront the abbess.

A dreadful thought occurred to me.

That was not the first time.

I was certain of it from the way they'd both behaved — as though it were a ritual they often practised. That was why the woman had been horrified when Claudine had offered to bathe her — the maid would have seen the marks on her back. And that was why she always went directly to bed in the afternoon, exhausted after her beating. But why, *why* would the abbess do such a thing? She must have been a wicked woman indeed. How could Eleanor have admired her so? I was terribly upset and confused. But more than anything, I was angry.

I swung down from the tree, my hunting exercise forgotten.

I slashed through the undergrowth carelessly with my knife, only sheathing when I heard voices and the baying of hounds. I hurried out into the open, where I saw a group of men in grass-coloured smocks with hounds at their heels coming towards me. I hid quickly, letting them pass. I stared after them a while, wondering, then turned and ran back to the abbey.

Brother gardener was still at his hives and I approached him, emboldened and emotional after the morning's traumatic events.

'Hello, brother.'

'Lady.'

I didn't let his cool manner deter me. 'I was surprised to see a group of men with hounds at the edge of the forest just now. Are they hunters?'

'Yes,' he replied curtly.

'Please,' I said, almost crying for want of warmth, 'I shall only keep you a moment. I don't mean to take you from your work. I only require a moment of your time, just to ask a question or two of you. Please?'

He set down the smoker.

'Thank you.'

'They are only monks and brothers hunting wild boar,' he said. 'The farmers have complained that the boars are breaking into their fields, trampling their crops. The abbess has given permission for them to be culled. Only the old males are to be culled.'

'I see,' I said. 'I didn't recognise them in their camouflage. I thought the abbess insisted that monks wear their white cowled smocks at all times? To be always recognisable?'

'Well, usually, yes. But the boars would spot them coming a mile away if they wore their whites. At times like this where the abbey's good name is at stake, the rules are relaxed. Also,' he added, 'the great estates pay a fortune for the meat.'

'So,' I said, more to myself, 'there is one set of rules for the monks, and quite another for us ladies.'

'Pardon?'

'Nothing. It's just that, when I went hunting with a few of the noblewomen here, we had to wear our everyday smocks, you see, which was so impractical, it spoiled our chances. I don't see why there should be two different sets of rules for us and the monks. Do you?'

His pea-coloured eyes stared into the mid-distance as he considered my question. 'I don't see why you shouldn't have the same advantage as the monks,' he decided. 'Either you hunt to succeed, or there's no point hunting at all.'

'My thoughts exactly,' I said, impressed. I hadn't expected him to agree with me. Perhaps he did have a mind of his own and wasn't just a brother, following orders. 'Thank you.'

'However,' he added, 'I am against the blood sport myself and would never practise it, Lady. I must get on with my work now.'

Just when I thought we were getting along.

'Please, call me Joanna. One other thing: could I purchase some of your honey? My aunt and I ... and the other woman we share a room with ... are growing so thin. We badly need to supplement our diet.'

'Forgive me,' he said, firmly. 'The honey is not mine to sell, but belongs to the abbey. You must ask the Holy Mother.'

Infuriating. 'Well,' I sniffed, 'that is as good as a no. I know it is not your fault, you are just following orders. Good day to you, brother. Thank you for your time.'

'You are welcome,' he said, carefully.

I went in search of the abbess, but to my vexation I couldn't find her anywhere. She was not in her apartment, nor was she at the church. The nuns were spilling out after Terce, but she was not among them. I thought she might have gone straight there after returning from the forest.

She suddenly seemed to me the worst of hypocrites — preaching to us of compassion, when she herself picked on the most vulnerable of women.

Downcast and disillusioned, I returned to my apartment. The smell of soup from the kitchen was nauseating, and I briefly regretted abandoning the hunting mission. Alice wasn't there — she must have taken herself to the church — but the dark woman was within, lying awake upon the bed. Nursing her wounds, I now realised. I just couldn't believe that such a gentle, mild-mannered creature could have done anything to deserve such treatment.

'I've something important to say to you,' I said, my voice shaking with emotion. 'I was just in the forest and I saw *everything* that passed between yourself and the abbess.'

She didn't move, but I saw her tense.

'I *know* you can speak,' I said, passionately. 'For you talked once in your sleep, and I heard you today when you begged the abbess for more lashings. Please, you *must* speak to me now. I deserve an explanation, as your friend. I went to the abbess first — but she was on her rounds. Hypocrite!'

I lay beside her, our heads together on the bed-rest. I suddenly felt weary.

'How could she treat you like that?' I murmured. 'It is intolerable.'

She spoke to me then for the first time, in a perfectly clear voice. 'I deserve it, believe me,' she said. 'The abbess is a good woman — she is not to blame.'

'Is that what she's led you to believe?' I said, in disgust.

'No. That's what I know to be true,' she said, firmly. 'There's no point in keeping silent with you; I see it's causing too much confusion. Let me therefore tell you my story and you can decide if you still want to confront the abbess. Is that all right?'

'Yes. That's all right,' I said.

'You must promise not to judge the abbess until you've heard the whole story.'

'I promise.'

I was fully alert now. She looked ahead as she spoke. I sneaked a glance at her profile. Her lashes were long enough to brush her cheeks, her cheek and lips were pale, chapped, from spending too much time indoors. I guessed her skin would be an even darker olive, if exposed to the sun.

'I grew up in the city of Collioure on the Catalonian border,' she began. 'I am the youngest daughter of Count Girard II and my mother was untitled, but refined and striking in that dark, Southern way. I was a disappointment to both my parents for not being born a boy. It was my mother's last chance to produce an heir. So, for the first few years of my life, I was kept out of sight by my Catalonian nursemaid, Alba.

'My two sisters were almost grown, so I had Alba to myself. She sang to me and told me stories in her native dialect. She was a very perceptive, caring sort of person and she gave me all the love my parents failed to demonstrate. Later, on the rare occasions that I was presented with my sisters to our parents, she always accompanied me, to protect me from our father's critical gaze. She'd always have a special treat in store for me afterwards, so I came to see the audience as a kind of performance, with a reward for good behaviour.'

She smiled, sadly. 'So, I grew up in two worlds: one the strict, reserved formality of the court where French was spoken; the other with Alba — which I believed to be my true place of belonging. In fact, the court world was like a game we played from time to time, featuring those strangers. My father was distant, and I don't have many memories of my mother. I believe now she was preoccupied with finding suitors for my elder sisters, who were reaching puberty. I didn't miss her, for of course I had Alba and that was all the security I needed. Then, on my seventh birthday, something happened which changed my life forever.

'The day began with Alba dressing me in a frock and ribbons to be presented at court. She led me out before the assembly, where Father was seated at the front, looking bored. I remember the next part as clearly as though it happened yesterday, for it was so distressing. Father's gaze turned darkly from me to Alba and back again and he spoke angrily. "She's as fat as a pig!" he roared. "She's a disgrace!"

'Soon all the assembly was talking and staring at me and I was most confused and embarrassed. They asked me to turn to be viewed from the side and back. Nobody wished me happy birthday. My cheeks were burning with shame and I burst into tears. Mother rushed over to hurry us from the room.'

'Oh, how cruel!' I said.

'Back in the nursery, Mother started arguing with Alba. "She is a disgrace," she repeated. "Look how fat she is! How could you let this happen?"

'Well ... I was mortified! I'd had no idea I was fat. I suppose it was no surprise, after all the treats and cakes Alba fed me. When Mother left, she tried to comfort me with a piece of treacle cake, which I slapped out of her hand. "Do you want me to get even fatter?" I bawled. "Do you want everyone to despise me?" She stared at me and looked so hurt, I immediately regretted my words. "It's all right," I told her. "I forgive you."

'She started laughing and it frightened me, for it was not real laughter. I know now it was bitter laughter. "You forgive me? We are a little countess with airs," she said, looking at me strangely. "It's your birthday," she shrugged. "You may do as you please." I was really frightened now, for Alba had *never* spoken to me so coldly. "Come here, Marguerite," she sighed, hugging me to her. "I've treated you as if you were my own, and this is the thanks I get. I have a son the same age as you," she confessed, "whose milk I gave to you, instead of him. I never see him, because I must work here and send food home. You are more my child than he is."

'From that day on, two things changed. First, I realised I was not Alba's whole world. Second, I started to watch what I ate. Those initial feelings of jealousy and fear kept growing inside me like a hidden tumour and changed the tone of our relationship. I could no longer be sure of her exclusive love. I asked her to tell me stories of her son, really to see whether she loved him more than me and to check if she was likely to leave me for him someday.'

'Your name is Marguerite?' I asked. She nodded. 'What a lovely name!'

Footsteps on the stairs startled us both. It was probably Alice returning, as Claudine wasn't expected till later.

'I shall continue another time,' Marguerite whispered, pressing her fingers to her lips. 'Don't breathe a word of this to anyone.'

'I won't, I promise.'

CHAPTER EIGHT

The next day after breakfast, I'd arranged to walk in the orchard with Heloise. We passed through the archway filled with a fiery morning sky. To my surprise, the orchard was buzzing with activity. Many women wearing smocks, veils and gloves were milling around with baskets.

'Today's the first day of harvest,' Heloise explained. 'The women do the fruit picking and the men harvest the fields out yonder.'

I was grateful for her quiet, easy companionship, for my mind was still busy processing Marguerite's story. I'd been badly shaken by the scene I'd witnessed yesterday between herself and the abbess, but when I considered telling Heloise, it felt like a betrayal. I had promised secrecy, at least till I'd learnt the full story.

Some nuns saluted us and I recognised Francine, the young nun I'd met in the dormitory on the day I arrived. She beamed at me.

'It's nice to see you again,' I called. It turned out she and Heloise were already good friends.

She insisted on sharing the contents of her basket with us. We happily took handfuls of apples, hazelnuts and almonds, and sat beneath the trees to enjoy them. Brother gardener was darting about, aiding and ordering the fruit-pickers, and I was conscious of his whereabouts all the while. Presently, he walked right by us and I stood to greet him, but he brushed past me.

'I believe he is the rudest man I've ever met!' I complained.

'Brother Ambrose?' said Heloise, surprised. 'Surely not. I'm certain he didn't see you.'

'You know him?'

'Ah, yes, very well. He grew up here. We played together as children.'

I was impressed that boys and girls had played together freely and pleased that she knew him so well. It gave me an idea.

'Please call him over, Heloise,' I urged. 'I've met him briefly before, but we've never been formally introduced.'

She was at once shy and reluctant. 'Oh, no, I don't think I could. You can see he is busy.'

'Please,' I begged. 'I know so few people here, and I am so lonely for Poitiers and Eleanor sometimes I could *die*.'

My passionate words did the trick, and she did as I bid and called after him.

'Sister!' he said, swinging around. It was the first time I'd seen him smile. 'I see you are taking some refreshment.'

Heloise smiled. I noted with a pang how disdainfully he had treated me by comparison.

'The fruits of *your* labour, brother.'

'My pleasure, Heloise,' he said. 'How may I help?'

At Fontevrault I'd noted it was customary for people to greet each other with this phrase. *How may I help?* Then he added, 'I hoped to see you walking here more among the trees you love so well!'

'Ah, so true! I meant to come more, Ambrose, but unfortunately I've been much occupied.'

I could tell they were old friends, despite the formalities.

'Brother, you are busy,' she said. 'I shall not detain you, but wished only to introduce my good friend, Lady Joanna.'

He glanced at me. 'Good morning, Lady Joanna. I hope your time here is productive.'

Productive! This too was a formulaic phrase I'd become familiar with. 'We've met before, of course,' I said, warmly, hoping for a more natural discourse.

To my vexation, he ignored my remark and turned to Heloise. 'I trust your work is going well?'

'Very well,' she said, her face lighting up. 'I consider myself both honoured and blessed to work in the service of God with those less fortunate.'

'They are truly blessed to have you,' he said. 'Not everyone would embrace such work.'

'What kind of work do you do, exactly?' I asked. She'd told me before that she worked with the sick, and I'd assumed she'd meant the old and infirm.

'I attend the lepers,' she said.

I was astounded. I knew there was a house at Fontevrault which housed lepers, but I'd never seen one of them. I'd *never* have considered putting my life at risk like that. I suspected that Heloise must have had a heart of gold. That's what brother Ambrose must have seen — and admired — in her.

The heart is the greatest treasure.

Yet again, I worried about the substance of my heart. 'Perhaps you could take me with you sometime?' I said, recklessly. I really only wanted to impress Ambrose. I enjoyed the fleeting look of surprise on his face.

'Oh, Joanna, I'd be honoured,' she said. 'Come with me on Sunday, after mass.'

So soon!

'I see your work is also going well, Ambrose.' Heloise gestured around. 'No better work than the sowing and reaping of God's great earth to feed the community. However, I have kept you too long, and you are busy.'

'I always have time for you, Heloise,' he said. 'We must drink an elderberry infusion together when the harvest is in.'

'And laugh like old times!' she added. 'I'd love that. Perhaps you would not mind if my good friend Joanna joins us?'

He paused. 'Any friend of yours is a friend of mine,' he said, smiling at both of us.

'My goodness,' I said, once he'd left, 'I didn't realise you had such good friends among the brothers. I'm surprised that you could be so friendly with a man.'

'Oh, I never think of Ambrose as a man!' She laughed. 'To me he is still the boy I used to play with.'

The only friend I had of the opposite sex was Jean, and he was my lover. I hadn't even realised it was possible to have a male friend who was not a lover...

'You should make friends with him, too,' she said, generously.

'I don't know if he likes me very much,' I sighed. 'He seems an odd fellow.'

'I don't think him odd. He's very ... smart and funny, once you get to know him.'

'Is he?' I was surprised. 'He always seems so serious to me. He was different with you, though, Heloise,' I allowed. 'He has a lot of respect for you. I didn't realise you worked with the lepers. Do you really risk your own health to attend them?'

'No,' she said, decidedly. 'We never come into direct contact with the poor souls. I merely carry their food and bring them new dressings for their wounds, wash their clothes, talk to them over the gates to try to cheer them up...'

'You are putting yourself at great risk, surely, by touching their clothes and linens?' I worried.

'There is always some risk, I suppose,' she said, 'but I am always careful to scrub my hands afterwards. If it is God's will that I contract leprosy, then I am happy to die in His service.'

I regretted my foolish offer to help on Sunday, but I was also curious to see the poor souls.

The bell rang out for Terce and we parted ways as she made her way to the church and I to the stables for the day.

After dinner that evening, I slipped back to the orchard to snip a few blooms for Marguerite.

Worn out monks and migrant workers were returning from the fields, leading oxen pulling carts full of produce and mules weighted down with grains and flax. Fontevrault boasted its own mill, where the wheat and corn were made into flour for our coarse, daily bread. The bread at Poitiers had been a refined, soft white in contrast, which I sorely missed, especially when I thought of how I'd spread it thick with apricot or strawberry preserve. The flax would be made into linen for bedclothes, towelling and tablecloths, and the oil separated for medicine. At Poitiers, I'd sometimes applied flax-oil to my skin and hair for a radiant glow. I wondered if I'd be able to get my hands on some here. I'd have liked to procure a fine-spun piece of linen, too, for Alice to embroider, to liven up our gloomy chamber. I'd noted spinning-wheels in the sheds behind the stables, so I guessed they would be occupied over winter.

When I found myself alone at last, I surreptitiously picked a bunch of open, highly-scented roses in shades of coral and strawberry, tying them with a Michaelmas daisy. I really wanted to do something to cheer up Marguerite and these were so pretty, I hoped they'd bring her pleasure. On such a beautiful evening, it was hard to imagine such a tormented soul.

When I arrived back at the apartment, she was asleep, so I placed the roses in water by her bedside.

Next morning, I rose with the call for Lauds and stole out again to the forest. Luckily, the morning air was chill, so I was able to conceal my knife easily beneath my cloak. This time there were no distractions, and I arrived back before breakfast with a fat pheasant to present to Cook. She eyed me, frowning, but although she made disapproving clucking noises, she took it from me — as I'd guessed she would.

'Come back after dinner when everyone's cleared off,' she grunted.

I could almost taste the succulent meat already.

Claudine was rising, sleepily, from her bed by the kitchen stove. She was more than impressed with my hunting skills.

'You are *so* clever and talented, Joanna!' she cried. 'Oh, but the abbess mustn't discover you went out hunting alone,' she added, her snub nose wrinkling with uncertainty.

'She won't find out,' I said.

Her little face brightened again. 'Let me help you clean up quickly,' she offered.

The exercise had given me a ferocious appetite and I washed down the bread with big gulps of milk. Alice only picked at hers and looked so miserable, a wave of pity came over me. I guessed she was terribly worried about Marie — it was strange we'd had no news from Chinon.

'You should try to eat something, Alice,' I said. 'Here, drink this.' I pushed a cup of milk over to her. 'You must keep up your strength...' I faltered, aware of the role reversal. 'It's what Eleanor would want.'

101

She cast me an amused, but grateful look.

'You're right,' she sighed. 'It is what Eleanor would want. I can't drink that, though.' She pushed the milk away. 'It would make me sick. Now, if it were ale, I'd drink it all right.'

We both smiled. Ale! The monks brewed it for sale — if only I could get my hands on a tankard. I'd managed the pheasant, so surely I could obtain some ale?

'I have a surprise for you this evening that should cheer you up,' I whispered.

Alice touched her hand briefly to mine. 'You're a good girl,' she said, affectionately.

If only you knew how I'm scheming to escape. I felt a twinge of guilt.

I ran back to the apartment after breakfast to wait for Marguerite. She arrived back presently, but when I jumped up to greet her, she shied away from me like a highly strung horse.

'I need to lie down,' she said. She looked desperately tired, circles round her eyes. I was suddenly aware of my own youthful energy by comparison, and how immature I must seem to her.

'Yes, of course.'

I wondered if the abbess had lashed her again this morning. The very thought sickened me. Loathing for the abbess was rising in me as surely as my admiration for Marguerite was growing.

She lay down in the same way as always, head against the bed-rest. I wanted to lie beside her — like yesterday — but she seemed distant, standoffish. I didn't know her well enough to read her mood.

'Would you like some … fresh water?' I offered. 'I could fetch some from the stream…'

'Goodness, no!' she said, looking alarmed. 'Don't dream of waiting on *me*, Lady Joanna. I assure you, I'm not worth it.'

'I only wish to make you...' *Less sad? Happier? More fun?* 'More comfortable.'

'It was you who brought the roses?'

'Yes, it was.'

'They're beautiful, thank you. So beautiful they made me cry.'

'Why?'

'Because beautiful things make me sad.'

I knew what she meant. 'Because of loss?' I suggested, quietly.

'Yes. Please don't bring me gifts again. Don't pity me, Lady Joanna,' she said. 'I've had every privilege in life, and I've abused that privilege and betrayed my loved ones.' She sighed. 'Let me continue with my story and then you will believe me.'

I moved the roses and sat on the footstool, a little too eagerly. She picked up the story where she'd left off.

'Once I'd learnt of Alba's son, I developed an obsessive interest in him. I asked her to describe him over and over. Whenever I was enjoying an activity — such as horse riding — or even tasting some new dish, I'd ask whether he'd like it too. It was as though an invisible third person had come between us. Alba spoke of him with such indulgent pride, my fascination would sometimes turn to jealousy, so I'd quickly change the subject. I was afraid that one day she would leave me for him. I imagined that if she did return to him, I'd run away with her, for in my mind we belonged together. At some point I asked if it would be possible to meet Albert.'

The pain in her voice when she said his name made me look up sharply. Her eyes were closed. She was lost in sorrow.

'Did you meet him?' I dared ask.

'Yes, but not till much later, when I was twelve. By then, I was considered more presentable and was allowed to attend my first banquets — accompanied by Alba. We'd sit at a special board reserved for the children of visiting nobles and I'd watch my parents and sisters and other grown-ups on the main benches. It felt like being an observer at a spectacle which became so repetitive, I was always happy to be led to bed early. My newfound independence included being taken to visit the linen shops in the city, and I enjoyed this more. I'd little interest in linens, but afterward, Alba and I would go to watch the boats in the harbour.

'It was on such an outing that I first met Albert. At the time, I thought we met by accident, but now I believe that Alba had it planned. I was struck by how grown up he looked and amazed that he was working aboard one of the vessels. We were the same age, but I was still a sheltered child. He was also … disturbingly beautiful. So beautiful he gave me a queer pain at first sight.'

Marguerite was crying softly, so I attempted to console her.

'You don't have to continue now, if you'd rather not,' I said.

'It's all right,' she said. She gave a little laugh. 'I'm ashamed to say that I behaved *dreadfully* that day. His beauty made me self-conscious and aggravated my jealousy, and I felt like hitting him. His manner was impeccably gracious and affectionate, by comparison, and when he looked at me, he looked directly into my eyes. A trait he never lost… Despite my bad manners, at the end of the day he hugged me warmly and said he hoped we'd meet again soon.

'After that I was more interested in him than ever, but more reluctant to ask about him. Around that time, my mother ordered that I move into my sisters' bedchamber. My eldest sister had left to live with her new husband and the next was engaged. Mother stressed I was to move in on my own, meaning without Alba. "Of course, you'll always have a home here," she assured Alba.

'Strangely — and this is something that haunted me after — I welcomed the change. I found the idea of my own chamber exciting. I often wonder if Alba was hurt by that... "You'll hardly be alone, even after your sister leaves," my mother had said. "All our unmarried young ladies sleep in that chamber. I hope you'll learn from them, Marguerite. Look and learn and I've no doubt you'll turn into as fine a lady as either of your sisters. Let me look at you." She regarded me. "She's dark like me," she sighed. "Pity she didn't inherit the flaxen hair of her father and sisters. Still, she has good, clear eyes."

"'She is excellent at needlework and with her hands in general," Alba said, loyally. My mother frowned at that. "Needlework is all right, but she mustn't ruin her hands with common work," she said. "They are already darkened by the sun, I see, and somewhat calloused. Her sisters have softer, whiter hands. You should make her wear gloves from now on." Alba had encouraged my love for growing things by helping me to plant a herb garden, which I loved dearly. She'd also taught me to use herbs in cooking, which was unheard of for a noble daughter, but I loved these pursuits and had begged her to teach me.

'My mother's unwholesome comparisons to my sisters wounded me deeply, and I remember Alba comforting me after. Now, it occurs to me that Alba disliked my mother, which is probably why she left...'

'She *left?*' I said, amazed — it would have been like Alice leaving me alone with just my father after Mama died.

'She left the court.'

'Oh! How awful for you. How could she just leave you like that?'

'It was never clear to me why she left. It seemed to happen overnight, though I'm sure that wasn't the case. I was quite distracted by my new surroundings and enjoying all the attention I was getting from the young ladies, but I always sought her out. It was a bitterly complicated and highly confusing time in my life. The ladies tried to soothe me with embraces, but their bosoms were puffed up with vanity — not love, as Alba's had been. They told me I'd forget about her in time, but they were wrong. I grieved for years. It was around that time I stopped eating.'

'Why did you stop eating?'

'I didn't stop eating entirely, but my relationship with food became problematic. I think it was something I could control, whereas I'd lost control of every other aspect of my life.

'The next time I remember seeing Alba was when she came to visit on my fourteenth birthday. It was as though spring flowers had arrived! Even then, I begged her to take me with her. Of course that wasn't possible, but she did promise to visit again soon. "Only," she said, "on the condition that you eat." She was worried at how thin I'd grown, even if no one else seemed to have noticed.

'I may have attempted to keep that promise, but by then I'd developed an unhealthy attitude towards food. Many other girls my age had become women with full figures and breasts — but I still looked like a child. I dreaded attending banquets, where I was forced to act grown-up. I preferred to work with my hands and spent much of my time making gloves for the ladies. I still loved to visit the harbour of Collioure to watch the boats. My sister, Gwen, and her husband usually escorted me. I loved to observe the boats and crew, but if anyone addressed me, I cringed with shyness. Happily, I didn't have the kind of looks that drew attention and could watch unmolested.

'However, one day, a sailor jumped from his boat and ran to embrace me, shouting my name. I froze in shock and fear, while my brother-in-law leapt to my defence. The sailor stepped back, holding his hands up apologetically. Only then did I recognise him as Albert. He'd grown into a tall man. "It's all right," I explained. "He is Alba's son, Albert. I know him." The others stepped back a pace, but scanned him critically as we spoke together. His eyes danced with warmth when he looked at me and despite my blushes, we spoke as naturally as if we'd known each other for years. When we parted, he said he'd come and see me with his mother.

'I confess that seeing him had kindled a passion in me and he began featuring, alarmingly, in my daydreams. Not long after, I was thrilled to receive both of them on a visit. I just felt more comfortable with them, more relaxed and like myself — even if Albert's presence initially made me giddy. He was so easy to talk to, just like his mother. He spoke of his work and dreams with a passion that I lacked, for I did not envisage a happy future for myself. His vibrancy and hopefulness affected me so much that I dared to imagine the possibility of a better life.'

'Why did you not envisage a happy future for yourself?' I asked.

'Oh, I don't know,' she sighed. 'I suppose I had a low opinion of myself. Whenever Albert's ship, *Abraham*, came into harbour in Collioure, he would call to see me at the castle and we'd walk the grounds,' she continued. 'The castle was practically in the city, so there were always knights and men-at-arms passing through on horseback. I remember all the artisans making their daily rounds on foot, pulling carts laden with heavy sacks and groups of boys — or women — carrying impossibly full pails and trays on their heads. Labourers would come down from the vineyards above Collioure, looking ravenous and dusty after a day's picking.

'The sun always seemed to shine when Albert came. When I dared cast my eyes up at him, his face always seemed to be bathed in light. Everything grew brighter in his presence. Even the dull wool smocks of the labourers seemed to take on a softer hue and texture. The richer costumes of the knights and ladies seemed as dazzling as new-spun tapestries. I suppose my heart was bewitched and I was falling in love.

'He told me his dream was to captain his own ship, and I had no doubt he would achieve it. He made me believe that even I had a spark of the divine and encouraged me to have dreams of my own.

'Alba was getting older and less willing to travel, so she sent her love and small gifts of food with him. He explained that she was weary from carrying sustenance to the labourers in the fields all summer. In their mountain village, everyone worked together in order to survive. His own father — Alba's husband — had been a chandler, though he was dead now. Albert explained that his clients often paid him in pork or eggs instead of money. Everyone — artisans and even the wealthiest families — depended on bartering with their neighbours. At harvest time, Alba and the older women worked together sheathing corn. In winter, they gathered around one hearth to swingle and comb hemp. I was amazed when he told me there was only one oven in the whole village where they all brought their bread to be baked.

'Despite the daily hardships, I thought that village life sounded idyllic and longed to see it for myself. When I'd say it to Albert, he'd laugh and say they'd put me to work in the fields. I said I wouldn't mind. The truth was, I enjoyed working with my hands and hated being idle. My mother had come from a family of artisans, so I suppose it was in my blood. Alba had taught me to spin cloth and to grow things for cooking, and I could even bake bread.

'After months of begging, Albert began to take my request seriously. It would not be easy to arrange, he warned. We would have to gain permission from my father, and it would be a difficult day's journey by mule up the mountain. We both agreed we should keep the plan a secret, to surprise Alba. He was worried about the cost of hiring a mule, as there'd be no question of my trekking up the mountain the way he did. Also, I wanted to bring a special gift to Alba. I persuaded him to take the pearl necklace I'd received for my fifteenth birthday to sell. I was growing more and more impatient and excited with every passing day.

'I have this one, crystallised memory of myself at that time, when I was the happiest I've ever been. One summer's evening after spending the day with Albert discussing our plan, I prepared for the evening banquet with uncommon enthusiasm. I tied the pearls at my throat — knowing it would be the last time I'd wear them — and I pulled on a new pair of felt gloves. Burning with secret passion, I told myself this was one of the last banquets I'd have to attend.

'You see, there was something I'd kept secret from Albert. Some things are just too sacred to confide, and I feared that this was too fragile to survive disclosure. I had made up my mind that when I went to Albert's village, I would not return. I intended to marry him and live there, as his wife. We had exchanged assurances — even vows — of love, so I knew he loved me. My family would never give their permission, for he'd be considered too low class, even though my own mother had been an artisan. If I wanted to marry Albert, I was convinced this was the only way. That's why I lied to him about obtaining my father's permission for the journey. I could tell the men at the gates we were going to the harbour for a picnic, and then I'd just disappear and be married before anyone would be any wiser.

'I have an image of myself that evening, strolling down to the banquet hall in my light, summer dress, smiling at everyone and glowing with secret happiness. I remember everyone taking a second look and smiling back at me, and for the first time in my life, I felt beautiful.

'Soon after, Albert took the necklace to sell at the sheep market and that's when all the trouble started. A poor, young sailor with such a costly necklace aroused suspicion and my brother-in-law was called down from the castle. I believe he'd always held a grudge against Albert since their first encounter, and he was only too eager to incriminate him. My sister, Gwen, verified that the necklace was mine and, before I knew what was happening, he'd been accused of theft.

'Early next morning as I prepared to meet Albert, my father summoned me to a meeting and I knew we'd been found out. The fear I'd always felt in my father's presence had never ceased and I remember my knees buckled under me, so I had to be supported by my mother and sister as I walked.

'My father ordered me to stand opposite where he sat lording it over his men. They were still dressed in their morning's hunting clothes. I've always abhorred the hunt — such a cruel sport — and the sweet smell of fresh blood filling my nostrils almost made me retch. As he spoke, my eyes were drawn to a dark blood stain on my father's tunic. Even his yellow beard was smeared crimson.

'At first, I was rendered almost speechless with fear — unable to defend Albert. Statements were made — by my brother-in-law, even by my sister — about how I had been preyed upon by a depraved sailor. When I found my tongue, I explained that I had given him the necklace to sell, but that only made matters worse. They decided that Albert had intended to kidnap me — either for sexual gratification, or for ransom, or probably both. Our innocent plan made Albert look greedy and sordid, while I seemed a naive fool. What tortured me most was that they'd got it the wrong way round. Albert was in fact the innocent one whom I had been planning to seduce. After factoring in his youth and Alba's loyal service, they passed a relatively lenient sentence. He would be locked up — for a period — and taught to reform. On release, he would never be allowed to set foot in Collioure and would be forbidden from making contact with me ever again.

'My mother was very angry and referred often to my "dangerous liaison". I believe they suspected that I was complicit in the plan to elope, but couldn't allow the scandal to ruin my future marriage prospects. Up until then I'd been treated as a child and allowed to roam about unattended, but that changed overnight. Suddenly, my every move was watched. I was forbidden from walking the grounds or visiting the harbour as I'd done before. It became compulsory for me to attend the evening banquets, where I'd be seated next to my mother for easy surveillance.

'She began inviting eligible noblemen with a view to marrying me off quickly. I realise this paints my mother in a cynical light, but she believed she had my best interests at heart and she was quite gentle with me, mostly. I refused to engage and managed to freeze off every suitor — much to my mother's vexation. She said she would not force me, but lectured me on being a dutiful daughter and one day, she hoped, a dutiful wife to a "deserving" husband. By deserving, of course, she meant wealthy. None of these suitors was as good or as beautiful as Albert. I continued to resist and racked my brain for a plan to rescue and be reunited with Albert.

'I was kept in total ignorance of his whereabouts the entire time. Had I been less solitary, I might have had friends to help me. I believe this character flaw cost me dearly, for nobody was willing to help. Alba was also kept in the dark and ordered to stay away. They even treated her as a possible conspirator. After they took Albert away, I heard her banging frantically on the outer door, crying for them to have mercy on her boy. My heart broke for her. Her radiant boy, the light of her life, cast down into the shadows. What would become of him? The scandal could ruin his prospects, which had been so bright. Their whole village would be shamed and it would mean certain poverty. It was all so unjust, but I've since learnt that life *is* unjust.

'I hatched a plan to get engaged. It seemed to me the only way to gain some freedom. If I appeared to have forgotten Albert, I'd not be watched so closely. My mother would be happy and distracted and I could take the opportunity to find Albert. I'd request to go on a trip to the best shoemaker in Carcassonne for my bridal footwear and somehow I'd escape.

'My plan made me bold enough to start seeking a husband. Unfortunately, my reputation for being standoffish preceded me, so my first attempts were misconstrued and failed. Two noblemen I recognised from my mother's matchmaking attempts regarded me frostily, with distrust. Finally, I managed to catch the attention of an older man named Eduard, whom my mother was pleased to introduce. He was at least twice my age and mostly bald with fat hands and pale, sweaty skin. My mother liked him because of his inheritance — some castle, somewhere. Despite his extreme shyness, we shared dessert and he offered to fill my cup. He seemed the perfect contender for the role I needed him to play.

'Over the coming weeks, I pretended to like him and feigned interest when Mother spoke of his attributes. As I'd hoped, she became less vigilant in her watchfulness and began to relax about my future. Before long, we were engaged. My mother asked my sisters to speak to me about the wedding night and I listened attentively — hoping I would soon be performing the act with Albert. Likewise, when they measured me for my wedding gown, I imagined myself as Albert's bride. They perceived my happy glow as a sign of love and so it was — but for Albert. My mother began treating me with some respect and perhaps I should have felt guilty for deceiving her, but I did not. I could only think of Albert and Alba. They were my real family with whom I couldn't wait to be reunited.

'A few weeks before the wedding, I broached the subject of Carcassonne. At first, my mother refused on the grounds that there had recently been an outbreak of plague in that city. I'd have to go on horseback, as we didn't own a carriage, but it was believed that the plague was airborne. My mother was adamant I mustn't put myself — or others — at unnecessary risk, so she ordered my brother-in-law to take me in his carriage. This ruined any hopes I'd had of acting independently, so I needed an alternative plan.

'When the scheduled day arrived, I pretended to be ill. My desperate need to see Albert was turning me into a scheming dissembler. Over the coming days, I feigned fever and loss of appetite in hopes that a physician would be sent for. When he came, I begged to be bled to relieve the pain and I saw his forehead crease with worry as I writhed and moaned. As I'd expected, he ordered I be removed to a chamber on my own, to avoid contagion. Incredibly, I was housed in the same nursery I'd once shared with Alba, which I read as a good omen. The door was always locked, to avoid accidental visitors, but it was possible to escape out the window. My meals were sent up three times daily — thin soup and dry bread, which I barely touched.

'My new plan was to flee to the harbour, find Albert's former captain and explain everything to him. His ship usually docked on Fridays, so I had three days to wait. I carefully stowed away the bread at mealtimes and managed to wash my hair surreptitiously. On Thursday, I dressed in all my clothes and lay awake all night, my heart pounding.

'I had every confidence the captain would side with Albert, for he knew his true character. I hoped he'd hide me and help me find him. He'd also know the location of Albert's village, so I could seek out poor Alba. I knew that if I didn't act now, Albert would be gone from me forever. I also knew that my actions would mean the severing of all relations with my family — a price I was willing to pay. I would find Albert, marry him and live in his village, where I would work with my hands like the rest of them. If we were married and I'd lain with him by the time they found me, they'd have to let me go.

'I did not know that I would never see Albert again. That our fate had already been sealed by black fortune. I was sighted climbing out the window — followed — and captured boarding the *Abraham*. My plan was doomed, my scheming exposed. Now they knew the truth, I'd never be let out of their sight.

'To my unimaginable distress, Mother arranged for the wedding to Eduard to take place at once. In a daze, I was married before a handful of men and sad-looking ladies. My sister, Gwen, cried the entire time — a fact I was grateful for afterwards. I shed no tears, only felt a coldness seeping into me that I now recognise as horror. The marriage was not consummated that night, for I screamed when he attempted to touch me. He left the chamber in the morning without uttering a word.

'Later that day, a cart arrived to take me to his castle. I was grateful he wasn't attending me himself, though mother was indignant. "You must obey your husband now, child," she said, weeping, despite herself. All decorum and logic abandoned me then as I clung to her and my sister, begging them to let me stay. I was only a girl of sixteen, after all. Grief-stricken and bewildered, I was bundled into the cart along with my wedding trousseau. It took four men to lift the trunk up, for it was made of gold-plated oak. The first thing I did when I arrived was take a hatchet to it — like a mad woman. Still, it made me feel better for an instant.

'I was Eduard's property now, as he perpetually reminded me. I could never love him. I pitied him eventually, despite the suffering he caused me. He forced himself on me, finally, though I fought tooth and claw to fend him off. Sex was a brutal, mortifying act that left me withered in body and spirit. The sight of him naked repulsed me and I believe he loathed me too, though he violated me constantly.

'His castle was merely a big, old, draughty house, and I accused him of deceiving my mother about his wealth. I'd torn up most of my bridal wardrobe on arrival and I went about in a peasant's smock. I felt ugly inside and out and I'd turned my back on God, so I never prayed. When Eduard and the household attended Mass, I refused to go. No wonder they thought me wicked. Naturally, the servants were loyal to him — they even liked him — and disliked me. They sniggered as I walked by, and I knew they could hear our wrestling at night and my face would burn with shame. I couldn't understand why he kept forcing himself on me when he hated the sight of me. He pounded into me with his sweaty belly slapping against my stomach, his face livid with the effort. I fought and scratched like a cat and sometimes he gave up — roaring at me. Mostly, though, he managed to overwhelm me and push into me with a force that almost made me faint with pain. During the day, I dragged myself around, sore and bruised, with not a single friend to offer comfort.

'I was convinced that God must think me very wicked to have cursed me with such a life. I endured the violations until I fell pregnant and then, thankfully, the nightmare stopped. Eduard didn't touch me again. I began sticking pins into myself, to relieve my anguished mind. I'd stick them in my feet and walk around all day on them. In the evening, I'd peel off my blood-soaked shoes with fascination. I grew fascinated with my own blood. You might think I didn't want the child, after how it came about, but I did. I really wanted the child. The unborn child was my only friend, my consolation.

'However, God took my baby away one night and left me drowning in blood. They found me in the morning nearly dead. I don't remember any of it. Weeks passed where I lay in bed being spoon-fed and watched over, until one day I sat up and took some soup from the concerned-looking matron who attended me. "My baby?" I cried. I vaguely remembered uttering these words, as in a dream. "Your little angel is with God, ma'am," she whispered. I bawled, for I knew that God was cruel.

'The matron was the first person who'd been kind to me, so I asked her to inform my family that I'd suffered a miscarriage. Not long after, my sister, Gwen, arrived with a tonic to help my recovery. She was startled by my altered appearance — afterwards, she told me I was like a wizened old woman. I'd lost so much weight, my bones were sticking out, fraying against themselves and causing me to bruise. Her eyes filled with tears whenever she looked at me and she apologised repeatedly for the part she'd played with Albert. At the time, she said, she thought it better we were separated, but now she saw that she'd been wrong. Poor Gwen, she's a gentle soul, really, but class-conscious like our mother.

'I clung to her with renewed hope, begging her to tell me of Albert's whereabouts, or, better still, to take me to him at once. "It's too late," she said. "Please, Gwen," I implored. "I love him! Eduard hates me — the marriage was a horrible mistake. We barely knew each other. I'm sure he'll be happy to give me up." She shook her head, tears streaming down her face, staring at the ground. "I'm sorry... I'm so sorry," was all she said. "It's too late."

'The way she said it made the blood run cold in my veins. Horror raced up my spine. I grabbed her and shook her. "What is it?" I cried. "What is it you're not telling me? Has something happened to Albert?"

'"I'm so sorry," she kept repeating, maddeningly. "I wasn't going to tell you, but Albert is dead.

'We both fell silent, just staring at one another. I knew she spoke the truth, for at once I felt his absence and I just knew he was no longer on the earth. There was a strange kind of peace in that. I let the silence fall around us like snow. The only sound was my heart ripping in two, heard by me alone. "He died by his own hand," she told me after. When he heard of my marriage and that I was with child.

'Gwen stayed and watched over me all winter, terrified lest I decided to follow Albert to the grave. She pleaded with Eduard to give me an annulment, but oddly, he would not. I don't know how my ripped and bleeding heart managed to keep beating. Finally, an agreement was reached that I be allowed to travel back with my sister to Collioure and stay there until my health was restored. So, I went to live with my sister and brother-in-law and I was grateful to be away from Eduard and his hellhole of a house.

'Time was somewhat suspended at my sister's grand, but disorganised estate. The large chambers were filled with the noisy, but joyous clamour of children and dogs. I became a beloved aunt, always prepared to mend or make things and easily persuaded to provide illicit treats. I pushed my recent, tragic history from my consciousness, but the trauma reared its ugly head every night, in my tormented nightmares. My disordered eating habit was ruthlessly scrutinized by the children, and I was forced to eat more regularly under their keen surveillance. I soon put on weight and colour reappeared in my cheeks. I brought them often to a little, secluded beach where we could swim. The breeze wafting gently off the sea was like balm to my troubled soul. Their energy lifted my spirits and I existed in a haze of forgetfulness, for a while.

'The following winter, Eduard sent his cart for me and my nightmarish existence began again. He grappled with me that first night and forced himself on me. After a while, I realised it was easier if I didn't resist, so I lay there like a corpse and let him pound away. I fell pregnant and, once more, the pregnancy ended swiftly, in a pool of blood. After the miscarriage, I was sent to my sister's to restore my health, until I was fit enough to return and be made pregnant again. I fell pregnant five more times, but each time the child was taken prematurely. I took this as a further sign of God's wrath.

'After ten years, it was clear I could not fall pregnant anymore, and Eduard never attempted to couple with me again, thankfully. Once he realised I wouldn't conceive, he became so embittered he inflicted every possible punishment on me. Now that I was no longer the vessel for his potential heir, there was no need to keep me healthy, so he put me to work in the fields like a labourer. In fact, I loved being outdoors and working in the cornfields.

'One hot summer's day, I worked without a break from dawn till dusk, until I collapsed. The kindly matron I mentioned before discovered me and took me back to her cottage. When I came to, she spoke to me sternly. She'd observed that I showed no care for myself. That I was determined to ruin my health. She said she'd not stand by and watch it happen. She'd heard of an abbey in the Loire where they took in women like me. Women who were abused or in danger. Someday, when Eduard was away, she'd arrange for my sister to come and take me there. Once I was there, I'd be under royal protection and Eduard wouldn't be allowed to enter.

'She asked me to think about it carefully and decide whether I'd rather live or die. "I'd rather die," I confessed. "My life is worthless. I killed the person I loved most in the world, and even God has forsaken me." My words were shocking to her, but even more shocking was the torrent of tears that followed. I cried for days. All of my unshed tears over Albert finally poured out. Despite my claims of wishing to die, she went ahead and arranged with my sister to remove me to the abbey — here, to Fontevrault.'

As if in response, the dinner bell chimed just then. I was amazed at how quickly the hours had passed listening to

Marguerite's story. We never normally walked to the dining hall together, but today she accompanied me.

'I suppose you will tell my tragic story to Alice?' she asked.

'Only if you wish it.'

'Yes, you may tell her,' she whispered. 'It would not be fair to confide in one of you and not the other. But please tell no one else. I still must explain to you … about the abbess.'

We parted ways at the dining hall, and I joined Alice in the ritual hand-washing at the fountain. Marguerite's story had left me filled me with unrest. I couldn't believe the injustices she'd had to endure and here was the abbess, continuing the abuse! It made no sense. Alice cast her eyes over me, anxiously, sensing my mood.

When the abbess began reciting grace, I warned Alice not to fill her belly, as I'd a surprise for her. She frowned, pressing her fingers to her lips, to silence me. I couldn't have cared less for the abbess's rules anymore. Not after her treatment of Marguerite. I told Alice to meet me back at the tower kitchen.

I raced back to the tower, where the cook was waiting. She pointed inside, to a rough board with a bench either side, where the kitchen staff ate sometimes.

'Set out the bread and things,' she grunted.

'Wait!' I said. 'I must ask Marguerite … and Claudine!'

'It's not a banquet,' she grumbled, but she shrugged, giving me leave.

After cutting some bread and setting out the bowls, knives and linens, I went to find them.

Marguerite could not be persuaded to join us, but Claudine was delighted. I asked the boy Arthur to join us, too, with his beagle, Coo, at his feet. We were already seated when Alice arrived. She sniffed the air cautiously, like a mouse. 'I smell pheasant,' she said, with a smile.

The cook plonked a pot down on the board. She lifted the lid to a big burst of steam. She'd only seasoned it with leeks — no spices or salt — but I praised her cooking, anyway, for she was a powerful ally. The meat tasted outstanding after such a long period of fasting. We all filled our bowls, took cuts of bread and ate in contented silence.

CHAPTER NINE

The days were dawning crisp and pale, and darkness was drawing in early. At Poitiers, the maids would have been carrying fleeces from the linen closets and beating them vigorously on the thrashing hearth. At Fontevrault, each apartment received a single sheep's skin — to be shared — while the farm animals were brought into the monks' house at night for extra warmth. The three goats, Debbie, Daisy and Lily, wandered into the tower kitchen one frosty evening, but Cook chased them out. Alice, Marguerite and I all crowded together under the single fleece at night, as our glassless window and doorless doorway created a terrible draught. Sometimes Claudine came up from the kitchen to join us, just for warmth.

The harvest was in and I too was taking stock for winter. Eleanor's resonant voice rang in my ears. *Hunt for your meat yourself, Joanna... You'll appreciate it more that way.* Every day, I rose before dawn to go hunting, often arriving back with a pheasant. The cook accepted my contribution without so much as raising an eyebrow, and our illicit meals became commonplace that season. The exercise and enriched diet improved my spirits and kept my worries at bay.

Jean was fading into the background as Marguerite — and even Brother Ambrose — began featuring more vividly in my thoughts. I'd never encountered anyone as intriguing as Marguerite — so wounded and mysterious. I wondered what the future held for her. I wished with all my heart that I could help her to recover. We'd rarely had the opportunity to speak alone since all of us had started sharing the same bed. Alice had been saddened by her story and told her so, but Marguerite insisted she'd caused her own misfortunes. At least she spoke to us now, even though she kept her vow of silence with the rest of the community.

'Why don't you accompany me to the sacristy to embroider the priest's vestments?' suggested Alice. 'Your needlework is so fine and it would help pass the time.'

'I cannot do God's work, Alice,' Marguerite replied, quickly. 'God does not love me... Nor am I worthy of his love. Not until I atone for my sins.'

Alice and I exchanged concerned looks.

'The abbess made the same suggestion, when I first came here,' Marguerite said. 'But I explained to her that I fell out with God a long time ago. I asked her to mete out God's punishment to me, so I may be worthy again of his love. At first, she was reluctant to do so, but she soon recognised it as part of her duty. If a sinner asks for flagellation, it must be ministered by the abbess.'

So, *that* was what I'd witnessed in the forest that day between Marguerite and the abbess. I still thought the abbess should have refused to do it.

'It is the only thing that alleviates my suffering,' Marguerite said. 'The physical pain diverts me from the torment of my mind. It is some atonement for the suffering I inflicted on Alba and Albert.'

Her philosophy sounded strange and dangerous to me. I couldn't understand how the abbess could condone it, for Marguerite was obviously a poor, wounded soul in need of friendship and guidance.

Brother Ambrose had also become part of my daily landscape. Like the wandering goats, I caught sightings of him on the horizon whenever I rose my head from my early morning landscape of forest, pheasant and undergrowth. On one of my earliest expeditions, I almost ran into him while returning to the abbey with a fat pheasant. He raised an eyebrow at my catch.

'I suppose you're going to accuse me of stealing,' I said, warily.

'The forest belongs to no one in particular, as far as I know,' he shrugged. 'Most of the community here are vegetarian, anyway. Just don't let me catch you stealing my fruit,' he added, but with a twinkle in his eye.

'I wouldn't dare! Would you … like some of the meat?' I offered.

'I am strictly vegetarian,' he said.

'You're sure I couldn't tempt you?'

'I'm certain. I take no pleasure in flesh of any kind.'

I took another meaning from his statement, for he continued to be impervious to my beauty. I hadn't realised that such men existed.

Another time, I consulted with him about some mushrooms I had gathered and found him most knowledgeable about which to eat or not. One type grew aplenty on the bark of trees.

'One of the old monks in my house adores those,' he said, 'and I'm partial to them myself.'

'Please, take them,' I offered. 'If it would please another member of the community, it would please me to gift them.'

He raised an eyebrow.

'I only ask for a few pots of honey in return…' I said, innocently.

We both threw our heads back and laughed. After that, we became friends.

One Sunday, I accompanied Heloise to the leper house where she cheerfully went about her ministrations. The first snow had fallen that morning and I skipped alongside her, nervously, enjoying the sound of our feet crunching over the exquisite, glittering snow. I chattered noisily and, I confess, I hoped others would observe me and be impressed.

'Many people think leprosy is a disease inflicted by God to punish wickedness,' I said. 'Do you think lepers are wicked?'

'Oh, no!' said Heloise, clearly stung. 'I've heard people express such sentiments, but I couldn't disagree more. The poor things are always so grateful and try to smile at me, despite their suffering and the pain even a smile causes them. Their skin is all dry and cracked where the lesions have formed, and even smiling can cause them to bleed afresh. I believe they should be treated only with compassion, not with distrust, or fear. You'll see for yourself, they are only people like us who have been unfortunately disfigured by their disease.'

We passed by the monks' house, where a few monks were conferring together outside. I was pleased to see how their eyes followed me as I walked by. Accustomed to such attention from men, I rather enjoyed it, but Heloise was embarrassed.

'Some of them are not *real* monks,' she explained, blushing. 'Only brothers who don't have a vocation. They're merely passing the time here, before coming into some future inheritance.'

'Really?' I was pleased to hear it. 'They haven't all taken vows?'

'That's right,' she said, 'and some of them never will.'

'Is Brother Ambrose not a monk, then?' I wondered.

She answered, fervently, 'Oh, he has not yet taken vows, but I've no doubt he has a true vocation and will soon take them.'

'Maybe if I kissed him, he'd change his mind,' I said, playfully.

Heloise looked shocked. 'Oh, you'd not do such a thing, Joanna. Not to Brother Ambrose!'

I instantly felt ashamed. And guilty, when I thought of Jean. Why, oh *why* did he not come?

My bravery evaporated at the gates of the leper house. A member of the colony approached with a willow basket, piled high with linens. I automatically took a step back and covered my face with my veil. I even held my breath, lest I breathe infected air. I felt panicked and vulnerable, as Heloise cheerfully handled the dirty linen. The house loomed ghostly quiet behind, an aura of sadness about it. The woman's deformed body was entirely covered, but she dragged herself along with the limp of the sick and I observed black lesions on her face and hands. I didn't hear the soothing words Heloise spoke through the gate, for my heart was thumping loudly in my ears.

As soon as we arrived back at the nuns' house, I tore off my veil and gloves and threw them into the nearest fire. Heloise looked at me with amusement as I gulped the fresh air like a fish out of water.

'You don't have to help me wash these,' she said, 'if you'd rather not. You can just help me carry the food bundles, if you'd prefer?'

'You're ... we're going *back*?' I gasped, horrified.

She laughed. 'Look at your face!' she said.

The two of us laughed till we cried — like when we were fourteen. It felt so good to laugh after so much heaviness.

'All right, it's all right, Joanna,' she said when we'd sobered up. 'Just help me to prepare them and I shall take them back alone.'

'Oh, are you sure?' I was so relieved.

'Yes! Besides, it's best not to show fear around them…'

It wasn't a criticism, but still I felt ashamed.

After we'd made up bundles of bread, cheese and fruit, I accompanied her part of the way — but I bid her farewell just before the monks' house. On a whim, I decided to call in on the monks and enquire about procuring some ale. I'd no currency to offer, but I did have a plan.

The brothers who'd leered at me earlier had disappeared — probably retreating indoors on sight of my bold approach. Perhaps they were alerting their superiors to my arrival. I was aware that I was breaking the rules (by not first seeking permission from the abbess) but my newfound abandonment of the abbess's rules had given me a reckless courage. Life would be more tolerable with alcohol. I preferred wine, but Alice loved ale and I could see she was suffering on account of Marie's silence. I therefore felt justified in my intention of making life more bearable for another member of the community. I was also deeply curious to see how the monks lived. I'd heard rumours that they enjoyed more freedom and were more industrious than the nuns and I wanted to see for myself.

Knocking tentatively, I waited and listened, my curiosity aroused. Imagining the male eyes watching from within, I preened and poised a little, just for fun. My thoughts flitted to Brother Ambrose, for this was where he lived. I felt momentary shame for having abandoned the leper house for the monks and their promise of ale. I pushed the uncomfortable thought aside quickly. The door creaked open and a tiny, ancient brother peered up at me.

'Sister, you are welcome. How may I help you?'

I hadn't thought this through, but his greeting prompted me.

Help. They always want to help the needy…

'Brother, thank you. I need some ale for medicinal purposes,' I said, smoothly.

'Ale … for medicinal purposes,' he repeated, slowly, registering what I'd said. He squinted at me. His eyes — even his pupils — were unnaturally pale. 'The Holy Mother sent you,' he added, more an affirmation than a question. His hand jutted out suddenly, seeking mine, and I realised he was blind. A wave of pity rushed over me.

'The ale is not for me, but for a friend in need,' I said. 'Is it true you make it here yourselves?'

'Ah, yes!' He broke into a delightful, toothless grin. 'I hope we can help you, sister.'

His hand gripped mine and I felt comforted and warmed by the touch.

'Wait here and I shall find our brother,' he said. The door clicked gently shut after him.

'Thank you, Holy Brother,' I said, smiling a smile he couldn't see.

I waited again and nearly panicked when I spotted Heloise returning from the colony. I turned my back, praying she'd not seen me. How would I explain this transgression? The same guilty shame rose in me when I saw it through her eyes. I'd reneged on my promise to minister to the sick and went instead to seek out pleasure in the monks' house. Eleanor's clear voice came powerfully to mind, dispelling any shame. *Run after your meat yourself, Joanna!*

I was determined to do whatever it took in order to survive and thrive. I'd already wasted valuable time following the abbess's rules. I had to act in accordance with my own nature now and what I'd learnt from Eleanor. I would hunt to feed my appetites.

Moments later, the door opened wide and two or three brothers stood regarding me. I suspected they'd already heard my request. I slipped inside quickly.

'How may we help you?' one tall, forward fellow said.

'As I just explained to the brother,' I said, pointedly, 'I need some ale for medicinal purposes.'

'Is someone sick?' he quipped. 'If so, I suggest cider vinegar.' Their laughter was barely stifled.

I looked blank. They relaxed into smiles.

'Come, we are joking. Follow us, sister.'

They brought me through the cold, bare hall into a large chamber which reeked of perfume.

'This is the scriptorium.'

I gazed about me. Skins were being stretched and prepared for parchment using special, curved knives. Fragrant bunches of crushed rose, hibiscus, lily of the valley, marigolds, artemisia and snapdragons hung from the walls, while countless jars of spices, bark and roots were lining the counter tops, for making inks. Some fellows were binding parchment leaves together, using bone needles with linen thread. Row upon row of parchment was lined up for the scribes to copy into finished manuscripts.

They led me through a chamber where some monks were busy weaving. I noted (with great interest) that the looms were set up with a whole variety of different coloured wools. Like the other chamber, there was evidence of all the herbs and plants used in the dying process. I recalled the grassy-clad hunting group I'd met advancing on the wild boar late last summer.

So they dye their own smocks. I was angry that no one had thought to mention this to me. What was Lady Sarah thinking, with her simpering, subservient attitude to hunting, when the monks were clearly taking a much cleverer approach?

We exited that chamber and I found myself in a vast courtyard with a number of stone beehive huts dotted about. The smell of wood fire hit me. And smoked fish.

'This is where we brew,' the tall fellow explained. 'Please sit.' He indicated some low stools placed around a fire. 'Now, tell us how we may help you, sister.' His eyes lingered on my face and my mouth. I was certain he found me appealing.

'I am not a sister,' I corrected. 'I am Lady Joanna. It is nice to meet you, Brother...?'

He took the hand I offered and pressed it to his lips, sending a shiver of pleasure through me. 'And I am not a monk,' he said, meaningfully. 'I am John.'

'John. It is nice to meet you.' I observed the brief flash of desire in his dark eyes. I was sure I could use my charms to strike a good deal with him. I used my sweetest voice. 'John, I will be candid with you. I told the blind monk that I needed some ale for medicinal purposes. In fact, I live here with my aunt and at present her spirits are much depressed. The ale is for her. I would like a supply of it, if possible. You see, we came from a court where we were allowed more freedom than here at Fontevrault. We are both finding it ... most difficult to adjust.' I almost cried as I stated this truth.

'Of which court do you speak?'

'I should not say, but it was Poitiers.'

'Ahhhh.' He gazed at me. 'You were at the court of the duchess, Eleanor. I was acquainted with her, during the time she passed here at the abbey. A remarkable lady.'

'Thank you.'

'You know,' he said, drawing closer to whisper in my ear, 'women are not allowed to enter here, as a rule, without the abbess's permission, so I'm afraid you won't be able to come here again. But, we can — you and I — make some arrangement among ourselves, which nobody need know of. I saw you passing earlier and I thought to myself, now there is a lady I would dearly love to meet! Now I have met you once, I would like to meet you again. But, back to your request.' He spoke normally again. 'So, you want some ale. Are you aware that we are not allowed to supply ale to the community? No alcohol is permitted at the abbey, so we sell whatever we make and the money goes towards other needs.'

His two companions chortled, gently.

'That's not to say we never test the goods ourselves,' he laughed.

'Well… Perhaps we could do a little bartering, then,' I said.

They leant forward with interest.

'What do you have in mind, Lady Joanna?' he asked.

'Pheasant,' I said. 'Pheasant for ale.'

They conferred together.

'That is acceptable,' he agreed. 'Meat you hunt for yourself?'

'Meat I hunt for myself.'

'Good.'

'Lady Joanna, our ale is good and we trust your meat is good also. For appearances' sake, we must appear to deny your request, but that's just a show in case the abbess discovers us. We must all deny that this arrangement ever existed in that case. Am I clear?'

'As ice,' I agreed.

'Very well, then,' said John. 'We have a deal. Very good, Lady Joanna.' Again, he kissed my hand. 'I shall bring the goods to you,' he whispered. 'You are not a nun.' He smiled. 'In which house do you dwell?'

'I live above the tower kitchen — with my aunt, Alice and another lady,' I warned.

He smiled again. 'I shall find you.'

'Very well. Thank you … John … and goodbye.'

'Goodbye, Lady Joanna,' he said, smiling broadly. 'It was a pleasure to see you.'

The meeting left me elated and filled with a renewed sense of purpose. Clearly, there was a whole network of clandestine activities already in place. I relished the thought of subverting the rules set by the hypocritical abbess. I was also enjoying meeting more people — especially more men. If I was forced to live here, I would do so on *my* terms. On the principles that Eleanor had taught me. I imagined her looking on me with pride, and my heart soared as I skipped over to the cloisters.

The cloisters were always busy on Sunday, but today's sunshine had brought the holy out in droves to pray. Winter sun was gently illuminating the remnants of this morning's snow. The benches were full, so I walked in single file behind the pairs of nuns. To my dismay, I suddenly found myself face to face with the abbess.

I'd avoided any close encounter with her since what I'd witnessed between herself and Marguerite. My heart skipped a beat and I, foolishly, considered fleeing. Now that I'd heard her story, the abbess's treatment of Marguerite seemed even crueller. How could a woman who'd had nothing but misfortune all her life possibly deserve such treatment?

Now the abbess stood before me, looking me straight in the eye. In an oddly abrupt gesture, she thrust her prayer book at me. True, I didn't carry one, but still I was confused and reluctant to accept it. She pressed it into my hands, firmly, and plodded off. I gazed after her, puzzled. When I glanced back down at the book, I saw there was a note in it. So, she must have sought me out on purpose! I grappled with mixed feelings of fear and guilt, worried she'd discovered my transgressions. Despite my dislike, it disturbed me to remember how Eleanor had liked and trusted her and how I did not. I took off to the orchard to read the note in private.

The orchard was noisier, but less populated, than the cloisters. I spotted Lady Sarah at the centre of her group and nodded briefly. A lot had happened since our uncomfortable encounter in the summer, and I felt less vulnerable than when I'd first arrived at the abbey. I settled under a pear tree and carefully opened the little brown prayer book.

Ladies A, J,

Please come to my apartment before breakfast tomorrow. Do not allow yourselves to be seen. Cover your faces and come as swiftly and silently as possible. I shall be waiting.

I read the note to Alice, quietly and seriously, my earlier sense of elation having evaporated. Alice's expression was grave. We couldn't discuss the situation, for Claudine was in attendance. Alice rose, turning her back, so I couldn't read her mood, yet I could tell she was restless by the way she paced about and after, how she fidgeted, unable to focus on her needlework. I was fearful lest the abbess had got wind of my transgressions and was about to mete out punishment, or even hand me over to Henry's men.

I busied myself with the task of hanging a heavy brocade over the gaping doorway. It gave me an occupation and, also, an excuse to visit the kitchen below to speak with the cook about the arrangement I'd made with the monks. I'd need to store the ale in the kitchen, after all. She'd get her share of it, of course. I found her preparing the sad, cornflower gruel they fed to the old and sick. I recalled how, at Poitiers, the same meal was made with much tastier, fluffier oats and seasoned with prunes.

I'll be hanged before I end up eating that stuff!

Cook scolded me for visiting the monks' house without permission. She said my boldness would get us all in trouble. However, I'd grown accustomed to her grumpiness and I let the criticism slide right off me. In fact, I suspected that Cook was fond of me, in her own way, for I noted how she scolded Claudine and Arthur in the same way, even though they were her pets. I could tell she admired my courage, and she looked grudgingly impressed when I told her I'd managed to strike a deal with the monks.

That evening, the lamps were lit early. Claudine and I were carrying the earthenware tub up from the kitchen when the bell rang for Vespers. I added some crushed lavender and rosemary to the water, to help ease my headache. The bathing ritual had become a crucial time to collect gossip, for Claudine and I chatted and she casually dropped juicy titbits of gossip into the conversation. When I asked if she knew of Brother John, her eyes grew big.

'Oh, goodness, *yes*!'

I was all ears.

'It was only last winter,' she began, 'there was the *biggest* scandal between him and one of the sisters. Seems he had been bedding her, without first wedding her, you know?'

'Brother John?' I gasped. 'Tall, dark eyes…'

'The very one! Brother John and Sister Therese, it was.'

'I can't believe he was bedding a nun!'

'Oh, but why not? They are flesh and blood, the same as us. She was just a novice then. The first time I saw Sister Therese, I thought her too pretty to be a nun. Seems they were seeing each other secretly for ages before they were found out. Oh, it caused quite a stir.'

Wrapped in a towel now, I listened with great interest.

'When they were caught, the abbess gave them an ultimatum. She said either they leave the abbey together at once, or they choose to stay on the condition they never see each other again. If she caught them again, she said, they'd be sent off in disgrace.'

'So, I guess they chose to stay and forsake one another?'

Claudine shook her head. 'It was not that simple. The priest gave this great sermon at Mass that Sunday all about fornication and those that take holy vows being married to God and how it was adultery for them to … you know. Therese ran out of the church crying and wailing like a demon. I remember it like it was yesterday, for the vow of silence was broken that day by more than one. Everyone was talking about it. I was only thirteen then, and it was the first time I'd heard of such carrying on and I was really shocked.' She grinned. 'Nothing shocks me these days. The things that go on and I hear them all, in my work. Rumour was that Brother John wanted them to get married and go away together to live on his brother's estate near here, but Sister Therese refused him. Said she never wanted to see him again and took her vows and that was the end of it. She had her hair cut up real short, even under her veil.'

I felt a surprising twinge of jealousy. Claudine's quick eyes were watching me, so I made my voice casual. 'What does Sister Therese look like?'

'Dark mahogany hair, fine, straight nose, lovely, dancing eyes and dimples… Soft spoken. She goes around with Francine, sometimes.'

'Oh, yes! She *is* lovely! She looks so young, though, and innocent. I'd never have guessed!'

So our Brother John has an eye for pretty women.

Afterward, I pulled a cloak on over my nightdress and we carried the tub down the stairs. The kitchen was deserted — save for Arthur curled up in his crate with Coo. The fire was burning low, casting warmth and an ebbing glow off the walls. We passed out into an indigo twilight and dumped the water into the bushes. I paused, sniffing the air, which carried the woodsmoke and incense fragrance peculiar to the abbey.

Claudine shivered. 'Come, let's go inside.'

'I think I'll go for a short walk. Would you care to join me?' I asked out of politeness.

'I'm so tired.' She yawned and stretched. 'I can't wait to get to bed.'

'Of course. You work too hard, Claudine,' I observed. 'The abbess shouldn't allow you to wait on so many.'

'Oh, I don't mind,' she said, cheerfully. 'The Holy Mother is kind to me ... and fair.'

'I'm not convinced she is so fair to everyone,' I said, 'unless it's to her advantage.'

Claudine's eyes widened in surprise. Perhaps also in fear? Everyone seemed afraid of the abbess.

'You go to bed, my dear,' I urged. 'I won't stay out long, I just need a little air.'

The bell sounded for Compline and all the nuns made a silent beeline for the church for the last office of the day, before being called again for Matins. What a miserable, regimented life! How could they bear it? And yet, they seemed to embrace it. I thought of Sister Therese, sacrificing love and life — for what?

Brother John. I recalled his dark eyes roaming over my body and felt a heated rush.

The bushes suddenly shook violently, and a voice out of nowhere made me freeze on the spot. It sounded like, 'Jonah! Jonah!'

It was too dark to see properly and I was too scared to go closer, so I stood my ground. Could it be Brother John, I wondered, come to seek me already in his ardour? The thought both alarmed and intrigued me.

'Show yourself!' I demanded, feigning courage. I was sorry I'd not thought to grab my knife.

'I dare not!' called a now-familiar voice. 'Joanna, it is I, Jean!'

'Jean?' Hot tears sprang instantly from my eyes. I pushed apart the bushes and fell, sobbing, into his arms. The sight, even the smell of him, unleashed a torrent of pent-up emotions. Love, yes, but also hurt and even anger, as I berated him for not coming sooner.

'You have no idea,' he retorted. 'I risked my life coming here. You are so cloistered in this place.' He gestured around. 'You don't know how dangerous it has become out there … in the real world. Besides, I came as soon as I possibly could. As soon as I learnt of your whereabouts.'

'The letter I gave to Marie? But that was months ago,' I complained. 'Why did you not come at once?'

'We… Henry… I cannot discuss it here. Is there somewhere safe we can go, some place private? If I'm caught… If Henry's men catch us here, we could all be hanged.'

'There is no place we can go,' I fretted. 'Fontevrault has no place for secrets. Oh, wait, there may be a place.'

'Good. Let us go there now.'

'We may need an axe to gain access,' I said. 'Wait here.'

In a few moments, I was back with an axe under my cloak.

I led him up the tower stairwell as far as our apartment. I thanked Fortune that I'd hung a tapestry over our gaping doorway that very day, so we could pass by unseen.

'There's a chamber up higher,' I explained, 'where no one goes, but it is blocked, you see?'

He frowned with uncertainty.

'This is the only place I know of where we can be alone.'

He began investigating. 'Maybe if I could loosen this bit,' he said, testing a wooden plank with a shake. 'We may be able to squeeze through the gap. I'll have to make some noise. Is there anyone by who could hear?'

'I think it's all right,' I said. 'The kitchen is too far away, and it's only Claudine and Arthur there. Only Marguerite and Alice are sleeping within the apartment, and Marguerite would not venture out for any amount of noise. Alice's eyes are starting to fail her, so it is unlikely she would risk coming out alone in the dark...'

I watched him as he worked, the perspiration building on his brow, his cheeks turning pink with the effort. I observed how thin he was and marvelled anew at his long, rich hair. So familiar was the set of his jaw, his long eyelashes and the definition of his arms under his faded, coloured shirt. I smiled to myself at his clashing red jerkin and orange leggings — so colourful, so Jean. I breathed in the familiar, earthy scent of him. I was really glad that I'd just bathed and thought with excitement of the pretty nightdress I'd thankfully been inspired to wear.

'There,' he said, at last. 'I think we can try squeezing through.'

We suddenly found ourselves alone in the secret chamber. I looked about with great curiosity. Yes, it was dusty, but it had better windows than ours, with shutters. It was empty, apart from a crate and a large board (though no chairs). The board had probably been too cumbersome to remove.

I was suddenly self-conscious and aware of our aloneness.

'I can go fetch some hay for the crate,' I suggested, 'and some candles. Food, too. I suppose you must be hungry,' I babbled. 'We'll have the place cheered up in no time.'

'Joanna,' he said, his eyes on me, intense.

I blushed. He drew me to him, holding my gaze. He undid the strings on my cloak and let it fall to the ground.

We made love then, on the floor, just like our first time in the kitchen basement at Chinon.

I'd forgotten how good it felt.

CHAPTER TEN

It was still dark when I shook Alice awake. A rendezvous with the abbess alone would have been enough to excite me, but Jean's arrival — and the fact I'd been up all night — had me jittery with nerves.

Alice groaned. 'Oh, my aching back,' she complained.

I was baffled by all of Alice's ailments, which seemed to flare up in random parts of her body in a whimsical and, frankly, inconvenient manner. Between her failing eyesight and her creaking bones, she relied on me more and more. I wondered, guiltily, how I would explain my absence last night.

'Where were you last night?' she whispered, crossly, as though she'd read my mind.

'Nowhere.' I was about to tell a tale, when fortunately the bell rang for Lauds. 'The community will be called for breakfast in another hour, so we'd better hurry,' I urged, as if nothing else mattered. 'The abbess cautioned us not to be seen.' I moved off to wash and dress, humming a tune to discourage conversation.

'Joanna,' Alice whispered, irritably. 'Don't wake Marguerite.'

The water was so icy, it made me gasp. Still, I needed to wash Jean's scent off me, especially before meeting the abbess.

'How can you bear to wash in the cold?' muttered Alice. 'The vanity of youth knows no bounds, I suppose.'

She had risen at a snail's pace and was groping her way awkwardly through the dark.

'Wait! Let me run down for a candle, first.'

'Oh, all right, thank you. Be careful on the stairs.'

I returned with a candle lit from the kitchen fire and placed it by her, but she still needed to steady herself on my arm. She managed to pull her smock over her head. 'I like these plain old smocks,' she remarked, 'so much more practical, and less mortifying for me than the fine costumes we had to wear at Poitiers.' I'd noticed (with dismay) that she'd also started wearing the same flat leather sandals as the nuns. Her feet would become so wide, she'd never again fit into a pair of fashionable slippers. I, by contrast, went about either barefoot, or in dainty, embroidered slippers.

'Let us go down,' she said, but I paused, deliberating between two veils.

'Which one?'

'It hardly matters.'

'Don't be silly, Alice, of *course* it matters! Here,' I decided, 'this one.'

'Let me help you,' she offered. I still hadn't mastered the elusive art of pinning.

She peered at me as she arranged the veil. I was grateful for the darkness hiding my flushed cheeks. She coiled my hair gently into a bun and drew the veil over it, tying it at my shoulder with a little pearl brooch. She left a little hair fringing my face — the way she knew I liked it. I could hardly be expected to wear it like a nun at nineteen.

'How your eyes sparkle in the candlelight,' she murmured. 'You look quite radiant this morning.'

'Come,' I said, quickly, fearful of her scrutiny. 'Oh, I almost forgot.' I reached for my phial of orange oil, which I hoped would disguise any remaining scent of Jean. I dabbed it all over and then offered some to Alice, but she recoiled. I hated how she rejected all these small luxuries. 'Alice, it is only orange oil, not snake's blood!'

'Apologies,' she whispered. 'It is so early and the fragrance is overwhelming…' She smoothed her hands affectionately over my veil. 'There,' she said. 'All ready.'

I flew down the stairwell ahead of her. She descended gingerly — I suppose she couldn't afford to take a tumble, but I wished she'd hurry up. I waited till she'd reached the bottom before snuffing out the candle.

We both peered out into the darkness.

'At least it will break the day's monotony,' I sighed. 'Whatever the tidings.'

'Restless girl. I find the structure of our daily life comforting, punctuated only by the bell's call for meals and offices. It is a veritable sanctuary.'

I allowed her to grip my arm as I led the way, moving deftly through the darkness. By the time we arrived at the abbess's apartment, the sky had lightened a shade and an early bird was twittering an ecstatic solo. The birdsong titillated a rare joy in my heart, making me feel almost giddy. A good omen, I hoped.

The nuns at the door were expecting us, and hurried us inside with conspiratorial discretion. The abbess attended us at once, sneaking us past some ladies sleeping in a curtained bed. When we came to her bedchamber, she cautioned us before we entered, pressing her fingers firmly to her lips. It was all very strange and mysterious.

A heavily veiled woman came towards us, holding a candle. For a moment I thought I was dreaming, for the woman was Marie! A fatigued-looking Marie, her stomach rounded.

'Oh, Marie, you are with child!' I blurted. 'How marvellous. Alice, she is with *child*!'

'Yes, I know,' said Alice, curtly. 'Princess Marie told me of the pregnancy when we last met.'

I was about to complain they'd not shared the happy news with me, but something odd in both their manners stopped me. Neither of them looked happy with the circumstance. Alice's eyes were fixed on Marie's face and she did not look at her rounded belly.

'You kept your word. You came back.' Alice's mood changed as Marie drew her into a hug — awkwardly, due to the princess's bulk. The abbess came between them, urging them to follow her at once. She always seemed most uncomfortable with such emotional displays. I could not understand why they seemed so upset. A baby was a joyous thing, surely?

The abbess pushed the panel behind her bed which led down an underground tunnel to the crypt. We followed, cautiously, listening to the pattering of the nuns' feet just above us, returning from Lauds.

I had been relieved on sight of Marie, as I'd feared that the abbess might have summoned us because of all my recent transgressions. Now it seemed we might be about to learn something of Eleanor. Marie and the abbess walked ahead, so I lagged behind with Alice.

'Is Marie not happy to be pregnant?' I whispered. 'What is wrong?'

'How could she be happy to lie with a man she does not love? It makes me so upset and angry even to think of it,' Alice whispered, through ragged breath.

It was news to me that Marie didn't love her husband, but it *did* explain why she had left him to reside at Poitiers.

Inside the crypt, the abbess illuminated the aqueduct, lending an eerie glow to the marble effigies on the floor and animating the diamond finials on the reliquaries, setting them glinting and winking. To me, it was a sad chamber, housing so many lonesome hearts, forever encaged like trapped songbirds. Hearts that had once cried out in love and loss, now silenced.

'Let us sit,' said the abbess, drawing a chair. 'Princess Marie arrived very early yesterday morning, under cover of darkness with only a few attendants.'

'The rest of my entourage went on to Champagne,' explained Marie, 'and Henry believes I travelled with them. The war between himself and his wife and sons has made him paranoid. And dangerous.'

'Do you have news of Eleanor?' I asked.

'I've not set eyes on Eleanor since,' said Marie, her breath laboured, 'though I travelled all over France in search of her. Please ... I must sit down.'

She almost fell into the chair, her colour high, with perspiration on her brow. New streaks of grey peppered her temples and I felt a wave of pity for her. Alice, always prepared, offered her a cloth to wipe her brow.

'Thank you,' Marie whispered, squeezing her hand.

'Alice always has an endless supply of kerchiefs,' I observed.

'Oh, she is a saviour,' said Marie, warmly.

We waited for Marie to catch her breath. She dabbed her face, neck and eyelids, which I saw were red. Not even a princess could be spared from suffering.

'As you know, I went to Chinon after I left here a few months ago,' she began. 'Despite rumours to the contrary, neither Eleanor nor Henry was in residence there when we arrived. Also, incredibly, nobody would attend us. First, the grooms disappeared, so we had to bed down our own horses. The atmosphere was hostile and sour and clearly we weren't welcome. Then, that evening, the cooks refused to cook for us; the chambermaids wouldn't set fires or air the linens. What hurt most was the musicians, for we had been so close and I thought there was much love between us. However, they were nowhere to be found and I concluded they must be hiding.'

I was appalled at such apparent disloyalty from the musicians whom she'd always nurtured and indulged.

'Typical courtiers, selfish to the core,' muttered Alice.

'I soon discovered they were terrified that Henry would accuse them of harbouring enemies in his absence. So much has changed, my dears, since our Christmases at Chinon. Everyone fled before us, for fear of being accused of treason. It was a terrible blow at first, but afterward, when we went on our way, I learnt it wasn't personal. France was at war and terrible atrocities were happening everywhere, so no man trusted his neighbours, or even his friends.'

'We had no idea that things were that bad,' I said.

'No, neither had I,' said Marie. 'Life is so cloistered, here at the abbey. You are fortunate to be here during these terrible times.'

'What did you do?' I asked.

'After three or four fruitless nights at Chinon, we decided to pack up and leave. Some of my men had overheard a conversation which hinted that Henry had been keeping an important prisoner at Chinon whom he was eager to move elsewhere. They gathered he'd taken the prisoner to one of his other castles, to Rouen or Falaise. So, we decided to try our fortune and travel to Rouen, via Falaise. Of course, it was both an arduous and potentially treacherous undertaking, as Normandy is swarming with Henry's men. I knew that — as Eleanor and Louis's daughter — I too risked arrest. Yet, I was driven by a kind of rage against Henry for daring to take my mother prisoner.'

'How loyal and brave you are!' declared Alice. 'Praise God for preserving you!'

'I was never in danger,' said Marie, quickly. There was new steeliness in her voice I'd never heard at Poitiers.

'How dreadful that you've had to suffer so,' said Alice, impassioned.

'I have not suffered anything like my mother, or, indeed the people of France. I never set eyes on either Henry or Eleanor at Falaise or Rouen. It was on this journey that we witnessed the devastation of the land by both armies — the rebel army, led by Louis and the princes on one side, and Henry and his supporters on the other. Throughout the Loire and Maine, black smoke from the burning vineyards and the stench of rotting farm animals forced us to cover our faces. There were terrible scenes, too, of women, naked and splayed and terrified, famished children everywhere. The dirt tracks were thick with filthy, starving peasants forced to walk for miles to find food and shelter. It's unlikely they'll survive the winter, after the uprooting of their crops. Worst thing was, on sight of our royal banners, they shrank back in terror, fearing for their lives.

'In Normandy, we learnt that Henry's side had been victorious over the rebel army. I must confess, I didn't care which side won, as long as the devastation came to an end. A far cry, indeed, from our court of love…' Marie stopped, her voice choked.

'It grieves me so, to imagine what you have witnessed,' said Alice, taking her hand.

'Such dreadful tidings and no word of Eleanor,' I observed.

'By the time we reached Falaise, a truce had been reached between the two sides,' Marie continued. 'We weren't treated as the enemy, but nor were we welcomed. They informed us that Henry was not in residence and turned us away. Luckily, I remembered that the abbey of St John was nearby. It is dedicated to housing travelling pilgrims and we received great hospitality there.

'The surrounding land had been scorched, but the abbey's land was miraculously spared. They'd preserved the crops and orchard and were helping to feed the town. As it was harvest time, they were grateful to my men for their help in the fields. They shared whatever information they had regarding Henry. It seems that Henry had met with King Louis and the princes, Henry, Richard and Geoffrey, at Gisors, under the ancient elm tree — a traditional meeting place for the kings of England and France. Henry treated his sons most leniently, offering them revenues and allowances, but they had rejected his terms, apparently under Louis's advice. Still, they agreed to maintain peace while they renegotiated the terms of the princes' allowances.'

'So it was all for nothing,' I said. 'Henry has won after all and Eleanor has lost everything.'

'The remarkable thing,' said Marie, 'is just how effectively Henry has managed to keep her whereabouts secret. During our entire sojourn in Normandy, we had no news of Eleanor. One thing is certain, however,' she added, darkly, 'he means to punish her severely for the part she played against him. He is prepared to forgive his sons, but not Eleanor.'

Her ominous words shook me to the core. 'Have all her friends forsaken her?' I uttered, angrily. 'Is no one prepared to rescue her from Henry's clutches? Why don't her sons help? Where is her favourite, Richard, now?'

The abbess cast a disapproving look at me. She disliked such emotional outbursts. Alice placed a warning hand on my arm, but I shrugged it off, irritably.

Marie smiled, sadly. 'Don't forget that Richard is as ignorant of her whereabouts as we are,' she said. 'Henry is really taking great pains to hide her.'

'Eleanor is Henry's wife, Joanna, remember,' remarked the abbess. 'She is considered to be his property.'

'No!' I disagreed, vehemently, to Alice's great alarm. 'Eleanor is no man's property!'

'Please,' Alice interrupted, worried now, for I was quivering with rage. 'This intelligence has upset us all terribly. Let's take a moment to calm ourselves.'

'On our return from Normandy,' Marie continued, 'we heard rumours that Eleanor had been at Chinon the whole time, in a secret tower. This made sense to us, for surely if Henry had moved her, somebody would have sighted her. So, we returned again to Chinon and this time, we found Henry himself in residence, but he denied that he was hiding her and demanded we leave at once. Needless to say, we left the next day. He commanded that we take no detours en route. But I'd made you a promise, and I was determined to keep it.' She bestowed her warmest smile on Alice. 'I knew you would be waiting for intelligence and I couldn't bear the idea of you thinking that I'd forgotten you, or was myself in peril. So, I came back to you as soon as I could.'

The abbess rose. 'I'm afraid I must end the rendezvous now. It's not safe for Marie to remain here; she must return to her husband. She came here at great risk. We must give our thanks and say goodbye.'

'You are not staying…?' Alice's voice rose, upset. 'Surely you could stay for a night, at least?'

'She cannot,' said the abbess, tersely. 'She has orders to return and, besides, she should not be travelling round the country in her condition. It is imperative that nobody learns that she was here, for all our safety. These are dangerous times, as you know. Please say goodbye and I shall escort her back to her men.'

I hugged her first, as Alice stood by awkwardly. I watched as Marie embraced her warmly, but she remained stiff and uttered no words of farewell. Her behaviour was baffling to me, especially as I knew how much she esteemed Marie.

We parted ways abruptly and Alice and I found ourselves outside the church, blinking in the pale, afternoon light, both of us forlorn and frightened.

'Women are so helpless in this world,' sighed Alice. 'I am worried about Marie. Childbirth is dangerous and, at her age, it is irresponsible to put herself in such danger.'

'No,' I disagreed. '*I* am not helpless, and neither is Eleanor. Besides, women give birth all the time, Alice. I do not understand why you are so worried.'

'Despite the bad tidings, I am greatly relieved that Marie has returned unharmed. Of course she must return to her husband — poor Marie — and make the most of it,' she said, obscurely.

'Are you certain she does not love her husband?' I wondered. 'Did she confide in you?'

'Yes, she did. You remember the night we spent together before she left for Chinon? She confided about her failing marriage and the fact she was almost a stranger to her children. She asked me if I'd guessed her secret and I ... I thought she was speaking of a different secret, so I said yes. But I had not guessed that she was pregnant.'

'What secret did you believe she was speaking of, then?' I wondered.

'Oh, nothing, it is of no consequence now...' Alice replied. 'But I could not believe my ears when she told me she was with child. Especially when she had just told me that she did not love her husband. It seemed ... like a betrayal.'

'A betrayal?'

'Of herself... Of her life. I have felt terribly ashamed for the way I reacted to her news that night. I turned away from her — from the *princess*. I turned my back on her. She beseeched me not to be angry, not to judge her, but I *did* judge her, Joanna. I could not understand how she could lie with him that way. When, finally, I turned back to her, I asked her how she could have become pregnant! She laughed at me, which hurt me terribly. She said, "How? Surely you know how. You must understand, Alice, this child is a blessing from God." I confessed that I had hoped she would leave her husband and come to live with us here, at the abbey. Only as I uttered the words, did I realise how mad it must sound. Nothing but my own fancy could have conjured the idea.

'Next morning, if you recall, she departed early, leaving me burning with shame for how I'd reacted. These past months I've been in torment, worried that she failed to return because of me. At least now I know she entertained no such thoughts and all is well between us.'

CHAPTER ELEVEN

At Fontevrault, preparations for Christmas involved fasting for the entire month beforehand. One dark morning, Alice and I walked to breakfast as usual, our cold feet crunching on the clotted snow. At the fountain, we lined up to wash our hands in the freezing water. The abbess and nuns droned a lengthy grace, during which we noted the absence of milk and porridge from the boards. We were then told that we'd be expected to dine on just bread and water till Christmas eve! I took the news badly, and even Alice thought the restrictions unduly harsh at a time of year when we needed more nourishment to keep warm. Our only meat, consisting of fish on Fridays, was to be replaced with nettle, or turnip soup. A sting, indeed. I worried that the poor diet would ruin my health.

Unfortunately, my reserve of pheasant ran out around this time, so apart from some nuts and the odd pot of honey, we'd nothing to supplement our diet and often went to bed with growling stomachs. Huddled under our sheepskin, we reminisced about the winter feasts and entertainments at Poitiers, only serving to madden ourselves into even greater hunger.

Alice said she felt purified after the month's fasting, but I didn't share her feelings. She told me to consider our good fortune, as, due to the war, half of France was starving. She suggested that, when we went hungry, we were in sympathy with our fellow pilgrims, fellow sufferers. Every night, we prayed fervently to God to preserve us all, but especially to preserve Eleanor. Since Marie's visit, a terrible fear pervaded us over the sinister fact that no one had set eyes on Eleanor for months.

Not until Christmas eve did the sanctions lift, with dairy reappearing on the boards at breakfast, to our great relief. After, gifts of food and other items sent by generous patrons were dispersed among us. We rejected most of the non-edible, or ornamental items, in favour of the edible, but we did procure some precious beeswax candles to brighten up our apartment. I managed to stow away some cakes of soap and a sage and salt mixture for cleaning my teeth (Alice's were already blackened beyond repair). That afternoon, Marguerite and Alice amused themselves by making decorations from leftover wool. When it grew too dark to see, they sat up eating ginger cake, listening to myself and Claudine's chatter.

Claudine was a good-natured little thing, though Alice disapproved of the way she gossiped. In fact, she blamed me for encouraging her, for I was the elder, better educated of the two. Alice couldn't understand my curiosity. She said Mama had been the same, always wanting to know everything that was going on.

'I'd just finished making up Lady Mary's bed,' said Claudine, 'so I said to her, I've just got two more beds to do now, Lady Sarah's and Gertrude's, and I'm off on my holidays. Well, Lady Mary's face darkened *so* and she said to Lady Agnes, "It's an absolute disgrace what that Sarah is doing with that young girl right under the Holy Mother's nose. It's the unholiest thing I ever heard of." Well, I wondered what she meant. Then, when I asked, she said that everyone knew that they were carrying on the way a married couple does! Imagine, two ladies, doing that!'

'I cannot believe it!' I exclaimed. 'I've never heard of such a thing, two ladies, in bed together... How unnatural. How *perverse*. I suppose it was naive of me not to have guessed.'

'Joanna, stop! Claudine, that's enough of that,' Alice snapped at us, angrily.

That night, I did what I'd been doing for the past few weeks: I waited for Alice to fall asleep, before sneaking off to Jean. Next day was Christmas day, so we were expected to attend three masses — the first at dawn.

After spending the night with Jean, I jumped up in alarm at the call for Lauds and dressed at lightning speed.

'Let me help you, Alice,' I heard Marguerite offering as I entered.

'Where *were* you? We are going to be late!' Alice chided me. 'Where have you been?'

'I rose early and went out,' I lied.

She peered at me, suspiciously. 'Went out where?'

'Nowhere in particular,' I said, airily.

'Really, I thought you'd grown out of this wandering about at night. Come, Marguerite, let me take your arm.'

Outside the church, a bonfire was spitting and everyone was lighting candles from it. The nuns were in a semicircle around it, their faces bright as children's. The monks were inside the church, chanting sacred songs. The abbess was also inside. It was my first Christmas at the abbey, and I wasn't familiar with the tradition here. I was surprised at how pagan the dawn mass seemed, with all the fire and chanting. As the fire grew fainter, dawn grew brighter and the mass ended in a crescendo of song which might have been moving, only any potential joy was eclipsed by my guilty conscience.

'It is Christmas, after all, Joanna, a time when we should be together. What were you up to last night?' Alice whispered.

'I shall explain later,' I replied, curtly.

'I hope you have not found some boyfriend among the monks or lay brothers?' Alice whispered. 'I have noticed your frequent disappearances at night, how you've been stealing out when you think I am asleep. I'll not tolerate it, Joanna. You cannot place us in danger here. Such behaviour is unacceptable in a holy community like Fontevrault.'

My cheeks were burning, and I could think of no reply.

We did not speak again all morning. My thoughts returned to Jean and how we'd met, that first Christmas, at Chinon. I recalled the Christmases we'd spent at Chinon and how different everything had been back then. I'd have given anything to have that time back now, with Eleanor. I did not miss the bawdy entertainments favoured by Henry at Chinon, nor the tough cuts of venison and fortified wine at the Christmas board. Nor, indeed, did I miss the tension that always ensued between the king and queen, but I missed the freedom. I even missed the *noise*.

After Nore, the community sat down to a modest feast of currant bread and platters of river trout — caught by the monks, apparently — prettily garnished with nettles and frozen flowers. Even on this day, no alcohol was permitted, though we now knew that secret stores would be flowing illicitly in certain quarters. I had such a cache in store for us. I noticed that Alice had not tried to stop my illicit supply of ale. All her life she'd been accustomed to a large cup at breakfast, to fortify her addled nerves, and another cup at night, to help her sleep. Also, ale or wine warmed the blood nicely in this cold weather and balanced the humours, so it was silly of the abbess not to allow it.

Some ladies at a far table were making so much noise I suspected they'd already been imbibing. They'd dressed up in their finery, but were eye-catching for all the wrong reasons with their overly bright costumes and painted faces. Fatigued after my nocturnal activities, their laughter grated on my nerves. Alice too was studying them and clicked her tongue in disapproval.

Lady Sarah, clad in a voluminous gown, practically enfolded little Gertrude who sat, as a pet dog, in her lap.

'I cannot bear to look at that Lady Sarah,' I said, finally breaking our silence.

'Really, Joanna,' Alice whispered, angrily, 'you are hardly in a position to judge! What were you doing all night?'

I was sorry I'd spoken at all!

'I do not want to argue with you on Christmas day,' sighed Alice. 'But I must caution you. If you are, indeed, having *relations* with one of the brothers, we will both be turned out. We have nowhere else to go. Fontevrault is our last place of refuge. Imagine, after all we have endured, if we were to find ourselves in such a predicament?'

'Alice, I am *not* having relations with a *brother*! I am...' I was about to confess about Jean, but suddenly the bells clanged loudly and everyone stood up. The boards were cleared aside for a 'concert', which was only the nuns' carol-singing. How innocent, compared to the rowdy farces and farting clowns of Chinon!

Lady Sarah approached us. I found myself shrinking in her presence.

'How do you do,' she said, extending a hand. 'Lady Alice. I am very friendly with your charming niece, of course. I couldn't help but notice that you have not walked the cloister of late, Joanna. You have been scarce these past few weeks, in fact. You are not ill, I hope?'

A feeling of dread swept over me. 'I assure you I am quite well.'

'Oh, well, in that case, we are having a small gathering at our apartment — nothing elaborate, you can be assured, just some small refreshments in honour of the day. I wondered if you both would care to join us?'

Under normal circumstances, I wouldn't have dared refuse her, but of course I couldn't accept, as Jean would be expecting me. She'd think me terribly rude, but what could I do?

'We cannot accept, Lady Sarah, unfortunately,' I blurted. 'I'm afraid one of our party *is* in fact ill and we must attend to her. It is Lady Marguerite, who lives with us.'

Marguerite had, thankfully, left the board early and she always looked fatigued, or ill. It was the only excuse I could think of. It wasn't exactly a lie, as Marguerite was ill, in a way.

But Lady Sarah's eyes narrowed and she seemed offended, suspicious. If only my manner had been less guilty.

'Excuse me... I'm terribly sorry,' I mumbled, avoiding her gaze.

'It is *I* who am sorry,' she whispered, moving in closer, 'that I have not set eyes on you for weeks and now you refuse to join my party. I hoped to cheer you up, for you must be terribly lonesome, this time of year. You told me of a musician at Chinon you used to spend Christmas with. What was his name? I suppose he would come here, if he could, but it is too dangerous now, with King Henry in residence there... You poor, poor things.'

The way she spoke made me break out in goosebumps. How foolish of me to have mentioned my relations with Jean to such a person!

'Please... Excuse us,' I muttered, taking Alice's arm.

When we reached our apartment, Arthur's little dog, Coo was scratching and sniffing at the wood leading up to the chamber where Jean was hiding.

'That is curious,' Alice observed. 'He has never done that before...'

I must have looked guilty, for she knew something was up. I tried to shoo him away, but the little dog was insistent and crept back, sniffing and scratching excitedly. Alice then noticed that the wood was loose. To her surprise, it lifted off in her hands.

'No, Alice, oh…' I covered my eyes.

Before we could stop him, Coo had dashed up the stairs.

'What is up there? Coo? Coo?'

I just stood by, mutely, as Alice ventured up after him.

She found Jean, of course, sitting on a crate. He would have been expecting me, so he cried out in alarm on sight of her. I entered on her heels, not daring to look at her. The dog had discovered a little pile of bones in the corner and was gnawing on them. My stomach flipped in dread.

'So, *this* is where you've been hiding him. Hello, Jean. You cannot stay,' Alice said, sternly. 'You're putting us all in grave danger.'

'Alice!' I cried. 'Be charitable.'

She sat down wearily. 'You've already stayed too long,' she sighed. 'I should have known! I believe Lady Sarah may suspect something.'

'I was going to tell you, Alice…'

'He has been here for weeks,' she considered. 'Did you come here with Princess Marie?'

Jean nodded. 'Marie didn't want to take me, but I begged. She said once I got here, I was on my own…'

'The abbess does not know?'

'Certainly not. Marie deposited me at the gates before they entered.'

'We must inform the abbess,' said Alice, to my amazement. 'Jean, you have to go. She will arrange safe passage, I am sure.'

'No, Alice! It is Christmas day, how *can* you? What if it was Marie? You'd not make *her* leave!'

'How dare you!' Alice shouted, startling us. Alice rarely lost her temper. 'You will do as I say, both of you.'

'Yes, Alice. Jean thinks Eleanor has been at Chinon all along,' I said, meekly.

'Oh! Did you see her, Jean? Marie said they'd overheard that she'd been taken to Normandy.'

'Yes, Henry purposely deceived the princess — I believe he placed some of his men to give a false report within earshot of Marie's men, to put them off the scent, so to speak.'

'But did you see her?' Alice urged.

'Nobody has seen her, but Henry's guards were overheard talking in the kitchens. That is why Chinon has been so closely protected. I would have come sooner, but the gates were watched and anyone who tried to enter — or to leave — was questioned or arrested. Henry was always paranoid, but his paranoia has become chronic, since his wife and sons betrayed him…'

'How is it you were able to come at all?'

'Henry is winning the war, so the defences have relaxed. That is the only reason that Marie was allowed to leave, I'm convinced. As for me, I was able to slip out of the castle with Marie's entourage, but the journey was frightening, as Henry's men were on the tracks. His spies are everywhere. Since he has been keeping the duchess such a close prisoner, he is vicious with anyone suspected of carrying intelligence. Never has he taken such pains to hide a prisoner — afraid, no doubt, that their sons will attempt a rescue.'

'Afraid of Eleanor's influence over them,' Alice agreed.

'What hope does she have if Henry is winning?' I almost sobbed.

There was a sudden, heavy tread on the stairs which caused us all to freeze.

Too late to hide — I held my breath as the door was pushed open, painfully slowly. To my horror, it was the abbess standing there — panting and angry. She had never come this way before.

'What is going on here?' she asked in amazement, staring from Jean to us.

'Holy Mother...' I started.

'Who is this?'

'Let me introduce the musician, Jean, from Chinon,' I said, defiantly.

The abbess frowned. 'A pleasure, Jean. Had I known you were coming, I'd have invited you for refreshments.' Her tone was angry.

'I am truly sorry, Holy Mother,' I said. 'I was going to tell you. He ... he came here from Chinon with Princess Marie.'

'Well — I am sorry for the intrusion, but one of the ladies came to me after dinner with claims that one of you was seriously ill,' she said. 'I'm relieved to find you in good health, at least.'

Lady Sarah had wanted her to catch us out, no doubt. I was familiar with such trouble-makers from my time at court.

'I am here to assist,' said the abbess, incredibly. 'Even if he is an uninvited guest.'

'He brings news of Eleanor,' I said, quickly. 'He believes she's been imprisoned at Chinon the whole time.'

'I believe she is there still...' said Jean.

'Do you indeed?' the abbess mused. 'Welcome tidings! But you are risking your life bringing them. Has anyone else seen you, apart from these ladies?'

'No, I think not. I managed to slip in on the back of Princess Marie's entourage, but I'm confident I was not sighted.'

'You cannot stay any longer, I'm afraid.'

'That's not fair! He has nowhere else to go,' I said. 'We cannot send him back to Chinon now.'

'Joanna, enough!' Alice hissed.

'Unfortunate fellow,' said the abbess, not unkindly, taking in his dirty hair, his tattered jacket. She cast a suspicious eye over Jean and I. 'You know one another from Chinon.' It wasn't a question. 'You used to spend Christmas there.'

'Yes, Holy Mother,' said Jean. 'I had to see Lady Joanna, for we have spent the last few Christmases together.'

Oh, Jean, keep your foolish mouth shut…

'I see,' the abbess said, frowning. 'Well… We give succour to the needy at Fontevrault, and this boy is certainly needy. He may stay a few days more, until the start of Epiphany. You must employ the utmost discretion; nobody must see him.'

For the next few days, I stayed in the upstairs chamber with Jean, while Alice kept our secret from everyone, including poor Marguerite. I was greatly relieved at the abbess's cool response to the Jean situation, but I feared Alice's wrath, once the time came for his departure and she had time to scold me properly.

The day before Jean's departure, I brought his clothes to Alice to mend. The abbess had written to Princess Marie, who'd offered him a place at her court. A safer option than attempting to return to Chinon, where Henry could have him questioned and arrested.

'He has asked me to go with him,' I confided.

Alice stiffened. 'I thought he might.' She'd stared at the rumpled bedlinen when she'd entered the chamber where Jean was hiding. In the eyes of God — and probably Alice — we were already married. 'What are you going to do?'

I was surprised at the coldness of her tone, even if I'd expected her to be cross. 'Well, I couldn't *possibly* go with him, as you know,' I said, defensively.

'Why not? You'd be poor,' she said, rather cruelly, 'but free.'

I was deeply affronted. Did she care for me so little? 'Go live with Jean in obscurity? Forget all about you? Forget about Eleanor and all that has passed these past few years? I'm not so foolish, Alice, to risk everything we've fought so hard for on account of a man.'

'Then you must tell him so, Joanna,' she advised. 'And put an end to it, once and for all.'

I winced as she said *end*; it was so sad, so final.

The next morning, Alice told me she'd almost fainted when she'd entered the secret chamber after Lauds and found it empty. For a moment, she'd thought I'd left with Jean. So, when I arrived back, just before Prime, my eyes red from crying, she threw her arms around me in relief and gratitude. 'Oh, Joanna, dearest … I could not have borne it, no I could not,' she sobbed, to my secret delight.

So, Jean had departed, after days of great discord and disappointment. I prayed there'd be no repercussions from the visit and that he'd have safe passage to Champagne.

'I was just trying to persuade Marguerite to join us at the board,' Alice said, hoping to distract me from my sorrows. 'Since the place across from us is empty… Would it not liven up our mealtimes nicely?'

'Oh, yes, you must,' I agreed. 'Do join us, Marguerite. Why should we three not eat together, since we sleep together? And we are friends, are we not?'

Marguerite's dark cheeks flushed darker.

'Oh, come, Marguerite, say yes!' I pleaded, tears in my eyes. I went to her, taking her hands. 'Please join us. I need something good to happen, or I'll go mad! It's nothing but doom and gloom all the time. I need some change — or I shall die!' I was barely holding back my tears.

'Are you ... all right?' she wondered, gently.

'Oh, yes, of course. I am not like you, Marguerite, I do not feel so deeply...' The tears came gushing forth, startling the poor thing. 'You...' I sobbed. 'You have a purer heart than I, for in the end, I chose not to elope and live a life of poverty. You were willing to risk everything for Albert! I thought my heart was steadfast, but I was wrong. What do I have to boast of now? Soon my looks will fade and I shall grow embittered living in this ... tomb of a place. My heart will shrivel up like a black prune. Unworthy of preservation even in an old shoe box!'

Alice turned away to hide her smile. She refrained from uttering whatever she was thinking.

They soaked some linen cloths in lavender water and bathed my hot forehead. Alice combed out my hair and arranged it under my veil. All the time, she spoke soothingly about winter's end and the start of the New Year, with a whole new world of possibility.

'In truth, this year couldn't have been any worse,' I sniffed.

'The war is ending now,' she said, 'and things should return to normal. Henry cannot stay in France forever, but will be expected to return to his kingdom in England. Perhaps — when he returns — Eleanor will be released. We must hope and pray for such an outcome.'

I was surprised. 'You really think Henry will return to England?' I asked.

'He has to,' she said, stoutly. 'It's only a matter of time.'

CHAPTER TWELVE

Spring arrived with all the usual fanfare of flowers and glistening leaves, but still no news of Eleanor. There was certainly no talk of her release, nor any possibility of her return to Poitiers. However, some restrictions had been relaxed and travel was once again allowed between castles.

I had managed to persuade the abbess to give me a patch of ground to grow plants which could be used for making dyes. Mottled grasses and ochres, camouflage for the hunting seasons. Brother Ambrose had gladly given up some land beside the physic garden past the beehives.

'You see, Joanna,' Alice remarked, 'the Holy Mother is not as unreasonable as you might think.'

It bothered her that I disliked the abbess. I suppose she thought me unwholesome.

'Oh, I don't think she's unreasonable,' I said, breezily. 'She is more capable of making quick, clever decisions than anyone I know. I just wish she would show some humanity. She is at all times removed and cold. But I wouldn't expect you to share my feelings, Alice, for you rarely show your true feelings. I imagine you admire the abbess enormously...'

My little speech annoyed her, though she did not deny she admired the abbess.

'You have no reason to dislike her,' she said, coldly. 'She could have thrown us both out after the Jean affair. Did she not treat him — and us — with the greatest sympathy?'

'Oh, I think she was most pragmatic, as always, in her dealing. She needed the extra time she granted him in order to secure a place for him at Marie's estate.'

She thought the abbess an impressive, fair woman and could not understand my criticism. She hoped the small concession of the garden plot would occasion a truce between us.

In contrast to my dislike of the abbess, I'd taken an intense liking to Marguerite, who was curled up on the bed, as usual. I'd never before been so drawn to another woman. The age difference was not as wide as it appeared at first. Poor Marguerite was only in her late twenties, or early thirties, despite her appearance.

My knees were tucked up under me, on the little stool, as I gazed at her adoringly. I was attempting to persuade her to help me sow my plot, but she would not be persuaded. The idea of planting a garden was too pleasurable, too rewarding. Marguerite was only interested in suffering.

'I'll help you, if I may?' Alice offered, to my great surprise.

'Oh, goodness, of course you may! Thank you, Alice, that would be wonderful. I thought with your eyesight ... but many hands make lighter work, as the Holy Mother says.' I rolled my eyes. 'Now, perhaps you can help me to persuade Marguerite.'

The prospect of a change from sewing vestments all day made Alice quite cheerful; the close needlework was becoming too great a strain on her eyes. However, the gardening proved more challenging than she'd expected and by the first evening, I regretted ever accepting her offer, as she complained and moaned.

After dinner, while Claudine gave me my bath, Alice lay groaning on the bed, rubbing her aching muscles.

'Really, Alice,' I remarked, eventually. 'I did almost all the work, anyway! All you did was plant that single row of meadowsweet. I believe you're dissembling because you're too lazy to return tomorrow.'

'I am not dissembling,' she retorted. 'I am indeed in pain! I suppose I can't expect any sympathy from either of you. What would you know about ageing?'

'If you don't want to do the gardening, that's fine. I can do it myself.'

'I'd help you, Joanna,' said Claudine, 'but I've to tend to the ladies over yonder. They're preparing to travel to Collioure, for the summer... I wish I could work in the garden with you instead, with this fine weather.'

'Wait!' I must have made a big splash, for Claudine cried out. 'Forgive me, Claudine, but did you say the ladies were going to *Collioure*? Alice? Did you hear that? Why, that's where Marguerite is from...'

Just then, footsteps on the stairs alerted us to Marguerite's arrival back from the refectory.

'Hush! We must change the subject,' I said quickly.

In bed, Alice complained and chided again. 'Really, Joanna, you've no idea what it is to grow old. Every single bone aches after today.'

'I told you, Alice, you need not come again tomorrow.'

'Well... I *wish* I could be of more help...'

'Where does it hurt most?' Marguerite's gentle voice asked.

'Oh, all around my neck ... my shoulders ... this point in my back.'

'Tomorrow, I'll prepare a hot rub that should help to ease the pain,' she suggested. 'I shall come with you as far as the physic garden, Joanna, for I'll need to find the right herbs to make the balm. I made such a rub before ... for Alba.'

The next morning the three of us went to the garden. Alice sat awkwardly on some moss, while I accompanied Marguerite as she wandered around the physic garden looking for herbs. She recognised — and named — every single plant and seemed immensely knowledgeable about the properties of each. It was the only time I'd seen her absorbed and relaxed, and I was amazed at the transformation. By this light, she seemed youthful.

'Why, Marguerite, you belong here!' I declared. 'How well you seem, like a butterfly among the flowers. If I were you, I'd come here every day.'

'But I don't deserve to be well.' She shook her head, sadly. 'You know I don't, Joanna.'

'How foolish people are,' I said. 'Wait till you are Alice's age, with all her irksome woes.'

Alice scowled at me. 'Thank you, Joanna. She is right, though, in a way. Life is short, Marguerite. Don't throw away what little pleasure there is. It is all over far too quickly.'

Marguerite smiled — the rarest of smiles that caught my breath! She stretched herself out luxuriously in the sun. 'I had forgotten how pleasurable it is to be out of doors. Alba taught me how to grow things, so I have her to thank.'

'Then, perhaps you could teach Joanna,' Alice suggested. 'I'm sure Alba would wish for you to pass on the knowledge and Joanna is keen to learn.'

That did the trick!

Thankfully, Alice returned to the apartment alone.

Evening's darkness was falling, and Alice had just lit the candles when we returned. Apart from a short break for meals, we'd worked all day and were happily fatigued.

'My goodness, you've caught the sun!' Alice remarked. She was stretched out, leafing through a pretty flower book that Marie had sent her. In it was a note with her new baby's name — Alice! A greater compliment she could not have received.

She took out an embroidered blanket she was working on for baby Alice — all gentle buttercups and harebells against a delicate pattern of pale sage leaves. An enchanting sunset transformed our dark apartment into a temporary golden shrine. 'What a glorious evening,' Alice sighed. 'At this moment, I believe I would be happy to live here at Fontevrault forever.'

'Heavens, Alice, do not say such a thing, in case it comes to pass,' I groaned.

I took the ginger and turmeric roots we'd collected to the kitchen to brew, while Marguerite smashed, ground and pressed almonds into oil. After she'd blended the oil with the spices, she rubbed it gently into Alice's shoulders, neck and back. Her tender touch brought tears to Alice's eyes.

When Alice and I said our prayers, later, we thanked God for bringing us Marguerite, for her nature was good and true — though wounded — and she was a blessing to us both. I was glad that she helped to disperse the tension between us.

The days grew longer and we spent the sunlit evenings in the garden, weeding and watering. We worked all through spring, Marguerite counselling on the best plants and flowers for dyeing. At one end, carrots, onions, beetroot and yarrow were shooting. Flowers were promising to burst out into varieties of marigolds, sunflowers, goldenrod, camelias, roses, hibiscus. We'd planted vines and blueberries on trellises along the orchard walls and set lavender, clover and meadowsweet in all the spaces in between, for Ambrose's bees.

One lapis-domed day, the sky alive with skittish young swallows, a group of us (Alice included) set out with baskets to pick some plants for dyeing. Making grass-coloured dye for camouflage was the first task at hand. Saffron and blood-rose or berry-crimson would come later in the summer, to dye linen thread for embroidery.

Sister Francine was with us, as well as Heloise and a few other nuns. Brother Ambrose even deigned to join us — secretly impressed with the crop. Wearing thick gloves, Alice and I tackled the stinging nettles considered such a pest in general, but particularly useful for making grass-coloured dye. We could hear Marguerite instructing the others — her vow of silence temporarily abandoned. 'You may pick the leaves of the goldenrods, but please don't disturb the blooms.'

'It's done Marguerite the world of good to be out of doors,' Alice remarked. 'Well done, Joanna.' I raised an eyebrow. 'Yes, you *do* deserve the praise.' She smiled.

I frowned, cutters in hand. 'I thought she was helping me.'

'She is. But you can tell she's in her element. This is good for her — helps her forget her troubles.'

'Ah, but she'll never forget her troubles,' I said, woefully. 'She speaks of Albert and Alba all the time — even while she works. It is so tiresome! Whenever I attempt to change the subject, she draws the conversation back to them, as if she cares for nothing else.'

'Yes, it's disturbing. Poor thing is haunted by her memories.'

'Alice.' I drew closer. 'I was thinking... Claudine mentioned that those ladies are going to Collioure for the summer. What if we could get a letter to Alba? If she's still alive, then maybe she'd be glad to hear from Marguerite and it could help her to heal, if they were to meet again.'

'But how would you get in touch with Alba? Remember, she doesn't live in Collioure, but in a rural village in the hills. I doubt the ladies would travel there...'

'No, of course not, but I've a plan. Remember the captain that Marguerite mentioned and his ship, *Abraham*? Marguerite said he knew Albert's village, and she'd hoped he could take her there all those years ago when her brother-in-law had her followed. What if we got our ladies to take a letter to the captain? He could bring it to Alba. I know it's a faraway target — but we could at least try. We mustn't let on to Marguerite that we're attempting to contact Alba, in case it doesn't work out and the strain of it is too much for her. That way, we've lost nothing if nothing comes of it.'

'I'm not sure that we should meddle in Marguerite's affairs,' Alice said, doubtfully.

'Oh, by God's teeth, Alice, must you always be so fearful and cautious? Think about it. Marguerite is almost as heartbroken over Alba as losing Albert. She believes Alba despises her for destroying her son, but what if she doesn't? What if Alba is just as heartbroken at losing Marguerite? She is such a wonderful person, I can imagine that Alba must grieve her as much as her son, can't you? She was like her daughter, after all. Don't you see, we *must* get to the bottom of this, before it's too late. Imagine if we could bring them together? It may already be too late, for perhaps Alba is dead, or the captain is dead, or any number of people may be dead… But at least we can *try*!'

Alice stared at me, my words lingering between us. 'My goodness,' she observed. 'You are becoming a person to be reckoned with! I shall support your scheme. Tell me what to do.'

'Don't worry, I'll take care of it.'

I had poached some rabbit, which I used to bribe the cook, who let me use her copper pans to heat the plants overnight over a low fire. Claudine kept an eye on them to see they didn't boil or burn. The nuns had collected a number of old woollen tunics that could be dipped in dye.

By now, we were all invested in the enterprise and waited eagerly for the results. I was disappointed with the colour, which turned out to be more a faint stain than the rich, verdant green I'd been hoping for. Still, it was a start and the very next day, a group of us ladies gathered, wearing the grass-stained tunics. We stood around, admiring our handiwork. They praised my enterprising spirit, and I was certain Eleanor would have been proud! Lady Sarah — unsurprisingly — was not among the group, but some of her friends attended.

Later that evening, I drew Alice aside. I'd broached the subject of Marguerite and asked the ladies whether they'd carry a letter to Collioure on her behalf. They'd seemed eager to help, but were also concerned, on account of Lady Sarah — whose permission they'd have to seek. Of course she was heading the party to Collioure.

'Well…' Alice said, gloomily. 'That ruins that plan. She'd never agree to help us, I'm afraid. Still, I don't see why one of the other ladies could not be persuaded to take it?'

'They are all too afraid of her,' I said. 'But I am not afraid! Not anymore. I shall speak to her myself.'

Alice knew that I would not be dissuaded, so she just sighed heavily and said, 'I'll pray for you.'

CHAPTER THIRTEEN

After breakfast, I borrowed Marguerite's prayerbook and went to the cloisters. I kept an eye out and soon enough I spotted Lady Sarah walking with Geraldine. I nodded to her, but she ignored me, bending instead to whisper something to Geraldine. I'd underestimated Sarah's height and poise, which made me shrink inside. I almost lost my resolve, but the thought of Marguerite bolstered my courage.

'Lady Sarah, I'd like a word, please,' I whispered.

She drew herself up taller still and rested her stone-cold eyes on me. 'I am occupied, as you see,' she drawled, half smiling.

'Any time you are free,' I said, politely. My heart was beating furiously.

'Well,' she said. 'We are planning a picnic this afternoon; perhaps you would care to join us?'

Some passing nuns cast us disapproving looks. Cloisters were for prayer, not conversation.

'Certainly,' I whispered. 'Thank you!'

'We'll be at the olive grove at the bell's call for Sext,' she said.

Back in the tower kitchen when I told Cook I was going on a picnic with Sarah, she cast her eyes up to heaven, but then she threw together some goat's cheese pastries without my even asking. She folded them in paper, along with a bunch of grapes.

Fearful, but determined, I arrived at the olive grove just on the stroke of twelve.

'Cheer up, Joanna, dear. That long face does nothing for your looks!' Sarah said, aggressively. She was in her habitual, antagonistic mood.

'Oh, I'm just a little tired!' I lied.

We'd soon left the olive grove behind, veering across the park, towards the forest, just before the entrance to the orchard. Brother Ambrose was a distant speck, but his voice drifted on the breeze, chastising the goats for their latest crime, I suspected. I glanced behind me, longingly, wishing I could spend the afternoon in the garden. Or hunting.

'Oh, I forgot something!' I said. 'I'll have to go back... I'll catch up.'

Sarah frowned. 'We have everything we need,' she said. 'Why bother wasting time?'

'I'll be back in a moment,' I insisted and ran off.

Back at the apartment, I grabbed my knife, concealing it in my pocket. On my way out, I spotted Arthur wheeling a pile of vegetables into the kitchen.

'Arthur,' I called — as an afterthought. 'Come here. I have a task for you, an important one — leave those down.'

He hesitated, before laying down his load.

'Cook won't mind it,' I said, 'if you come with me. She knows where I am going.'

'Oh, all right,' he said, uncertainly.

'I am going on a picnic with two ladies and I need to borrow you. Can you follow us, but at a distance, so you can see and hear what is said? You must keep yourself hidden at all times, Arthur, am I clear? Only if I call you should you reveal yourself. Do you understand?'

'Yes, Joanna,' he said, willingly.

A smart boy, was Arthur. Eager to please, too. I grabbed a handful of raisins. 'Dried fruit!' I said, cheerfully, when I caught up with them.

Sarah gave me a scalding look.

I followed them into the forest, deeper than I'd ever dared go alone. I was so glad I'd thought to bring my knife.

'Over here, my pretty ones,' said Sarah, unfolding a rug. She patted a spot each side of her and we both sat down like obedient pets. It felt far too close and uncomfortable.

We laid out the edibles and removed our veils.

'You are beautiful girls,' she began. 'Look at each other.'

We did as we were told — Geraldine regarded me sulkily and I almost laughed out loud.

'There's nobody here but us,' Sarah said. 'You may kiss each other, if you like. I don't mind.'

It was clearly an order. We avoided eye contact.

'Go on,' she said, more forcefully. 'Kiss each other. You must be starved for it. Do it!'

Geraldine bent forward suddenly and pecked my lips with hers. Again, I almost laughed.

'You are smiling, Joanna, eh?' said Sarah. 'You'd like more of that, wouldn't you? Perhaps you'd like *me* to kiss you, no? Like this, maybe.'

She planted her mouth on mine and pinned me with her strong arms. My whole body clenched. I felt heat and wet in my mouth. I managed to pull away, and wiped my mouth, disgusted.

'There,' she said. 'You liked that, didn't you? I wondered if you liked me, or if you were just pretending.'

I stared at her with contempt. 'On the contrary,' I said. *I detest you.* 'I thought I made it clear before that I don't want anything like that between us. What you have with Geraldine, that is your business. I, on the other hand. I. Don't. Want. That.'

'Well, my dear Joanna, I don't think you know *what* you want! Maybe you're still thinking of the musician you left behind.'

'Oh, I know what I want,' I said. Inside I was shaking, but I summoned all my willpower to appear cool. 'I want to ask you a favour. I heard that you were travelling to Collioure in the summer and I want you to carry a letter for me to a woman, an esteemed friend of Lady Marguerite, with whom I live.'

Her eyes had narrowed in that calculating way of hers, a shrewd look replacing the sensuous one of a moment ago.

'I ask this of *you*, Sarah, for you are the only one with the power and connections to carry it out.' I hoped to appeal to her vanity. 'It's just a simple task, but it would mean the world to my friend.'

'This woman — in Collioure — she is high-born, like your friend?'

'No, she is a peasant woman who was like a mother to Lady Marguerite. She lives not in Collioure, but in a village in the surrounding hills. There is a captain in Collioure harbour, though; I believe he would deliver the letter to her... Or, failing that, Marguerite's sister.'

Sarah was shaking her head. 'A peasant woman living in a mountain village? What possible good could come of renewing such a connection?'

'Believe me,' I said, my tone pleading now. '*Much* good could come of it. If you only knew the suffering it has caused both of them, to be parted...'

'A romantic notion, my dear Joanna, but mistakenly so, I'm sure. I speak from experience. You are still only a girl, so you don't know any better.'

'Please,' I begged. 'Say you will do it?'

'Well... What favour would you grant me, in return?' At this, she lunged at me so suddenly I gasped.

I twisted about to free myself, but she was too strong. Her hands moved under my smock, against my bare thighs.

I remembered my knife and I pulled it out on her. 'Stop mauling me!' I hissed, through gritted teeth.

She drew back, and paled on sight of the knife.

Geraldine took off running.

'Your girlfriend has deserted you,' I said. 'I'm sure you forced her, as you tried to force me.'

'You little fool,' she said. 'Don't you realise I could hand you over to King Henry's men in an instant, if I chose to? You are right about one thing: I am powerful and I do have connections. I know about your friendship with Princess Marie, and I know you have spies at Chinon. I suspect — as Henry will suspect — that you and your aunt are using your contacts to plot Eleanor's escape. Do you have any idea what I could do to you?'

'Do *you* have any idea what *I* could do to *you*?' I said, pressing the knife against her throat. I enjoyed the look of fear in her cold eyes. 'You touched me and wanted me to lay with you. What would the abbess say, if she knew? Do you think she would let you stay another day at Fontevrault? What is the punishment for such a crime, I wonder? I don't know, exactly, but we both know it must be severe.'

'Who would believe you?' she said. 'Your word against mine? Believe me, Geraldine would not speak against me. She *loves* me. And your reputation has preceded you, Joanna.' She leaned in close. 'I hear you are no longer chaste.'

I was stunned and thrown off guard. She tried to grab the knife and we had a scuffle.

'Arthur! Arthur, are you there?' I called, desperately.

Little Arthur came running from his hiding place, ready and willing to fight, bless him.

'You!' he cried. 'Release Lady Joanna!'

Startled and confused, Sarah pulled away, guiltily.

'He was witness to everything, weren't you, Arthur?' I said, crying now. 'He can prove you tried to kiss me. Prove what you said about turning us over to Henry. Can't you, Arthur?'

'I heard everything,' he confirmed.

'Ha! Children, both of you... You'd better not breathe a word against me. I was only joking, don't you see? Play acting, all of it, just for fun...'

'So, we are agreed then,' I said. 'You'll carry the letter to Collioure, in exchange for my silence?'

I'd cornered her and she knew it.

She shrugged. 'I don't mind carrying your letter,' she said, 'so long as it's not out of my way.'

'I owe you, Arthur,' I said, as we walked back together. 'If there's anything I can do for you, just let me know. Is there anything you need?'

He blushed furiously, shook his head, and cleared his throat. 'All those nice meals we've had since you've arrived — we had nothing like that before, and we never talked in the kitchen the way we do now...' His words warmed my heart. 'Besides,' he continued, 'that Lady Sarah has always been mean to me and Claudine. She made me cry before, when I was young.'

I smiled, for Arthur couldn't have been more than ten or eleven.

'How came you to live at Fontevrault, Arthur?' I asked.

'Oh, my house burnt down and Mam and Dad died,' he said, matter-of-fact. 'I'd nowhere else to go.'

'Do you ... want to be a monk?'

'Oh, no! I want to get married and have a family of my own. I want that more than anything. I'm to learn to cook here first, I hope.'

'Oh!' It seemed an ambitious plan for one so young. 'Do you like it here?' I asked. 'I see how Cook orders you around all the time, and you're always labouring at something. Not much of a childhood, is it?'

'Childhood? Lost that anyway, when my family died. Cook is all right. And the abbess is so very kind to me,' he added, grinning.

I was surprised. 'You don't have to say that, you know,' I said. 'You can trust me, Arthur. I'd never say anything back to the abbess or anyone else.'

It was his turn to be surprised. 'No, truly, the abbess is really kind to me. When I came here I had nothing, and it was she who gave me Coo, as a puppy. It was her idea. She asked if I'd like to live in the monk's house as a brother, but when I asked her if brothers could marry, she laughed. She said she'd find another place for me and she did!'

So young, I thought, *yet sure of what he wants.* At nineteen, I was still unsure if I wanted to be a wife, or have a family. To have freedom, yes! To live in a grand estate and have beautiful things, oh yes! But, to be a wife? I thought of Jean and winced with guilt. I was grieved after he'd left, but I'd also been relieved, for I'd felt like I was suffocating. I'd wanted to be free...

That evening, at sunset, I went to my plot. Buds were appearing on the rose bushes and I stroked them tenderly, guessing at the colours of the blooms. I noted that the earth beneath them had been enriched with horse manure — probably by Brother Ambrose, or Marguerite. I'd thrown myself into the project as a distraction from Jean and the confusion I'd felt on his departure.

The bell rang for Vespers. I leant back against the wall to watch the slow procession to the church, as the lamps were lit, one by one, casting gentle light on the fading evening. When

I'd first come here, I'd hated the bell's forlorn punctuation of the days. Now, I found the sound both comforting and a useful reminder of the time. When Jean was here, it had become an invaluable warning of who would be where and when.

I'd been relieved when Jean was finally discovered. The prolonged secrecy had been tearing at my nerves, and the relationship itself was too intense, in the end.

If that's what being married feels like, I want no part in it!

It was frustrating spending all my days with him, and his habits had begun to vex me. But even now, my body craved his touch. I feared I must be wicked, to enjoy the love act so much, while feeling so detached. When we'd first met, we'd been friends and I'd badly needed a friend. I'd made better friends over the past year at Fontevrault than I had during all my years at court, I realised. Poor Jean. He'd *begged* me to go with him, to marry him. His pleas had only irritated me further. As he admitted, he had nothing to offer me except his love. For Marguerite, Albert's love was riches enough, but when I searched my heart... It wasn't enough for me.

I won a rare smile from Alice that evening when I said, 'I don't think Lady Sarah will bother us again.'

'Did she agree to take the letter?'

'She did.'

'Of course, you'll have to ask the abbess's permission,' she said.

I scowled; I hadn't thought of that!

.

CHAPTER FOURTEEN

The next morning, I steadied myself to wait in line for the abbess. She was bestowing a blessing on a laywoman I recognised from the stables. The woman's eyes were shut, her lips moving in prayer, while the abbess muttered in Latin, a stout palm resting on the woman's crown. When my turn came, the abbess gazed at me intensely, solemnly. I'd avoided her since Jean's departure, so perhaps her curiosity was aroused.

'Holy Mother,' I began. 'Forgive my intrusion. I have an urgent request to make.'

'No intrusion,' she said, but I thought I caught a flicker of interest in her eyes.

She listened impassively as I told her my plan to help Marguerite. I found myself growing breathless and, as I spoke, I grew less confident and had that feeling of shrinking with insignificance in her presence.

'I see,' was all she said.

'I've already found some ladies willing to take the letter to Collioure next month,' I added. 'However, I… We won't do anything without your blessing.'

Was that a little smile? I squirmed under her scrutiny. I meant I wouldn't do anything further to vex her, after the Jean affair…

'Alice approves the plan?' she asked.

'Oh, yes!' I said, emphatically.

'Something needs to be done about the woman,' she muttered, to herself.

Does she mean about me, or Marguerite? I wondered anxiously.

'This was your idea, Joanna?'

I was afraid to admit to it, but more afraid to lie. I nodded.

'I see. Then see that you carry it through properly. Do you have parchment and ink to pen the letter?'

I did not.

'Go to the monk's house this afternoon,' she said. 'Tell them I sent you for the materials.'

'Yes, Holy Mother, thank you!'

I turned to flee.

'Joanna? Bring the finished letter for me to look over and amend, if needs be.'

I waited till after Terce to go to the monks' house. I freshened up with rosewater, chose a light, summery veil to wear over my hair and dotted my cheeks and lips with cherry paste. I applied a little orange oil to my pulses, to boost my mood. My spirits were oddly low, despite the sunny day and the positive response from the abbess. Since Jean's departure, I'd been gloomy and easily upset.

I hoped I hadn't looked too irritated when she'd asked to look over the letter, but yet again, she'd laid claim to the one thing that was mine. I'd had to bite my tongue to refrain from asking why *she* had not written the letter to Alba. She was the only other person who knew Marguerite's awful story. The ugly thought occurred to me that Marguerite's family must have been donating richly to the abbey, to house her there... Perhaps the abbess didn't want to lose their patronage? All holiness aside, the Holy Mother's greatest interest was in building up the treasury...

I'd seen Brother John only fleetingly since our meeting in winter. I'd asked the cook to deal with his deliveries, as I'd wished to avoid him, after all. I felt only a faint interest now at the prospect of seeing him again.

The same ancient, blind monk as before opened the door. He cupped my hands warmly and smiled his toothless smile, his white orbs unblinking, as he listened to my request. I was admitted directly and led to the scriptorium.

Brother John appeared, looking taller than I'd remembered, his dark eyes lingering on my face. He greeted me more warmly than I deserved, but I remained aloof — I was not in the mood for flirting. I was offered mint tea with honey and an exquisite ginger bread. I noticed with amusement that the scribes kept sneaking glances my way, distracted from their work.

I couldn't help gazing about at the sumptuous arrangements of dried flowers hanging from pegs in the stone walls, like the floral tapestries that had decorated the tower at Poitiers. My own gardening enterprise seemed paltry by comparison. The fragrance in the chamber was almost overwhelming and the scribes with their ink-stained fingers reeked of it, not to mention the animal stink off the parchments.

'They work from after Matins until Vespers every day,' proffered John.

So, they worked from dawn until dusk! 'Then they work almost as hard as I do in the stables,' I joked. 'What kind of manuscripts...?'

'Books of Hours, mainly, commissioned by the nobility.' John pointed out the shelves of finished manuscripts. 'Fontevrault books are in high demand for the quality of the illustrations. Only at Fontevrault do they make such variable shades, like the palatinate, the cyan and the turquoise you see here.'

'How do they make these shades?'

'Crushed gemstones such as lapis lazuli, cactus plants… Look there.' He pointed to a flowering cactus. 'Many exotic plants are gifted to the abbey by crusaders, as thanksgiving for their safe return.'

'They must be very wealthy, the people who commission these books.'

A shadow crossed his brow. 'Eleanor of Aquitaine commissioned one, just before…' He blinked, unable to finish, and cast his eyes away. *Before her disappearance…* 'It was to be a gift, I believe, for her daughter.'

A gift for Marie, to acknowledge her unfailing support. Tears came to my eyes.

'She is the most impressive woman I have ever met,' he said. 'So well educated. You remind me of her.'

I recognised that he was being sincere, not just attempting to flirt. I was flattered, but uncomfortable. 'Oh! I wish you would tell my aunt,' I smiled, blushing. 'She worries over my learning, especially my Latin, which I find especially irksome…'

Poor Alice, who'd never had an opportunity to learn letters or languages, was deeply disappointed by my lack of learning. Still, I was grateful that both she and Eleanor had insisted that I persevere, until I could read and write at least.

'Eleanor, though, is the most well educated person I know,' I confirmed. 'Her father recognised her insatiable appetite for learning from a young age and nurtured it, they say. He gave her an education equal to any highborn son and more, for he took her with him on his travels round the duchy when she was only a child.'

'It must have been a great privilege to attend such a person,' John said.

'Oh, you've no idea!' Tears caught in my throat. 'She ... understands the value of women and promotes us at all times into bettering ourselves and becoming independent.'

'That is a great gift to have bestowed on you,' he said. 'I see her mark on you. You have suffered a great loss,' he added, most gently.

It was the first time anyone had said this to me. I couldn't stop the tears rolling down my cheeks.

'Ah, Joanna, I apologise, I did not mean to upset you...' he said, concerned. 'Please ... sit over here.' He led me to a quiet closet, hidden from the scribes. He gave me a linen cloth to dry my eyes and left me a moment, only to return with more tea. 'I've brought the writing materials you requested,' he said, setting them down.

'I must go,' I said, not wishing to be alone with him.

'Please do not rush off,' he said. 'I shall leave you to drink your tea in peace.'

'Thank you.'

'You never received me when I called at the tower kitchen,' he said. 'I asked for you every time, but the cook said you were busy...'

I squirmed. 'I'm sorry... I could not.'

'I understand,' he said, though I sensed that he did not. 'I shall leave you now. Please don't worry about anything... I apologise for making you cry. Take as long as you like to compose yourself. I apologise again. Goodbye.'

He'd been so kind, I was embarrassed.

'John?' I called after him. 'I apologise too. Perhaps I shall see you next time, when you call.'

His face brightened into a smile.

I took the parchment, feather quill and ink back to the apartment which, thankfully, was empty at this time of day. I didn't have a writing tablet, but I found the pretty flower book from Marie made a decent substitute. I inspected what the monks had given me — there was both black and lapis ink — the latter normally used for illustration. They'd placed the parchment leaves in a small, leatherbound cover for protection. They'd also given me some burgundy wax and a stamp for the seal. I ran my fingers over the silky parchment, admiring its unblemished smoothness.

I knew I'd better be careful not to make mistakes that would cause me to blot or even ruin it. I began writing, *Dear Alba ...* and stopped. It struck me for the first time that Alba wouldn't be able to read! Would the captain of the *Abraham* have letters? Probably not. The best person to convey the letter would therefore be Marguerite's sister, Gwen, rather than the captain. I closed my eyes. *I will persevere. This letter will reach Alba.*

Now, what to say? I tickled my face with the feather quill. If only Eleanor were here, she'd know exactly how to word it. John's compliment drifted into my mind.

You remind me of her... I see her mark on you.

How extraordinarily perceptive of him! Perhaps he wasn't just interested in me for my pretty face, after all. Had he guessed that Eleanor was my heroine, the person I most admired in the world? *The only person I've ever looked up to.*

After my cry, I felt lighter and less gloomy than I had these past months. I couldn't rid myself of the thought of those awful soldiers who'd taken Eleanor — bound her slender wrists, weighted her neck with irons, like jesses and anklets on a hooded falcon. That diplomatic head, that sparkling wit, that bright little girl who'd travelled round Aquitaine freely with her father.

Where is she now?

Perhaps in Chinon, as Jean had said, but what if she'd been moved? *What was Henry planning to do with her?*

Her own husband had made a prisoner of that precocious little girl who'd grown up to rule Aquitaine. The woman who'd turned Poitiers into a court of such sophistication that it was renowned throughout Christendom... How had this been allowed to happen? How could her sons allow it? Why all the secrecy over her whereabouts?

John had seemed to understand my grief in a way that nobody else had — not even Jean. I tensed, thinking of the night before Jean had left.

'Joanna, come away with me,' he'd pleaded, over and over. 'Be my wife. I can get a position as musician in some minor court. If we're married, we'll be allowed to share an apartment. I'll provide as best as I can for you and our children. You'll not have to work or hunt anymore...'

The idea of not hunting was abhorrent to me. 'Jean, believe it or not, I want more out of life than that!' I'd told him.

He had misunderstood me. 'I know you'll not have the fine things you were accustomed to before,' he said, 'but surely it wouldn't matter? Surely it would be better than living here, like a nun with all these women? Having to scrimp and scrounge for your basic nourishment? I could provide more than that...'

'I don't *want* you to provide for me!' I'd snapped. 'I want to run after my meat myself!'

'What? How can you be so selfish, Joanna? I risked everything to come here and now you are rejecting me? I'm offering you all that I am and you tell me... You tell me *what?*'

'How typical of a man to believe that he's all a woman needs to be fulfilled.'

'Why are you speaking of "men" and "women" in such terms, when I refer only to *us*? We are friends and equals. It is not unreasonable, I think, to suggest that if we love each other enough, our love will sustain us. I'm only saying that I'll care for you and our children, as I hope you'll care for me. What is wrong with that?'

I could find no counter argument. I had turned away, to hide my confusion.

'Joanna... Please don't turn away from me. It is *I*, Jean. Do not torment me with this uncertainty. Either come with me now, or we must say goodbye.'

'But *why*? When we were at Chinon, we said that we didn't need to prove our love by getting married like other people. You said you'd be content just to know that I am yours.'

'Times have changed, Joanna. Our country is at war. Once I leave here, I'll not be allowed to return — the abbess has made that clear. Unless you come with me, we may never see each other again.'

I had felt a panic rising. How could I just leave everything behind? Yet, a few weeks back, I'd wanted to escape with Jean — but that was when I thought we could return to Poitiers.

'*Are* you mine, Joanna?'

'I belong to no man!' I said.

His eyes flashed with hurt surprise. 'Well ... I am yours,' he said, quietly.

'Why are you forcing me to make this impossible choice?' I said. 'You are only going to Marie's estate. Surely you'll be able to visit again in the summer, when the tracks are clear...'

'No, Joanna. I've witnessed first-hand what Henry does to traitors.'

'Well, of course I wouldn't want you to take a risk on my behalf,' I said. I had sounded petulant, when really I was addled and trying to work out what to do.

'Henry is *dangerous*, Joanna,' he said. 'If he can make Eleanor disappear, what do you think he would do to me, if he suspected me of carrying intelligence from Chinon?'

I hated him saying that Henry had made Eleanor disappear. 'She hasn't disappeared. She's somewhere, Jean. She will emerge like a butterfly from her cocoon. I know she will. You don't know her as I do, so you shouldn't speak about her so carelessly.'

'Not carelessly, Joanna, truthfully. We don't know what the future holds for ourselves, or for Eleanor.'

'All right, then. Let's say she is imprisoned — as is likely — in one of Henry's castles. You said yourself the war is coming to an end. When Richard is reinstated in Aquitaine, how long do you think it will be before he appeals to Henry to have his mother freed, so she can rejoin him in Poitiers? It is likely, is it not?'

'I honestly don't know — and neither do you. I know that Henry has become extremely paranoid and likely to capture and punish anyone suspected of loyalty to Eleanor. I presume you don't want to waste your youth away in some freezing cell in England?'

'No, of course not. Nor do I want to be a prisoner in my husband's house, with no freedom of my own.'

'How can you even suggest that? We have been friends and equals all this time. I'd never keep you under lock and key.'

'Oh, Jean, I know.' I had felt utterly drained. 'If only it hadn't taken you so long to come... I thought of nothing but leaving with you when I first came here.'

'I told you why it took so long...'

'Yes,' I said quickly. 'I'm not blaming you.'

He had been studying me. 'You want to stay here,' he judged.

I had thought of Alice and Marguerite; even the meals shared with Cook, Claudine and Arthur sprang to mind and, oddly, the hearts in their jewelled caskets.

'You want to stay here,' he had repeated, incredulously. 'You'd rather stay here in this religious community than come away with me.'

'Oh, Jean…' I couldn't contradict him. My brain had been searching wildly for some excuse. *I didn't love him enough.* 'It's not just a religious community, you know. My aunt, Alice, she is my only relative, and I can't just disappear into obscurity where Eleanor won't be able to find me when she returns.' I was relieved to have hit on a reason. When I uttered it, I found I meant it. 'I need to stay here until she returns, however long it takes. I must be here, waiting to attend her. I swore fealty to her, for life.'

He had nodded. 'What about your fealty to me? Never mind… At least now I have my answer; you will not be my wife.'

Shame and disappointment had risen in me — and anger. I hated that he was making me decide like this. 'I suppose you think I'm heartless,' I said, bitterly.

'I suppose I was vain to fancy I could win the love of someone like you. I shall miss you and our friendship, but I think it's better if we do not meet again.'

Eyes closed, I ran the feather quill over my cheeks. An hour must have passed since I'd sat down, and I'd written no more than two words: *Dear Alba…*

I placed it carefully back in the leather binding and jumped up, deciding to take it outside for inspiration.

CHAPTER FIFTEEN

A young, April sun frolicked in rolling clouds, appearing intermittently to brighten the afternoon. I wove my way through the olive grove until I reached the archway to the orchard, which looked like a pool of fresh water. The temperature had grown crisper, and I regretted not wearing my cloak — Alice would not be impressed. I caught sight of a group coming my way and steeled myself. I'd expected to have the orchard to myself at this hour. My spirits sank when I saw that the abbess herself was leading the group. Ambrose was just behind her, with a party of brothers in Fontevrault smocks. I stepped aside, hoping I'd not be noticed.

'Joanna?' It was the abbess. 'What are you doing here?'

'I came here for inspiration, Holy Mother, to write…'

'Oh, I see… You should not wander about on your own.'

I was embarrassed at the reprimand, especially in front of the men.

'Ambrose, you may lead the group on,' she said, waiting with me. I felt utterly trapped now.

'Oh, please, Holy Mother,' I said. 'Don't tarry on my behalf. I don't mind going about unattended…'

She frowned to let me know she disapproved and looked at me until I blushed. 'I hope you won't object to my keeping you company?' she said.

'Oh, of course not, Holy Mother!'

'Very well.' She began walking, briskly, her heavy lower body swaying from side to side. I fell into step a pace behind. 'We were just finished, actually.' She waved towards the men. 'They were consulting over next year's crops. We've had so many calves born this year, I hope we've enough to feed them...'

I murmured hopes for the same, though I couldn't have cared less. I would not be here next year, I hoped.

I thought of the two calves I'd witnessed being born since my arrival, and the urgent bleating of snowy lambs which had been a touching ode to spring. At Poitiers, it had been all about the higher breeds of animals, like horses, hounds and falcons. Here, the animals were domesticated, givers, homely, their presence more solid than noble. They were always munching in the meadows, or huddled together under the trees. After smelling their muck all winter, though, I found nothing to admire in them apart from their coats.

I didn't really tend the horses here, as there were people far more qualified than I, but at least the expansive stables bore some resemblance to those at Poitiers, with the warm scent of hay and the horses nuzzling their nose bags of oats. They were nervous animals, which I appreciated, with sensitive, intelligent eyes. I liked to feed them apples and see the warmth in their eyes, and I often snuck a treat for my Smokey and Alice's Dappled, come with us from Poitiers.

I'd understood the animals at Poitiers better, had a natural affinity with them. I thought of the young falcon I'd trained at Poitiers that had gone wild and felt a terrible pang... So much *loss*.

'I have some time to spare, now, to look over your letter.' The abbess interrupted my thoughts.

'Oh! The letter! I'm afraid it's not finished. I was going to compose it in the orchard.'

'Well, I can help you compose it then. Come.' Her steps fell heavily on the cobbles and I trailed her, reluctantly. 'In here, please,' she said, as we approached the church.

She went to the altar and lit a candle off the eternal one, with the curious, split-heart mould. I lit one too, enjoying the sweet smell of beeswax. The candles we'd stowed away at Christmas were nearly all used, so I hoped to squirrel this one away.

As we descended the steps to the crypt, I felt deeply uncomfortable at finding myself alone with the abbess, but I was also curious.

Once inside, she tipped her candle to the aqueduct, which instantly caught flame. I gasped again in sheer wonder at the gold leaf walls, but I remembered to pocket my candle.

Perhaps I'll sneak another on the way out.

My eyes were drawn to the mysterious, glowing caskets of hearts. I suppose it was all those jewels reflecting the light. I so badly wanted to touch one.

'You may take a closer look, if you wish,' said the abbess.

I walked towards them in a trance. So much treasure! I ran my fingers lightly over a casket of the brightest carved ivory, which was studded with the tiniest gems.

'*Exquisite*,' I breathed, almost pained by the beauty.

'Yes. Of course, that's only on the outside. The real treasure is within — as you know.'

I thought of the decaying hearts inside and had a queer, giddy feeling, like I was in the presence of something otherworldly, macabre, even menacing. I tried, but failed, to pull my gaze away.

'Have you found peace here at Fontevrault, Joanna?'

The abbess's voice seemed strangely far away. The question seemed to hover just out of reach as I continued to stare at the treasure. I opened my mouth to reply, but no words came.

Each casket was more ornate than the last; it really was a remarkable collection. I'd seen plenty of treasure at Fontevrault, so why did I find this so moving?

'They contain stories,' came the abbess's voice. 'No two stories are the same. Remember I told you that most of these hearts belong to bishops and other clergy? Well, that's true — in this chamber. But just behind, there are rows and rows of hearts belonging to laypeople of all classes, each containing an individual story of love and suffering.'

I thought of Jean and flushed with shame and fear. I had been terrified of facing the truth as soon as I entered here. *My heart was not a priceless treasure, for I had not loved well.*

'Like the story of Marguerite and Albert,' I said, my voice trembling.

'Yes, exactly. But no two stories are the same,' she said. 'We mustn't compare our story with another's. Just as each casket is exquisite — as you saw — each story is individual and therefore priceless. Even yours, or mine, or your aunt's. Even if you do not believe it, each story is perfect in itself. It is *your* story, therefore it is beautiful.'

I believed she spoke the truth and I went weak at the knees with relief.

'Even an old lady like me has a story!' She smiled. Her first attempt at humour. She pulled out the folding table and a chair. 'Do sit.'

I laid down the leather notebook. 'I wasn't sure how to word it,' I confessed.

'Well, then, I shall dictate.'

'Once I started, it occurred to me that Alba probably cannot read.'

'Of course not. The letter must be read aloud to her.'

'By the captain? Or…'

'No. I shall ask Marguerite's sister to carry it personally, once it's been delivered to her. I've already had much correspondence and I'm confident she will approve the plan. She feels in part responsible, for the tragedy.'

'But this was *my* plan,' I mumbled.

'Yes, and it's a good one,' the abbess replied, matter-of-fact. 'Even you, Joanna, could do with a little help sometimes, from your community.'

I blinked, irked. *Was she mocking me?*

'You did well, Joanna,' she said. 'I hoped some good would come of placing you and your aunt in the same living quarters as Marguerite. She has many good qualities, but they are hidden under her melancholy. I believe she has helped to bring out the good in you.'

I disliked her patronising tone. *What was she suggesting? That she thought I needed reforming as much as Marguerite needed help?*

I didn't contradict her, for we were alone in a crypt, after all.

'Poor Marguerite,' she said, shaking her head. 'She only wants to be punished for her past. I could never persuade her otherwise. Between ourselves, Joanna, the one duty of being abbess I could never abide was having to administer flagellation. If a member of the community requests it, I must comply, you know.'

Duty-bound, like the nuns following orders. I'd much rather make my own decisions. Beating someone because they ordered it did not justify the act. I preferred to use violence only in self-defence. Or, for the purpose of self-preservation.

She proceeded to dictate the letter to Alba with a fluency and confidence I failed to possess.

Marguerite's family acknowledged the part they had played in the tragic circumstances of her son's death. They apologized unreservedly and admitted his innocence. Could she ever find it in her heart to forgive them? Marguerite had remained devoted to Alba — and to the memory of Albert — her entire life. Her marriage had been enforced and she'd finally procured a separation, after many years of abuse. She was living in penitence with the nuns at Fontevrault. Her life — like Alba's — had been marred by heartbreak and suffering.

The abbess melted some wax onto the envelope and used her fat ring to seal it, with the inscription, *In Deus Noster, Quem Colimus; In God We Serve.*

Marguerite's sister would therefore know that the letter was authorised by her, and Alba would know that the church sanctioned the communication.

That was helpful.

CHAPTER SIXTEEN

The forty days of lent dragged on and all dairy — and eggs — were again forbidden. If it hadn't been for the occasional poached rabbit, we'd have starved. I counted down the days till Easter, eagerly anticipating the first Sunday after the full moon of the March equinox.

On Easter Thursday, I found Cook grumbling over the fact that Arthur had been removed to the main kitchen for the festival. Smoke was billowing out of the multiple chimneys of the main kitchen, and my stomach flipped with excitement — and hunger — as I made my way to the dining hall for breakfast.

The morning was hazy, but promising. Since the nuns were still at Prime, I decided to sneak into the main kitchen, to see what I could pilfer. I wasn't expecting the blast of heat that hit me in the face, nor the sight of nuns in aprons, rushing around shoving trays into stoves. Arthur was nowhere in sight and I found myself pinned against the wall, looking conspicuous, so I left, empty-handed.

I was seated in the dining hall when the nuns began filing in solemnly after Prime. Alice arrived late, looking like a bent and withered stick. I supposed I should have waited to assist her, but I hadn't the patience. Absolute silence was imposed during Triduum, so we barely nodded, before tasting our bland, unsalted porridge. The smells coming from the kitchen were maddening, but we'd have to wait a few more days.

After breakfast, we walked and prayed with the nuns in the cloisters, enjoying the birdsong. We stopped to observe the large wooden cross which had been specially carved by the monks and erected outside the church. They were drawing a veil over it, to be removed the morning of the resurrection. Many other monks were milling around, chopping wood for the fires, or cutting and carting yew and willow branches for the Easter procession. I spied one monk with a bunch of fat trout slung from each end of a stick. The morning air was clear and the atmosphere so full of suspense that I regretted having promised Claudine that I would help her to paint eggs. I'd much rather have stayed out of doors.

Inside, the tower kitchen was both cold and dim, for no fires or candles were permitted during Triduum. Even the nuns had to make their way in darkness to the church for Matins and the only light in the church during the daily services came from the eternal candle on the altar.

I didn't mind Triduum, for it signalled the end of dreary lent and the start of the New Year. Even at Poitiers, we'd observed the Thursday, Friday and Saturday before Easter Sunday, by abstaining from meat and alcohol. Eleanor had fasted the entire forty days before, but her courtiers were not forced to do the same. Children and the elderly had not been encouraged to fast as they needed their strength to survive, so I was surprised when Claudine told me she'd observed it even as a little girl.

'Maybe that's why I'm so small for my age,' she lamented.

'Well ... I'm small too,' I remarked, 'and I never observed it!'

She'd been collecting eggs all lent, as was her custom, and had a fine stash. They were already boiled and cooled, their pale shells crying out to be painted. At Poitiers, the eggs had been painted scarlet — to symbolize Christ's blood. I recalled that sometimes at banquet, they were even painted with gold-leaf. Here, we had to make do with pale lemon, muddy earth and a watery grass. Still, I enjoyed making patterns of colour and incorporating any speckles or blemishes into the design.

On Easter Sunday, the bell's jubilant chimes woke us before dawn. I lit the beeswax candle I'd been saving and inhaled its sweet aroma as I poured water for washing. The air was warm as silk on my bare arms, and the fresh water cleansed away the remnants of sleep and left me fizzing with energy.

Alice and Marguerite had risen and were moving with — I thought — irksome slowness in the shadows. I'd no cause to be excited, for Palm Sunday at Fontevrault didn't promise much merry-making. At Poitiers, we'd awoken to new clothes and dawn Mass had been an occasion to parade them. I thought wistfully of the sage silk dress I'd worn this day last year — a colour that suited the spring. Here, everyone would be dressed in tedious uniform.

I reached for my coarse, wheaten smock, but touched something soft instead. 'What's this?'

My stomach fluttered with excitement. Alice and Marguerite had stopped to observe me as I held the garment up to the candlelight. It was a veil of rich, snowy cotton, embroidered at the edges with tiny scarlet and leafy flowers. The best thing was that the fabric hung from a thin circlet of gold, to place on the head.

'It's so beautiful,' I said, almost crying for joy.

'Do you like it? Oh, I'm so glad! Marguerite helped *so* much with it,' said Alice.

'I only cut the threads…' Marguerite protested.

'The *gold*,' I said, stroking it.

'From Princess Marie,' Alice added. 'We wanted to surprise you.'

'Oh, thank you, both! I'm afraid I've nothing to give you in return.'

'We're all to receive new smocks today, I believe,' said Marguerite. 'At least, we did last year.'

Alice arranged the veil, with the gold circlet shimmering like a crown and the soft, bright fabric draping down over my shoulders. 'You look like a princess,' she declared.

'I feel like one!'

The entire community — except the lepers — attended the dawn Mass. We all stood around the big wooden cross holding candles, as Mass was sung. The first streak of light was accompanied by tentative birdsong, which rose to full chorus with the rising sun.

The priest emerged from the church in magnificent robes of cherry and gold, with the abbess at his side, dressed in her habitual white smock and starched veil. Had I been in her place, I'd have dressed to rival the priest! They each took a corner of the veil covering the cross and swept it off, efficiently, before folding it ceremoniously in a few fluid movements and handing it to the prostrate nuns at their feet. Many monks were in attendance, ranging from mischievous boys to venerable elders. They carried palm fronds and Easter lilies from the altar, placing them beneath the cross.

We all crept forward to take pieces of palm, as the priest, abbess and monks lifted the cross up high on its stand and began a slow procession around the park. We circled around a few times in silent procession before halting at the bonfire, which had been set up outside the church. The cross was again laid down and the priest led us in Latin prayer. After far too many Amens, the priest fell silent and a boyish monk came forward to light the bonfire — to signify the resurrection. Joyous hymns erupted from the gathering and as the fire grew hotter and began to spit, we raised our voices higher.

Only when the bell called us to the dining hall did we begin to trickle away in small groups.

Coloured eggs decorated the boards and — lo and behold! — each place boasted a neatly folded smock as well as an individually wrapped gift. I tore off the linen cover and found a fabric image of the Virgin Mary, which made me smile. Later, I swapped it for Alice's sandals.

The abbess's face was beaming, her colour greatly heightened as she addressed the hall. After thanking everyone who'd helped in the procession and thanking the nuns for making the special Easter gifts, she raised a goblet to officially break lent and we began feasting on boiled eggs, salted mackerel and freshly baked bread. I'd never remembered an Easter breakfast tasting so good.

After Easter, the stables were a hive of activity as so many noblewomen chose this time to make their annual pilgrimage to Fontevrault. For many, it was like a moral cleansing after the excesses of Easter. The roads were also finally passable after the thick mud following the November rains and the black ice of the February freeze. In another month, it would be less comfortable for riding in the growing heat and dust of summer.

I found myself busy in the stables from dawn till dusk, fetching water and hay for tired horses and showing the owners to their apartments. These visitors were often wealthy widows dressed in crow-coloured fabrics, travelling with a small entourage, or young women accompanied by their mothers, seeking nuptial blessings for their wedding day. All of the lavish (and normally unoccupied) apartments beneath the nuns' dormitories suddenly came to life.

I enjoyed chaperoning the new arrivals, as I was eager to break the monotony of my days and curious to meet new people. They were grateful to have a lady — refined, like myself — to show them around. Mostly, they arrived in a spirit of contrition, ready for the prayer and silence of the abbey. Sometimes, though, I sensed reluctance on their part and I relished terrifying them with stories of the abbess's austerity. I observed them casting glances back towards the stables, wondering whether it was too late to gallop off. It was entertaining to alarm them, but I always told them (finally) that they were not expected to follow the same rules as the community and could enjoy every luxury in their own apartments. They would only have to observe mealtimes and the silence of the dining hall and cloisters.

With some bitterness, I thought how I could have come to the abbey under such terms, had I married the knight who had proposed to me at Eleanor's court, Hugh de Montel. I wondered now if I should have married him when I could, considering where I'd ended up, but I had not been in love with him. I'd have been a rich, pampered and important lady, though.

It struck me that, if I ever returned as a wealthy countess, I'd not want to stay in one of the lavish apartments so close to the abbess's chambers. At least we were lucky to have been housed at some distance in the tower kitchen, where we could enjoy a little more freedom. Yet, I loved to imagine myself returning to Fontevrault a great lady — the cooks and stable hands running around nervously before my arrival and the abbess fussing over my comfort!

Exactly one week after Easter Sunday, the countess Matilda arrived with her daughter, Amandine. I was warned to be especially attentive, as the daughter was marrying this summer and a generous donation to the abbey was forthcoming. Amandine either hated the idea of pilgrimage, or hated being with her mother. She was a well-padded girl, with dark indigo eyes, a sallow complexion and full, sensuous lips. Her mother had the same, unusual colouring, but with sharper features and pursed lips. Both wore rich, burgundy robes, with delicate black lace veils barely covering their well-groomed hair. The countess was wearing heavy gold earrings with matching necklaces.

I was bitterly disappointed when my attempts at conversation received only cursory replies. I'd been so excited about their coming and had hoped to win some trinket of appreciation for myself.

'Dinner is served in the dining hall after Nore,' I said. 'You are obliged to attend, but you may have anything you like served to you here in your apartment. Your maid may want to take a list to the main kitchen, for quail or venison, mead, or wine... Or, I could take it, if you like?' My mouth was watering. I could sneak a little something away...

'No, thank you. We had enough wine in Chinon over Easter,' the countess sniffed.

'You have travelled from Chinon?' All my attempts at decorum fell away, I was so desperate for news of Eleanor. 'Did you stay long at Chinon? Have you...' *Have you seen Eleanor? Have you news of my beloved queen?*

I knew I mustn't say it. My head was dizzy and my mouth went dry.

They stared at me, suspiciously. Two bright red spots had appeared on the girl's cheeks.

'Thank you, you may leave us,' the countess said, coldly dismissing me.

I rushed back to the apartment. 'The countess, Matilda, has come from Chinon, Alice!'

Alice froze, her needlework suspended, peering at me. 'Oh! Did you recognise them?'

'No. They happened to mention it.'

'That's good — thanks be to God. We must hope they did not recognise you either, as Eleanor's lady.'

I paced about. 'I acted … strangely, Alice, when they mentioned Chinon. I had to bite my tongue to stop myself from asking about Eleanor.'

'You didn't say anything, did you?' Alice was panicked.

'No. I bit my tongue just in time.'

'Oh — thanks be to God.'

'Don't you think we could ask them, Alice? I could try to gain the girl's confidence, perhaps, and ask her… They may know something. They may be able to help!'

'Don't even think it, Joanna.'

'So, again we do nothing?' Tears of vexation stung my eyes. 'Must we always live in fear? This is intolerable. We are prisoners here — I cannot bear it! Must we keep creeping about silently, saying nothing, *doing* nothing? Are we not complicit in Henry's actions by doing nothing? Her own son doesn't even know Eleanor's whereabouts, thanks to our silence and … weakness.'

CHAPTER SEVENTEEN

I didn't even taste the rabbit stew Cook had prepared for us after Nore, so upset was I. The countess and her daughter had sat next to the abbess at dinner and after, the Holy Mother had escorted them back to their apartment. I was certain that she was still there with them, for the candles were still burning in their window.

What if they could answer the questions which tormented me? I felt a headache coming on. Was Eleanor being kept at Chinon? Was her life really in danger? Or was Henry prepared to release her now, after the truce at Gisors? It was, after all, a promising sign that the ladies had been allowed to travel here from Chinon. Perhaps Henry's paranoia was lessening and his grip was relaxing? Perhaps he was prepared to release her and she — all of us — would soon return to Poitiers? Or, had Henry sent these ladies purposely to spy? Their manner *had* been odd, especially the girl's, but that was not so unusual, if she was at odds with her mother...

'Aren't you going to clean those bones?' Cook said, startling me. I normally sucked them dry.

'You or Arthur can have them,' I said, absently.

She dumped them into Arthur's bowl. 'Don't you give them to that stinky dog,' she grumbled. 'There's good meat on 'em.'

I couldn't bear the thought of returning to the apartment, so I set out walking. I passed through the archway of smoky-white sky into the orchard and scanned around for Ambrose. I walked briskly past the pear and apple trees and took the winding path through the fig and nut trees, before stopping dead at the vision before me.

Two people were courting beneath the old cherry tree. I quickly hid myself, but kept spying. They were holding each other in a tight embrace and whispering. I recognised the man as Brother John. The lady in nun's smock I was certain was Sister Therese, though I couldn't see her face. So, they'd not ended their relations after all! I felt surprisingly slighted, for he'd flirted with me and I'd thought of him with interest since.

The cherry tree was resplendent with blossom and the petals swirled in the air like pink snow. Their clothing was sprinkled with them and they coated the patch of ground beneath them. He gazed at her with such intensity it made me catch my breath. The romance of the scene filled me with sadness and longing. Almost every man who looked at me desired me, so why was I alone? Why could I not settle in marriage?

I pulled my eyes away and went off to brood. I reminded myself of how much trouble they'd be in when they were discovered. Also, their mutual enchantment would be short-lived when faced with life's realities. He was a brother, after all, and she a nun. Once the abbess forced them to leave, they would live in obscurity and he'd likely take comfort in the arms of other women.

Why, then, was I sick with envy?

I'd come to the orchard seeking solace, but found only more upset. The sight of the nuns filing back after Vespers was comforting, and I trailed behind them as they progressed to their dormitories. I sat on a seat in the cloisters as the evening torches were being lit. I was amused to see Sister Therese running in just after the other nuns, all rosy-cheeked and breathless.

Unkindly, I hoped the abbess would catch her.

Just then, the door to the visiting countess's apartment creaked open and the abbess stepped out. She saw me and walked over. 'What good fortune that you are here,' she said. Normally so composed, she seemed a bit flustered. 'I was about to go find yourself and Alice. Please come to my apartment tomorrow, at the dawn bell for Lauds. I shall be expecting you both.'

She was gone again — like an apparition — and I wondered if I'd dreamt it.

I stayed seated, fixated on the torches taking flame and melding with the burning sunset which was casting light on the abbey walls, the archways and the grounds. I watched as the daytime shades of grass and stone turned all molten and the alchemy made me giddy, turning my bitterness and despair to hope.

The abbess must have learnt something from the countess. She must have news of Eleanor! I jumped up and tore back towards the tower.

Brother John startled me then, by steeping out of nowhere, arresting me on my path.

'How do you do,' I managed. 'It's late…'

'Lady Joanna, wait!' He kissed my hand. 'Don't go… I need to speak with you!'

'I must go, good night!' I called back, running off.

I was confused. Why had he been waiting for me at the tower? Playing two ladies at once, I supposed, the scoundrel — nothing new in that. I'd make sure to avoid him from now on.

By the time the bell rang for Lauds, I was already up and pacing around. Alice was still snoring gently, so I shook her, impatiently. She got up and began moving around at her usual, land-turtle's pace.

I noticed Marguerite watching us, but she was too sensible to pry. I wished I could tell her what was happening, for she knew of my great bond with Eleanor and how I yearned to be reunited with her. I hoped I'd have good news for Marguerite later.

We stepped into the half-lit dawn in time to watch the nuns trailing towards the church, their chanting monotone but powerful, and their candles twinkling like little stars. I reached for Alice's hand and squeezed it with excitement.

The door to the abbess's apartment pushed open at a touch and she ushered us inside. She took us to her bedchamber and opened the panel which led into the secret passageway. As we followed her down the underground route, I had the impression of being exclusively privy to weighty events. It struck me that we'd often been privy to such events at Poitiers, but were less accustomed to it now. Since living at the abbey, I had developed a greater sense of apprehension. I was suddenly aware of Alice's palpable nerves and was irked by her obvious fear of bad tidings. Eleanor was in peril and any intelligence of her whereabouts was essential, if she was to be helped to freedom. Unless… But, no, *that* was unthinkable. Henry would not be capable of murdering his own wife…

We emerged inside the crypt and the abbess lit the aqueduct, which illuminated the gold-leaf walls and made the jewelled caskets sparkle. We drew our seats and waited for her to break the tense silence.

'We have a situation,' she began.

My heart was thumping in my ears. Alice and I both leaned forward.

'I have received intelligence that King Henry is to come here — to Fontevrault — on Whit Sunday, so just a few days hence. He is travelling to Poitiers and plans to break his journey here.'

'Henry is to come *here*?' I exclaimed.

'Yes. No need to be alarmed. He is coming to pray and do penance, as was his custom in the past. I need to ascertain ... to avert any danger... Is there any chance that he might recognise you from Chinon?'

'Chinon is a huge estate and we were so rarely in his company there,' said Alice. 'I doubt he would remember us, though he did dance with Joanna once.'

The abbess turned her gaze on me.

'Only because Eleanor wanted me to distract him,' I said, quickly. 'He danced with all the pretty young ladies.'

'I see. Good. Then hopefully we have nothing to worry about. He'll be residing in the monks' house and using their cloister, so it is unlikely you'll meet. He will, however, be observing the communal meals with us.'

'Perhaps we should avoid the dining hall during his stay?' Alice suggested.

The abbess looked uncomfortable. 'It is important that the entire community observes mealtimes. However, if you think yourselves in danger, we could make a concession this once. You may decide as you wish. You have no enemies here; no one is likely to betray you.'

Except Lady Sarah... How foolish of me to make an enemy of her! 'Any news of Eleanor, Holy Mother?' I asked, my palms all sweaty.

'The countess did not mention her,' said the abbess, 'and I thought it wiser not to bring it up. She came with a message from Henry, so we can assume her loyalty lies with him.'

We are residing with the enemy! 'Did Henry's men not murder Thomas Becket?' I muttered, angrily. 'He should be refused entry here...'

Alice cast me a warning look, but the abbess only nodded vaguely and did not disagree.

'Is there nowhere safe?' I said.

'You are safe here,' said the abbess. 'Do not fear. These may be strange and unpredictable times, but the abbey remains a sanctuary.'

Her words failed to reassure me. Alice, too, looked badly shaken.

'I must see to my rounds,' said the abbess, rising bulkily. 'I shall be announcing the king's visit at dinner, but until then, keep it to yourselves.'

'Lady Sarah is not to be trusted, Alice,' I whispered, as we walked back. 'I don't know what to do.'

'There is nothing we can do — only hope and pray.'

CHAPTER EIGHTEEN

The day before Henry's arrival, Alice was occupied embroidering new vestments from dawn till dusk, while I was shooed out of the stables for causing too much distraction. It vexed me that Henry's visit was considered such a great honour, after what he'd done to Eleanor, but I dared not voice my anger. Being idle, I grabbed my gilt-handled knife and headed towards the forest in hopes of finding some rabbit or woodcock to liven up our diet.

The afternoon was mild and domed with lapis and the spring grass richly verdant. The strains of bleating lambs, cow bells and humming bees were so sweet and harmonious, it was impossible to imagine that Henry and his violent men were due tomorrow.

I spied a figure standing beneath the rose trellis, whom I recognised as the countess's daughter, Amandine. I sidled over with interest. She'd removed her veil and her lustrous hair had tumbled down her back.

'Hello,' I greeted.

She looked up, startled, and her forget-me-not eyes fixed on me.

'They're lovely, aren't they?' I said of the roses.

'Excuse me,' she said. 'I must go.'

'Wait, don't go,' I pleaded. 'Wait a moment!'

She watched while I cut a few blooms off.

'A gift for your chamber,' I said, offering them with a curtsey.

Her hands remained by her sides.

'Do take them,' I said.

She reached out, slowly, but then her full lips trembled and she burst into loud sobs.

'What is it? What is the matter? Don't cry… It can't be that bad.'

'How would *you* feel if *your* mama was forcing you to marry an old man rumoured to have murdered his own wife?' she wailed. Then she slapped both hands over her mouth, as if to take back the words.

'That is very wrong of your mother and I would refuse, if I were you!'

'Refuse? It's impossible for me to refuse… I should not have said anything. I have to go.'

If the poor girl's fortune was to be sealed by her mother, no wonder she was so unhappy. I wished she'd stayed longer, though, for I ached for news of Eleanor.

By Whit Sunday, the kitchens had been well-stocked with beef, venison, pigeon and oysters and the casks were full of Henry's favourite Bordeaux. There were rumours that fighting had broken out again in Poitou and Henry was on his way there to try and crush the rebels. I was overjoyed to hear that Eleanor's duchy was staying loyal to her.

Alice was keen for us to keep indoors all day, but I managed to catch a glimpse of Henry's entourage from the tower kitchen — I shuddered on sight of those familiar crimson and gold banners, the lions with bared teeth. I beheld the men's armour with both fear and fascination. Their glinting swords and heavy crossbows looked so menacingly close and out of place here. The jet, metal-studded saddles and blinkers made their war horses look ferocious. The chainmail livery of the knights was invariably grim. There were so many of them and they were mostly wearing visors, which made them anonymous. I wondered if any of them would recognise me, if they could see me.

Henry was riding up front on a big brute of a jet stallion. He wore a plain woollen shirt over leggings, with a sleeveless tunic bearing the emblem of the lions. He looked older — and less robust — than when I'd seen him last.

'He brought his whole court with him,' said Claudine later, with much excitement. 'Except for the women, of course. Many of them are knights from noble families, aren't they? Oh, I wish they weren't to be cloistered with the monks. I'd give anything to see them fencing. I wish I was allowed to wait on them.'

'It's not as exciting as it seems,' I said. 'Believe me. I've attended many tournaments and the fighting becomes tedious and … just bloody.'

'Is that so? I wouldn't mind seeing such a tournament with my own eyes. Are they very handsome, do you think, the knights? It's so hard to see their faces through the armour, isn't it?'

'They are just like any other men,' I said. 'They are neither more nor less handsome than any other group, I suppose.'

'Oh, but look how they *carry* themselves,' she said. 'How masterfully they ride! I know I would swoon, if one of them looked my way.'

I smiled, then sighed. 'Yes,' I said. 'Some of them might be worthy of your swooning, Claudine, but many of them would not be. They are men of violence.'

That first evening was unbearable, as everyone — even Cook — disappeared to attend the king's men in the dining hall and Alice and I were left abandoned, anxious and miserable. Marguerite had been warned to say that Alice was unwell if anyone enquired, and that I was attending her.

By the time the bell rang for Terce the next day I was starving, so I went down to the kitchen to forage something.

'Be careful,' Alice warned.

'Don't worry, I won't go outside.'

I couldn't hide my shock when I entered the kitchen and found Lady Sarah sitting at the board with some of the king's men. I gasped in alarm. It was clear she had been waiting for me. I looked about wildly for Cook, or even Arthur, but found myself defenceless, as they were not about to protect me. She looked striking in a dress of crushed emerald silk, and the three young men were wearing the king's badge on their tunics. I was aware of how vulnerable I was in my plain, wheaten robe, with nothing underneath.

'Lady Joanna!' she gushed, gleefully. 'I was just telling these friends from Chinon how you and your aunt used to keep Christmas there.'

I felt the blood drain from my face. They would guess that we had attended Eleanor.

The three knights were studying me, so I tried to compose myself.

'Ah, yes, well, it was a long time ago,' I said. 'I hardly remember…'

'I cannot believe it was *that* long ago,' said one fellow. 'You look no more than sixteen or seventeen.'

They all laughed.

'Almost twenty, my lord, but thank you for the compliment.' I'd collected myself enough to smile. 'Sarah … a word?' I drew her aside. 'What are you doing?' I whispered. 'You know I have the power to disclose your secret … if you endanger us with the king.'

'I don't think Henry would be nearly as interested in my secrets, as he would be in yours. I warned you, Joanna, it is within my power to have you taken away. All it would take is one word from me and you would be summoned...'

'Please,' I whispered. 'Don't.'

'Why shouldn't I?' she sneered. 'I would enjoy getting rid of you and your nasty allegations.'

'There are no allegations,' I whispered, almost crying. 'Please, spare us.'

'If I spare you, you will do something for me.'

'Anything.'

'What a serious discussion you two are having,' said the fellow who'd commented on my age. 'It must concern us!'

'Do not flatter yourself, Serge. Us ladies live rich lives with or without you men!' Sarah quipped. She turned back to me. 'Meet me later at the forest, at the stroke of Vespers,' she whispered, 'and bring the boy with you.'

'Arthur?'

'Do not dare to come without him.' She swung off to rejoin the men. 'We are going hunting, Joanna. Would you like to come? She is a fine hunter, you know,' she smirked, 'but is rarely satisfied with her catch...'

'I'm afraid I must decline. I must go; my aunt is sick,' I said, hoarsely. 'It was a pleasure to meet you...'

'The pleasure was ours.' The two men bowed.

I stumbled, breathlessly, into the apartment. 'Oh, Alice! Oh, God!'

'What is it? What has happened?'

'Lady Sarah was waiting below in the kitchen!'

I told her everything, starting with how I'd got Arthur to hide and bear witness to Sarah's perversity. How I'd tricked her into promising to deliver the letter to Alba and how, now, she was threatening to inform on us, unless I did her bidding.

'I was a fool to treat her as I did,' I said. 'God only knows what she'll force me to do.'

'Yes.'

I hadn't expected her to agree with me. 'Well ... I was just trying to help Marguerite,' I complained.

'You should not have got yourself involved with Lady Sarah in the first place,' said Alice, sharply. 'Also, it was underhand of you to use her ... *weakness* in that way.'

'But she is *unnatural*, Alice!' I protested.

'Who are you to judge what is unnatural?'

I stared at her in amazement. I'd been certain she would think the same as I. 'Everyone must know how morally perverse it is for a woman to ... do things with another woman? It is not even a matter of opinion.'

'Again, I say, who are *we* to judge? Let God be the judge of what is morally right or wrong.'

Her response made me angry and confused. I'd been so proud of how I'd dealt with Sarah. 'Besides,' I said, 'even if it was not morally wrong, she tried to force herself on me and *that* is a violation. I'm frightened, Alice. The least you could do is comfort me, not ... not reprimand me!'

'Shhh, calm yourself. We do not know what fortune has in store for us, but we must face the consequences of our actions. You are hungry; let us eat now and forget for a while.'

'I couldn't get any food,' I whined.

'Then I shall go; they will have left by now.'

I was a bundle of nerves all morning, until Marguerite arrived back and calmed me down. Her gentle manners always seemed to ease the tension. I dearly wished I could confide in her, but

Alice forbade it, as it could implicate her in our troubles. Alice played sick and kept to her bed. All the secrets I had to keep were starting to weigh me down.

My loyalty to Eleanor and our secret meetings with the abbess in the crypt. Jean. My strategy to reunite Marguerite with Alba. Lady Sarah and her hatred of me. My terror of Henry and his awful men.

The last two were such a real threat, they set me quaking once again.

'If you like,' suggested Marguerite, 'I could collect some herbs for you from the physic garden? Perhaps something to calm the nerves...'

'Oh, yes, please! Marguerite, may I ask another favour? Please ask Arthur to meet me at the back of the kitchen before Vespers.'

Her discretion prevented her from asking any questions, but I almost wished she had. She'd already gone to bed by the time I made my way to the grim rendezvous with Lady Sarah.

'Joanna?' Arthur's expression was puzzled.

In an attempt at disguise, I'd pulled my hood down so low that only my lips were visible. 'Thank you for coming, Arthur; I know how busy you are.' I was sorry I had not thought to bring him some trinket of appreciation.

'It's not so easy to slip away.'

'I wouldn't have asked you to come, unless it was urgent.'

'I am at your service, Joanna,' he said, bravely.

'Spoken with the courage of a true knight,' I said, making him smile and blush.

'Is it the same as before?' he asked.

I paused. 'Yes,' I decided. 'Yes, it's the same as before. Only this time, there is no need for you to hide yourself from Lady Sarah.'

He nodded with understanding — and with touching, earnest trust.

Oh Arthur, how sorry I am!

Sarah was waiting for us at the edge of the forest. I'd hoped she'd come alone, but she'd brought the tansy-haired, tongue-tied Geraldine with her. We listened to the bell sounding for Vespers and, with a sinking heart, I glanced back at the distant, robed figures of the nuns and monks entering the church bearing candles. Never before had I felt so unprotected and had such a strong sense of foreboding. I prayed to Mama to protect me from heaven.

Sarah looked impossibly tall and lean in her long, emerald robe, with her hair piled into a russet-dyed scarf on top her head. Her pale eyes glittered coldly, but her mouth was twisted into a smile. 'Ah, good, I see you brought the boy again.'

My mouth was too dry to speak, as we followed her to the same glade in the forest where I'd witnessed the abbess flogging Marguerite some months before.

She ordered Arthur to undress.

I cried out in protest, but she shoved me aside with such shocking force that I was left half-dazed.

'You just watch,' she said. 'Watch.'

I was winded and petrified. *She's not just evil, she's mad!*

'Undress, boy!' she ordered.

I watched helplessly as poor Arthur stripped off all his clothes and stood there, shivering, too ashamed to look up.

'He's only a boy,' I pleaded. 'Please, leave him alone...'

'Ah, *now* you say he is only a boy! Why did you not think of that before, when you had him spy on me? You considered him grown-up enough then, didn't you, when it suited you? Do you know what I call that? I call it hypocrisy! If there's one thing I *hate*, it's double-standards.'

'Please,' I said. 'Don't hurt him.'

'I'm not going to hurt him,' she said. '*You* are.'

She drew a willow whip with a leather strap from beneath her robe. I shuddered on sight of it. I'd often heard their crack used on horses. Suddenly, it dawned on me what she wanted me to do.

'Oh, no! I won't do it!'

'No? All right, Joanna, here is your choice. Either you whip the boy, or else you come back with me to Henry's men and tell them who you really are. You decide. Arthur can be returned to the hearth unharmed if you simply come with me and tell the truth.'

I took the whip.

Afterwards, I couldn't remember flogging Arthur, but I knew I did it. I remembered the look of disbelief he gave me when it was over.

'She made me do it,' I told him, but he still looked incredulous. 'I had no choice.'

'She *had* a choice, dear boy,' laughed Sarah, cruelly. 'She chose to save herself and punish you. She is a *lady*, after all, while you are only a servant boy.'

'No, Arthur, that is not true!' But a part of me *had* deemed him less important than Alice and I.

'Not true that you whipped him? We witnessed it ourselves, Geraldine, didn't we? Not true you had no choice? We all witnessed you choosing to spare yourself. A lady will *always* sacrifice a servant, Arthur. Let that be an important lesson!'

After taking her revenge, Sarah left us at the tower kitchen. I couldn't bear to look at Arthur, nor him at me. Our relationship would never be the same again. He'd never trust me again.

'I know she made you do it,' he said, eyes on his feet. 'I'll not tell.'

I was so ashamed, I couldn't even reply.

Alice was awake when I got back, her candle burning low. 'Well?' she whispered, urgently. 'What happened?'

I didn't even undress, but lay beside her fully clothed. 'She made me flog Arthur,' I said, wearily. I heard her pained intake of breath.

'Oh, no! That is terrible. Oh, you poor things…'

'I can't bear to think of it.'

'I understand. Oh, that wicked woman. You were right, Joanna, she *is* perverse and this is proof of it. I hope that is the end of it, now.'

'You should have seen him, Alice. He looked so helpless…'

'I hope he is not badly hurt?'

'He'll be sore for days.'

'Well. He is as fresh and springy as a young sapling and he will recover. Your own inward scars may not heal so quickly, poor girl,' she said, too kindly.

I let her hold me as I cried into the sheets.

CHAPTER NINETEEN

I couldn't bear to go downstairs the next morning, in case I bumped into Arthur.

Cook had greeted Alice with some surprise, for of course she was supposed to be ill. 'She kept these for us,' said Alice, holding out a cloth with boiled eggs and cheese. Normally, I'd have been thrilled with the food, but it only made me bubble up again with shame and guilt.

'She'd never have been so generous, if she knew what I'd done,' I said. 'Arthur is an orphan, Alice...'

Alice spoke as she laid out the food. 'Now, Joanna, it was a terrible thing to happen and I hate to think of it, but you mustn't punish yourself. Sarah placed you in an impossible situation, and at least we have been spared.'

I'd never in my life known what it was like to feel ugly, until now. At that moment, I'd have swapped all my beauty to get rid of this awful feeling of shame. I'd have given anything to recover my innocence. And Arthur's.

'We do not know what is in store for us,' said Alice, 'but hopefully we have averted danger, for now. Why don't you eat something? You should eat...'

Alice's solution to everything — eat! I began slowly peeling an egg, but when I tried to swallow it felt like a tasteless lump of clay. 'Was Arthur there?' I asked, torturing myself.

'No.'

'Did Cook mention him?'

'No. Have some cheese. She did mention that Henry is due to leave for Poitiers tomorrow, so one more day and we are out of danger.'

'I wish I *had* given myself over to Henry's men!' I said. 'It would have been better than feeling like this.'

'Nonsense, Joanna,' said Alice, adding, darkly, 'do not trifle with your life. Think of the violence those men would inflict on us...'

Violence I'd brought on Arthur's head instead. I shook my head, to release the horrible thought. Sarah was right, I *had* had a choice and I'd chosen to save myself. And Alice.

Marguerite arrived back and I deeply regretted that I could not unburden myself to her. Shame would prevent me from speaking of what I'd done to anyone. I was certain that Marguerite would have given herself up before hurting anyone else. Eleanor, I was sure, would also have given herself up first. She *had* given herself up. Never before had I felt so alone and disconnected from everyone, even from myself, or the person I'd thought I was.

I wanted more than anything to stick my knife into Sarah's gut and watch the blood gush out and drain from her face... I was a person of violence.

The next morning, Henry and his men attended Lauds, setting off for Poitiers after their last meal. From the tower kitchen, I watched with relief as they mounted their horses and adjusted their weaponry. Claudine was waving furiously; she even blew some kisses. With growing surprise, I watched the countess and her daughter, Amandine, being escorted into a carriage with their luggage, to travel alongside Henry. For Henry to have ladies in his entourage was aberrant, unless it was his wife, perhaps, or daughter. My burning curiosity caused me to run out of my hiding place quite recklessly, before the dust had even settled after their horses.

I was waiting in line to see the abbess, when Lady Sarah brushed past, with her leech, Geraldine.

'Henry seemed quite charmed by you last night, Geraldine,' she said, clearly for my benefit. 'His new fiancée looked quite plain beside you! Still, you know, the countess is related to half the barons of Poitiers and Anjou... What an *opportune* match.'

His new fiancée? I was confused and incredulous. Luckily, the abbess noticed my stricken face and came to my aid. I followed her back, silently, to her apartment. She brought me into her study, with the stained window casting warm light, and ordered some tea to be sent in.

'It is no secret now,' she said. 'Henry is requesting an annulment of his marriage to Eleanor from Pope Alexander. His ulterior motive in coming here was to court the countess's daughter, Amandine, with the blessing of the church. He intends to parade the countess and her daughter around Poitiers, in hopes of currying favour with the barons there.'

An old man rumoured to have murdered his own wife. Amandine had been speaking of Henry! 'Eleanor is not dead? Please tell me she is not dead?' My hands flew to my mouth.

'No, most certainly not! Oh, if anything, we can believe her to be more alive than ever. Henry would not go to such trouble to have the marriage annulled, if she was dead. The fact that he has chosen a new match with such strong bloodline connections to Poitiers proves how much of a threat Eleanor's duchy remains for him.'

The tea arrived and I held the clay cup with both hands gratefully, for I was shivering.

'Do you think he will succeed in having the marriage annulled? How is it possible?'

'He will certainly do his best to prove the marriage was void. He cannot claim that their marriage was not consummated, given the number of their offspring. I believe he means to plead that the prior relations between Eleanor and Henry's father, Geoffrey, render their marriage incestuous.'

'This is shocking intelligence,' I said. 'Do you think Eleanor knows what Henry is up to? But what about Henry's mistress, Rosamund Clifford? Would he not wish to marry her if their marriage was annulled?'

'Gracious, no, he could not afford such a foolish luxury. The duchy could — and should — revert back to Eleanor if they are separated, so he takes a great risk, unless he has the barons on his side.'

I felt a twinge of pity for the girl, Amandine, with the forget-me-not eyes. 'Why is the countess willing to sacrifice her daughter?'

'For power, of course. Besides, who would dare to refuse Henry?'

True.

I returned, half-dazed, to share the news with Alice.

'We must just wait and see what comes to pass,' she advised. 'Perhaps an annulment would be good fortune for Eleanor, though I can't imagine Henry ever letting her take up the duchy again. Still, I suppose she would be happy if Richard was made duke.'

The rest of May was a season of endless, lapis-domed days, but my spirits were too depressed to benefit from the fine weather. I was so worried that Arthur would confide in Cook or Claudine about what had happened that I tried to avoid them all. I dreaded the thought of bumping into him in the kitchen, so we took our evening meals of rabbit stew or pheasant up to our apartment. One good thing was that Marguerite kept us company while we dined — though she'd not touch the meat.

'Alba used to make a delicious lamb stew,' she reminisced, 'with spices. All of her recipes were Catalan.'

I wished she'd speak of something else. 'Don't you ever imagine your future, Marguerite?' I couldn't help saying.

Alice frowned at me.

Marguerite only cast her eyes down and shook her head.

'Well… You are still young…' I wished she'd eat our food, as her thinness made her look haggard and older than her years. 'Do you ever think of visiting Collioure?' I persisted.

She shook her head.

'I can't stop thinking of Poitiers,' I sighed, deeply. 'Especially now that it's summer. Imagine, we've been here almost a whole year! I used to *adore* this time of year at court! I'd spend the days either dancing out on the green, or hawking with Eleanor. Then, the banquets in the evenings were *magnificent*. You should have been there, Marguerite! Each dish was more exquisite than the last, and the clothes! You should have seen those silks and the dainty, embroidered shoes. The perfumes mixing with the spices in the air. Not to mention the entertainments in the halls. The beating of the drums! The troubadours' compositions and Chretien's plays! My heart is aching with longing to return…' My voice was loaded with self-pity. I glanced up to catch them both looking at me.

Poor Marguerite — trying to cheer me up — said, 'Claudine mentioned that there is to be a celebration here this Saturday, June the first, in honour of the abbey's dedication to the Sacred Heart.'

'How thrilling,' I said, my voice flat.

'Now, Joanna, we are fortunate to be here, as you know…' Alice began.

'Oh, I *know*.' I cut her off. 'It's just so hard being cooped up here all the time. I don't mean to offend, Alice, but I feel like I'm half-dead. I just want to feel alive again!'

I'd never have exposed such strong feelings had Marguerite not been present, for she was like a shield between Alice and I. Once I had expressed myself, I felt curiously better, as if some internal pressure had been released. The fact was, I'd felt more confined since the incident with Arthur. I was too ashamed to roam around as freely as I'd done before and everything seemed spoiled. I wished I could just run away to another place and start afresh.

On the eve of the festival of the Sacred Heart, as Claudine was helping me bathe, she confused me by winking with exaggerated suggestion, before finally slipping me a note, which read: *Lady Joanna. Meet me in the orchard at the call for Vespers.*

I looked at her quizzically, but she just shrugged. 'Perhaps it is from an admirer,' she whispered, gleefully. 'Don't worry, I shan't tell.'

I was intrigued and I dressed with special care in preparation, though I couldn't guess who the note was from.

The archway to the orchard was empty, apart from the deepening sky. I leant against the stones and listened to the sound of distant chanting. I watched some bats diving among the fruit trees and marvelled at their speed.

A figure then emerged from within the orchard and, with mounting dread, I recognised her as Lady Sarah. I had not even thought to bring my knife, I realised. It was too late to flee.

She strode up with her usual confidence. 'Lady Joanna, I'm so glad you came! Would you care to take a walk?'

'I would prefer to stay here,' I said, frostily. 'What do you want, Sarah?'

'Forgive me for summoning you at this late hour,' she began, 'but I have been busy these days, in preparation for Collioure. I wanted to ask you for that letter I promised to take for you and the details of where to deliver it. I leave the day after the festival. Are you sure you do not want to walk? The evening is so fine…'

'We can talk here.'

'Ah, I see you are still angry with me, Joanna. Please, I only wish to carry out my promise. Do you have the letter?'

I was in a dilemma now, for I wasn't confident anymore that I should meddle in Marguerite's affairs and I *certainly* did not trust Sarah. *What was she up to now?* 'What are you playing at, Sarah?'

'Nothing! As I said, I gave my word to you and I mean to keep it.'

'How can I trust you, after what you did?'

She blinked her stony eyes at me. 'I do not trust you, either,' she said, finally. 'You led me to believe that you liked me, Joanna, but you only wanted to use me, for my connections.'

'What?' I suppose I *had* wanted to use her for her connections…

'Thankfully, I am not one to hold grudges and when I make a promise, my word is good. The incident with Arthur, well, that was in recompense for how you had him spy on me. That is all over now, and I am here for your letter.'

I suppose I *did* still want her to carry the letter… 'It is written,' I said. 'Hold on here and I'll fetch it.'

CHAPTER TWENTY

The festival of the Sacred Heart was happily uplifting. All the laywomen — including Alice, Marguerite and I — were requested to dress in snowy linen robes and gather roses to bring to the church after Prime. The nuns and monks chanted as we decked the altar in roses and made little garlands with the leftovers to wear in our hair, like brides. After a service which involved the lighting of a great many coloured beeswax candles bearing the abbey's curious insignia of the split heart, we were invited to visit the crypt in twos and threes.

The first thing that hit us when we entered the crypt was the strong fragrance from the scarlet roses bobbing up and down in the aqueduct. The jewels adorning the exquisite caskets of hearts were winking and sparkling at us like stars, and we were invited to kneel before them and meditate on a verse placed there, of love and of loss. On our way out, two nuns came forth to anoint our foreheads with rose oil and press ginger bread hearts into our palms.

We emerged again into another glorious summer's day, nibbling on our ginger bread. Everyone was strolling around the park, mingling, and some nuns were even strumming on harps. I spotted Heloise, Ambrose and Sister Francine and waved to them.

'Come,' I said to Marguerite, 'let's join our friends.'

'No, no,' said Marguerite, 'I am tired and need to go rest.'

I couldn't have been more displeased, but when I saw the tears welling in her eyes, my annoyance turned to pity. She did look fatigued and sad. I was so glad I'd given the letter to Sarah yesterday and my heart swelled for her. 'Of course,' I said. 'I'll tell you all about it later!'

She smiled at me gratefully.

'Please hold my arm, Joanna. I am a little unsteady, I'm afraid,' said Alice.

I wished she'd gone back with Marguerite, but I hid my impatience and guided her over to my friends.

It was so unusual to see everyone out chatting and enjoying themselves. We stayed in our little group all afternoon and, the more we laughed and joked together, the more my chest expanded with joy. During the course of the afternoon, I even managed to speak to Arthur and he let me feed some ginger bread to Coo. I was so relieved that he did not appear to hate me, though we were both awkward and he left as quickly as he could. Claudine was also there and we admired the pretty garlands in each other's hair, and I even taught her some steps of a court dance. A few of the laywomen from the stables watched and clapped us on. Alice sat in the midst of it all, smiling calmly and seeming relaxed and content, for a change.

I forgot to give Brother John a frosty reception when he approached and asked me to dance a step with him.

'I am glad to have caught up with you, at last,' he smiled.

I lifted an eyebrow in response. At least he was a good dancer.

'I have something important to tell you,' he said.

'Oh?'

'I am leaving the abbey at the end of the week.'

I wished Claudine wasn't watching us and winking suggestively! 'You are leaving?'

'Yes. It was my father's intention that I follow the religious life, but it was never my desire,' he explained. 'My older brother has just come into his inheritance and he has invited me to help manage his estate.'

'Happy tidings indeed,' I said and meant it. 'I suppose … Sister Therese will share this new life with you?' I whispered.

He looked at me, puzzled.

'I saw you together,' I said. 'In the orchard the other night.'

'Ah! That! No, unlike me, she *is* destined to follow the religious life. We … we were saying goodbye.' He sounded so sad, suddenly, I was lost for words. 'There!' he said, as our dance ended. 'I hope you shall visit me soon, on the estate. There is a lovely wood, and I'll see that it is well stocked with pheasant.'

I smiled. I was a little sorry he was leaving.

'It is not far from here and, of course, your aunt is welcome, too. I must say hello to her.'

'Yes! We shall come soon, I hope,' I said. It was thoughtful of him to go speak with Alice, for she'd been alone all day.

When the bell rang for Nore, we went to take some rest before the evening meal.

'What did you think of Brother John?' I asked Alice.

'He seems … well bred.'

'He has invited us to visit him on his brother's estate, you know,' I said. 'He said it's not far from here.'

'Ah, yes. I don't think we'll be able to go.'

'Of course we'll be able to go, Alice! We've not set foot outside the abbey for almost a year. It's not natural!'

Alice was winded after climbing the stairs, so I held my tongue until she caught her breath. Wisps of thin, faded hair were sticking to her head with perspiration and she reeked of body odour.

'When is the last time you washed, Alice?'

'I cannot remember.'

I wished she'd take more care of herself. At least when we'd lived at Poitiers, a certain standard of hygiene was maintained, but here, apart from all the hand-washing before meals, bathing was sadly neglected. The older Alice grew, the less she attended to herself. The thought of having to help her wash was too abhorrent to entertain, but what would she do, when her eyesight failed even more? I'd not be the one to attend her!

'You should lie down, too,' she said, stretching herself out on the bed.

'Oh, no, I am too restless!'

'You must be tired after the dancing. Why don't you soak your feet? It may help you relax…'

'Alice, I'd *really* like to take John up on his offer. He said we should visit soon.'

'Oh, I don't know. It is so complicated, you know.'

'No, I *don't* know. How is it complicated? It would only be a day trip for a few hours…'

'Well… The fighting has broken out again, you see. I suppose it suited the rebels to be quiet during the winter months, but now that the weather is good…'

'We cannot live our whole lives in fear, Alice. We must live while we still have any life left in us!'

Looking at Alice, half-dead on the bed, I realised she was a hopeless cause.

'If we do not travel anywhere this summer,' I said, trying a different tactic, 'another year may pass before we have the opportunity again.'

'Please, Joanna, I'm trying to rest… Yes, all right, you may take up John's offer, so long as it is safe and the abbess gives us leave.'

'Thank you, Alice!' In gratitude, I went and soaked a cloth in rosewater to lay on her forehead.

'Oh, that feels wonderful!'

'Yes, and you can use it to wipe the dust off your face.'

In another minute, she was snoring lightly. I felt an unexpected rush of affection for her, but also vexation with her weariness. Her physical — and mental — lethargy was slowing me down. It was impossible for me to imagine life without her, but I was growing convinced that I needed to distance myself from her. Physical distance was impossible, given our circumstances, but I would somehow need to carve out my own, independent path. I was convinced that this would be healthier for both of us. Otherwise, I'd only grow more resentful, as she grew more dependent on me.

'Alice?' I shook her, gently. 'The dinner bell just rang.'

A lovely surprise awaited us when we entered the dining hall. The fountain where we washed our hands had been filled with rose petals, and the boards had been decorated with heart-shaped kerchiefs in shades of crimson and coral. Even the nuns had garlands of roses around their necks and were wearing shy, girlish smiles, as they dished out glasses of rose and cinnamon sorbet. Our faces glowed by the light of the split-heart beeswax candles which burnt with carefree abandon around the hall.

I waved to Heloise and Francine, who had been given the privileged position on the top board with the abbess as a reward for all their help with the preparations. Such an honour was all their ambition in life, and their beaming faces made me more painfully aware that I was not fulfilling whatever my purpose was.

Today was a special day, but tomorrow life at the abbey would return to its usual banality. I wished I was happier here and not so restless all the time. How much easier everything would have been if I had felt content to lead a quiet life of contemplation like Heloise and Francine.

Sarah and her companions left the hall early and she caught my eye as she passed, patting her inside pocket, as if to say my letter was safe with her. They were getting an early night ahead of their journey to the South in the morning. If they could travel the significant distance to the South, there was no reason why we would not be able to take a day trip to visit John.

Jean had been floating in and out of my mind all day, and I wondered how he was faring at Marie's estate. I caught myself hoping that he'd meet someone who'd distract him and, eventually, make him happy. The more I thought about it, the more I realised that I'd never truly loved him. If I had really loved him, I'd have suffered his loss more deeply. The friendships I'd made at Fontevrault seemed to compensate for any sorrow I felt over him. I would always think of him with great fondness and I was really grateful for our time together, but I was relieved that I'd chosen not to spend my life with him. We'd have been dependent on Marie's charity for our future and, more importantly, Jean did not understand my appetite for hunting.

CHAPTER TWENTY-ONE

Just a few weeks later, an invitation arrived from John. When we went to seek the abbess's permission, we were vexed to find ourselves at the end of a long line. Some laywomen from the stables stopped to wish us good fortune. They knew how much I wanted the trip, for I'd spoken of little else since the festival. I wished there were not so many needy people seeking the abbess's charity. She looked fatigued, and it would be better for us if she was in good form. With the war intensifying, hungry people were walking for miles for bread, and sick people came looking for herbs from the physic garden. Others just came for a blessing.

When our turn came, I did the talking, as Alice didn't share my enthusiasm.

'Holy Mother.' I bowed my head, piously. 'We have a request. Brother John has sent us an invitation to visit his brother's estate not ten miles hence, this Sunday. We would dearly like to go, with your blessing.'

'This could have waited, ladies,' she said, irritably. 'Surely you can see that there are many people here who are really in need. I don't think it's a good idea. These people bring terrible tales of fighting in the land. Anjou is rising again along with Poitou, and Henry's men are thick on the roads between Chinon and Poitou.'

'John has promised to send an escort,' I pleaded, 'and it is only for one day.'

'I do not have time to consider it,' she said, waving us away.

'Well! That was most *rude* of her,' I said, peeved.

'You saw how occupied she was.'

'We are going, anyway, Alice,' I said. 'She did not forbid it.'

On Sunday, I had risen before the bell for Lauds. It was already uncomfortably warm, so I stripped off my night gown and soaked my towel in rosewater. I dressed in the wheat smock that all laywomen wore, but I placed the beautiful gold circlet I'd received at Easter on my head and arranged my hair under the embroidered veil.

Dawn was entering through the narrow window and, using the shiny steel of my knife, I lined my eyes and brows with coal and smudged my lips with cherry paste.

After breakfast, we found a horse and cart waiting for us and John surprised us by stepping out to greet us.

'Ladies! I am here to escort you!'

Already, he looked different, more relaxed. It was the first time I'd seen him in a tunic.

'Please,' said Alice. 'The Holy Mother was too busy to see us. Would you speak with her on our behalf, John?'

We watched, bemused, as John quickly charmed the abbess into giving us her blessing. After, he jumped up and took the reins.

'She was not rude to *him*,' I observed.

'Don't be unjust, Joanna,' said Alice. 'She knows we are in safe hands now that he is escorting us.'

I was too happy to be cross and when we passed out the gates, my spirits soared. It was another bright, midsummer's day and I felt beautiful with my veil fluttering in the light breeze. Even the bumpy unevenness of the track did not dampen my spirits, and I laughed as we were jerked from side to side. By the time we arrived, though, Alice was looking green.

John jumped down and introduced us to his maid and cook, who were standing outside a neglected-looking cottage with roses climbing the facade.

'Is this your home? How charming!' I declared.

'It needs some work, like its owner,' he laughed. 'Please, refresh yourselves first and then I'll show you around my brother's estate.'

The maid led us into a low-ceilinged and rather dark chamber where water and dried fruit had been set out for us. Unappetising. I wished they'd thought to leave a bowl and linen for washing the dust off our faces and hands. The place smelt of damp and animal skin.

We sipped a little water politely as we looked about the chamber. The cook had disappeared through the door of the adjoining kitchen and I caught a glimpse of hanging fowl, bunches of garlic, onion and sheaves of corn. Apart from that, there were only two small chambers which appeared to be for sleeping. These had skins covering their doorways. In all the chambers, the walls were lined with shelves containing dried flowers, leaves and roots, as well as glass jars of fruit preserve and bottles of beer and cordial. The overall effect was messy and homely, but a little crude for my liking.

The cook reappeared with a herbal brew served in a black, clay pot and mismatched cups. We'd barely taken a sip when John addressed us from the door.

'Have you finished taking your refreshment? If so, let us go!'

I jumped up, eagerly, but Alice was slower and I had to help her out of the low stool.

We surveyed John's brother's fields of golden barley, his crops and pigs. John strode about proudly, clearly intimate with every tree, every stone, for this was the landscape of his boyhood. He told us his plans for making wine and for cultivating the apple trees, which he assured us were the sweetest in the country. He brought us to a gorgeous wood which reminded me of my beloved wood at Poitiers. It was teeming with wildlife and prey, he said, grinning at me. His manner towards me was familiar, but he was always polite with Alice. I was glad, for if Alice enjoyed the day, we would be able to return.

Just as I was regretting not having filled my pockets with fruit, John steered us towards the big house for the midday meal. Set in the wood, with its small turrets and sandy-hued stone, the house reminded me of a mushrooming tower from a fairy tale. I couldn't take my eyes off all the wood carvings lining the avenue and porch. The entrance was decorated haphazardly with tiles of every shape and colour, and seashells tied on long strings hung over the doorway, making delicate, clinking sounds. Gazing about at the surrounding trees, I had the sensation that I *belonged*. John asked us to wait outside, as he disappeared through the tinkling shells.

'Intriguing place!' said Alice, clearly charmed.

Two ladies welcomed us in, introducing themselves as John's sister, Mathilde, and mother, Anne. They were both tall, thin and serious-looking in dark clothing with crosses round their necks. Mathilde's head was covered, so she must be married.

The floor of the hallway was strewn with hay and marigolds, which looked gay and smelt sweet. Again, there were wood sculptures everywhere and I'd dearly have loved to inspect them, but they brought us through to the dining chamber.

John's brother, Alain, stood very tall before us and welcomed us with a shy smile. There was no sign of his wife, if he had one. He had been carving a side of pork and I noticed his beautiful hands. His face seemed to shine with an inner light, so I could hardly bear to look at him. I was startled to find my heart was beating fast.

Alice and I were seated at the far end of the board with the two ladies. After a long grace, my attempts at conversation were met with only cursory replies, so we ate our meal mostly in silence, only murmuring our appreciation of the food. The meat had been seasoned with garlic and thyme and served with their sweet apple sauce, and I'd not tasted anything as delicious since Poitiers. I was also grateful that John kept refilling our goblets with beer. Every so often, I stole glances at Alain and wondered how such a graceful man could be without a wife…

'You must ask John if his brother is married,' I whispered to Alice, who smiled and pressed a finger to her lips.

There was no need to ask, for after the board had been cleared away, drinks were poured and the talking began, as was their custom.

'I promised Joanna she could hunt in our wood,' said John, looking at me fondly. 'She was a brilliant hawker at court, you know. Apart from the duchess of Aquitaine, I've never met anyone so resourceful.'

'Marvellous! Indeed you must,' said Alain. 'It is well stocked. You'll find spotted hart if you venture into the middle, where the trees are thickest. Or, if you prefer guinea fowl or smaller prey, closer to the old walls is best, or so I'm told… I don't go myself.'

'You don't hunt?' I asked.

'Not when I live among so many superior foragers,' he said. 'My sister is quite skilled at it.'

I looked with renewed interest at the meek girl by my side.

'She is truly skilled,' said John. 'She takes after our mother… Alain, on the other hand, has other pursuits.'

'My eyesight is not as good as it was,' said Anne.

'My husband does not like me to hunt anymore,' sighed Mathilde, 'and I miss it.'

'They never do,' murmured Alice.

'*I* would *encourage* my wife to hunt!' said John, stealing a glance my way.

'The wooden sculptures I see around the house, who makes them?' I asked, to change the subject.

'Ah, that is Alain's workmanship,' said John, 'and I'm glad of it, for if he spent less time carving and more time managing the estate, he'd have no use for me!'

I was impressed. 'They are lovely; I must inspect them further.'

I smiled at Alain. For a moment our eyes met, and I almost couldn't bear the brightness of his gaze. I felt so light-headed, like I was hurtling through the air and could crash down anywhere. I wished we were alone together, so I could talk to him.

John had been speaking to me while I'd been daydreaming, and I looked up to find him regarding me closely.

'Alain is getting married this Christmas,' he said, 'and his wife will expect certain standards of husbandry. We're praying he is up to the task...'

'With your help, brother,' said Alain, warmly, modestly.

I was devastated by the tidings. I tried to arrange my face so my disappointment would not show.

'I could never manage without John,' he said, pointedly, to me. 'Everything I lack, he makes up for with his prowess. I am convinced the estate would run to rack and ruin if it weren't for him.'

'Alain would never bother to collect his rents and the house would crumble into a pile of stones in no time,' joked their mother. 'But at least we'd have wonderful furniture.'

I saw what they were doing. They were praising John for my benefit, because he needed a wife and had set his hopes on me. How torturous it would be to live so close to Alain, but be married to John.

Alice must have sensed my discomfort, for she asked if we could tour the house and view the sculptures.

Apart from some feminine touches, like the bouquets of flowers in the windows and the freshly laundered linens, there was nothing comfortable about the house. In fact, the furniture was monastic and there was no glass in the windows, nor any embroidered wall hangings or silk fabrics, so I was surprised at how homely it felt.

When we were leaving, I thought Alain's eyes lingered on me awhile.

I wanted to know everything about him. *What was I going to do?*

On departure, John lifted me off my feet and held me a moment in a tight embrace.

'My goodness, I was not expecting that!' I forced an awkward laugh. His eyes were dancing all over me, so I could be in no doubt of his attraction.

He squeezed my hand, as he helped me into the cart after Alice.

'You'll come again soon for the hart? My home is your home. Your aunt's, too.'

'Ask about Alain,' I urged Alice, as we bumped about in the cart.

'Your brother has an impressive gift with wood,' she called out. 'How did he come by it?'

'Oh, Alain has been wood crafting since he was a boy. You saw where our house is positioned in the wood. Our father worried that he was an idiot, for he used to spend hours staring at barks. He said he was trying to see the shape in them.'

'Well, I'm sure your parents must be proud, now. Of you both.'

He made no reply.

'Go *on*,' I whispered. 'Ask him something else.'

'He must be very glad to have you home,' she shouted. 'I'm sure it was difficult for him to manage the estate without your help.'

'Yes, as you saw, it is a significant estate.'

I rolled my eyes. I wanted him to speak more of Alain, so I nudged Alice. 'Ask about his fiancée.'

'I suppose his new wife will help him manage?'

'Ah, well, perhaps. I am not well acquainted with her, for I was at Fontevrault when they met. It was my father, I believe, who encouraged the match.'

'When is the wedding due to take place?'

'At Christmas, we hope. The estate looks magical in the snow. You'll love it, Joanna! I hope you will both come for the celebrations?'

'Ah, yes!' I called. Alice shrugged.

It was hard to imagine snow, looking out on the lush fields. How far away was Christmas? I felt panic rising.

'It's a disaster!' I said, tearing off my veil.

Marguerite sat up in alarm. 'What happened?'

'John's brother, Alain, is so *very* lovely. I believe he is the loveliest man I've ever beheld, and he's about to be married! Then, to make matters worse, John is courting me. What should I do?'

Alice picked up her sewing under the window, and Marguerite joined her to cut the threads. A brilliant ray of dying sunlight entered the chamber and turned their faces ochre just as the bell rang for vespers. It was baffling how things could carry on as normal when my whole life had changed…

'*I* found nothing very extraordinary about him,' said Alice, 'but his estate is quite lovely. You should have seen where the house is set — right in the wood, Marguerite.'

'Are you implying that I like him for his house?' I said, frostily.

'I am simply describing the estate for Marguerite. The house, you know, was like something out of a story…'

'He seemed such a gentle, decent person and so *graceful*,' I said. 'What am I to do?'

'It is a blessing to fall in love,' said Marguerite, wistfully. 'You are so fortunate.'

'No! I am most *unfortunate*,' I complained, 'for he is to be married!'

'It is not set in tablet,' said Alice. 'Where is your spirit? If you desire him, you should fight for him.'

I stared at her in amazement. *Such advice from Alice!*

'Don't look so shocked,' she said. 'You told me once that when the right man came along, you would not be in two minds about him. Don't you remember? If you are sure about him, then you should fight for him.'

'Oh, thank you, Alice,' I said, flying into her arms. 'I shall!'

'Wait,' she said, sternly, holding me at arm's length. 'Unless something has already happened with John?'

'No, of course not! Why do you always think the worst of me, Alice? Never mind… I'm going out.'

'Be back before dark.'

Matching my mood, the archway to the orchard was full of fiery sky.

I thought of Alain's woodland house and how I'd love to soften the stone floors with sumptuous Eastern rugs and find vibrant silk cushions for the benches. How I'd love to embroider slippers for those long feet! I thought of him touching my naked form with those beautiful hands and was overcome with longing.

The orchard leaves were drenched with dew and seemed to quiver with excitement as I wandered over to the cherry tree. Its great boughs reached out like a pair of arms in welcoming embrace. There I nestled and watched the sun's chariot riding out of the sky as the moon rose up in the east. A sprinkling of stars were dashed across the indigo sky. My heart thumped with longing, but my spirits flew about like a coven of brazen witches. I was spinning out of control.

What was I going to do? I had to see him again.

I arrived back just as the nuns were settling to roost for the night, like white crows, after Compline. Poor things would soon be up again for Matins. Perhaps they felt about God the way I felt about Alain!

I knew I'd not sleep a wink that night as I slipped in beside Alice. 'Are you awake?'

'No.'

'Alice, what did *you* think of him?'

'I must warn you, Joanna, not to get your hopes up. Perhaps I was wrong to advise you as I did. He *is* betrothed, after all.'

My head clouded with doubt.

'However,' she continued, 'there is a big difference between betrothed and married, and if anyone could change his mind, it would probably be you.'

Her words were like lemon balm to my anguished soul. 'Do you think he could love me too?'

'You've only just met,' she sighed. 'But I trust your judgement, Joanna.'

It was the greatest compliment I'd ever received from Alice.

'Whatever happens with Alain, I *know* I will regret it if I do not fight for him. Like you said.'

'Yes, I think you're right. One word of caution, though: you must tread very carefully with John. He'll be disappointed and he could become angry.'

I felt a pang for John, but then I recalled that I'd not been his first choice. If Sister Therese had not rejected him, he'd not have set his hopes on me. 'Perhaps I should tell him?' I suggested.

'I think that would be wise.'

'Alice?'

'Yes?'

'It's what Eleanor would have advised, isn't it, to fight for him? She would have been happy for me, wouldn't she?'

A terrible sadness and wretched guilt came over me, for I had not thought of her once all day.

CHAPTER TWENTY-TWO

On the last day of June, the abbess summoned Alice and I to a secret meeting at dawn. We slipped out before Lauds, inhaling the woody aroma of smoke from the newly lit ovens.

I didn't recognise the two nuns who stood sentinel at the abbess's door, their faces grave under their wimples. My stomach flipped with that unpleasant sensation of anxiety.

The abbess brought us straight through to the bedchamber and bolted the door. She pushed at the hidden panelling on the wall and we followed her through the secret passageway. I had the familiar, recurring feeling of being an unworthy, and, increasingly, unwilling, witness to critical events. Unworthy, because as a woman I was powerless to help. Unwilling, because as a former attending-lady to Eleanor, my safety was compromised. It was only *because* we had been her attending-ladies that we were made privy to these affairs. I welcomed the possibility of news of Eleanor, but I dreaded the awful intelligence regarding Henry's intrigues.

The abbess lit the crypt's aqueduct from her candle. The last time we were here, it had been filled with blood-red roses, and the fragrance of rose still lingered. The jewelled caskets shimmered and twinkled like tiny fires, and I thought of the hearts encased in them.

'Let us sit,' said the abbess. 'So,' she began, 'it is not yet common knowledge, but I wanted to inform you first.'

I leaned forward in trepidation.

'The pope has refused to grant Henry's annulment.'

Amandine's tragic forget-me-not eyes. The girl would be spared. I didn't know whether this was good intelligence or bad. I looked to Alice, whose face was an impenetrable mask.

'He will appeal the decision, of course, but that is how it stands for now. We can safely assume that, for the time being, his mind will be occupied with greater concerns. It seems that fighting has broken out across the water in Scotland and England. The Scottish king has taken up arms and invaded Carlisle, and young King Henry has joined forces with Philip of Flanders to send an army to besiege the city of Norwich. Henry's position is extremely unstable. He is in difficulty...'

I recognised that this was excellent news indeed. 'Then there is hope for Eleanor!' I cried.

'Perhaps, yes, one would hope so...' the abbess agreed. 'Another thing. It seems that Henry is convinced that this fresh bout of bad fortune has come as punishment from God for the murder of Thomas Becket. Apparently, he is much haunted by the memory of Becket and has recurring night terrors. They say that Henry has dropped arms to go and do penance for the murder.'

'Well, well...' Alice murmured. 'There may be resolution yet.'

'Yes,' agreed the abbess.

'There may be *justice* yet,' I corrected.

With gayer hearts, we surfaced into another glorious, lapis-domed day and joined the community for breakfast. Afterward, Alice and I strolled together in the orchard.

'Eleanor shall be released, Alice,' I said. 'I can sense it! Oh, do you think she will come here on her way back to Poitiers? I think she will... Can you imagine it, Alice? How glorious!'

'There is no going back to Poitiers now,' Alice said, quietly.

'Why do you say that? Why should Eleanor not reclaim her title? It is she who is duchess of Aquitaine. Henry has no right to usurp her land…'

'Don't, Joanna. That is not what I meant.'

Alice's outlook was maddeningly dreary. 'Come, Alice, we should rejoice! These are happy tidings!'

We wandered as far as the ancient cherry tree and sat under its shade out of the hot sun. Alice's back was growing more bent every day and, as I helped her sit, I caught an unpleasant whiff of perspiration. I worried what Alain's pristine mother would make of her and of me, by association.

John had invited us to dine with him again on Sunday. I was to help him cull the deer on the estate. I'd never before hunted such large prey, so really he'd be teaching me to handle a spear. I hoped with all my heart that Alain would join us. At least I had better camouflage for hunting now.

We looked up at the abundance of perfectly rounded cherries which were ripening to brilliant scarlet. I knew that Ambrose would be watching the fruit like a sparrow hawk, for the starlings would descend the very instant it was ripe.

'It is so peaceful here,' said Alice. 'I would like to be buried beneath this tree.'

This part of the orchard had a few gravestones, half buried under moss.

'What a morbid thought,' I said. 'I hope we shall not be here *that* long! I'm very much looking forward to Sunday. We'd better ask Claudine to help us bathe on Saturday… We *need* to make a good impression, Alice.'

'Our manners and breeding are every bit as good as theirs,' she said.

'I wish I didn't have to work this afternoon,' I said, stretching out lazily. 'I could stay here forever.'

'What are you doing this afternoon?'

'We are harvesting the roses.'

I hoped to dye one of my wheaten smocks the kind of rich fuchsia shade that flattered my hair, to wear at Alain's some Sunday. I'd wear my hair down, with only a garland of flowers. Why not? I was not married and I *certainly* was not a nun. I'd make some rose oil and gift it to Alice to help cover up her odour. At the back of my mind, I knew that wherever I was going, Alice was coming too, so they would have to accept her. John seemed to realise this, but how would Alain and his mother feel about it? But, of course, I was worrying prematurely. Still, I needed to make sure poor Alice did not repulse them.

Marguerite had been withdrawn lately, so I was delighted to find her chatting with Heloise and Francine when I arrived at the plot. I stood by to watch them a moment.

My friends. I would miss them when the time came, but there was no future for me at the abbey.

My joyous mood bubbled over and infected everyone, and we spent the afternoon picking away in merry abandon. Francine, with her big hands, was by far the best picker and she delighted us all by telling us stories of the animals on her childhood farm. Heloise's glorious laughter rang out like silver bells, and even Marguerite was distracted into smiling her rare and dazzling smile and making the odd shy comment. By the time Ambrose and Claudine joined in, we were in full swing and I was singing.

The sky was stretched overhead like one of Eleanor's royal silks. I was certain that all the omens were good for her release. *A Christmas wedding with Eleanor in attendance! Imagine that house and all those surrounding trees in the snow!*

On Sunday, Claudine came to help us before her other chores, and she kindly brought ribbons for me to weave into my hair. I was more concerned over Alice's appearance, though, so I was relieved when she allowed Claudine to wash her hair and dress her in a new, snowy smock I'd borrowed from Heloise. I dressed in a grass-dyed smock for camouflage, but I regretted not having any protective leather to wrap over my sandals. Thankfully, I had salvaged a delicate pair of embroidered slippers from Marie and I placed them in my saddlebag along with another gay-coloured smock, to change into for dinner. Even the idea of changing for dinner had me fizzing with excitement.

As we rode along, John's high spirits invoked some guilt in me, for I knew that his cheer was based on false hopes. I decided not to disillusion him — yet. Nor would I encourage him.

Alice opted to stay at the cottage while John and I went into the woods with a small party of men carrying spears. I had brought my precious knife, of course, which I could use to slit the hart's throat. I was struck by how different this kind of hunting was from hawking on horseback, for the men moved so stealthily. I wasn't given a spear on this occasion, but I observed how they handled it with fascination. It seemed to me more like a courtly dance than a hunt, and I fancied how much I would come to enjoy it.

At times, it was difficult not to be distracted by the beauty of the wood. The light filtered through the leaves of the trees from behind and there was such great variety of woodland, it was like meeting a beautiful lady and her entourage wearing exquisite clothing and sparkling jewels.

We tracked an old male hart with antlers matching the gnarled branches of its habitat. The men danced around the prey in strange unison and moved in together, suddenly, to rain their spears on its back. They avoided the head for, as they later explained, that would be displayed and could not therefore be maimed. The hart lay shivering on the ground and they called to me to slit its throat.

It was a great honour to kill such a noble beast.

Back at John's cottage, I wiped the blood of the hart from my face and hands and felt my veins coursing with renewed life. *Hunting made me feel so alive.* 'What a wonderful day!'

Alice was looking at me strangely.

'What is the matter?'

'I had forgotten how much you loved the hunt.'

Was that dislike? I talked about the hunt, as she combed my hair. Even without a glass, I knew that my cheeks must be pink, my eyes shining. It was just like old times. 'Isn't this a marvellous place?' I said. 'And so close to Fontevrault! How fortunate we are, Alice.'

She made no reply, and I sensed a heaviness about her.

'Don't you think we are fortunate?' I pressed.

'What is fortunate?' she said, strangely.

I was afraid she'd be in bad humour during dinner. We both needed to make a good impression.

'Look, we are about to feast on venison. *That* is fortunate!'

The men were setting the beast on a spit over a bonfire. The head with the magnificent antlers was missing.

'So sad to think it was alive only this morning,' Alice brooded.

'You'll not say that when it's covered in apple sauce! Why are you so gloomy?'

'I am thinking of all we have lost,' she said.

'Oh, Alice, *why* did you have to say that!' I pushed the comb away, upset.

I was suddenly ashamed of myself. How selfish of me to be happy when Eleanor's life was in danger. Yet, how could I go on being miserable forever?

Tears spilled down my cheeks.

'Oh, no, don't cry, you'll spoil your lovely face!'

I swatted away her attempts to comfort me. 'Eleanor would have wanted me to be happy,' I said, my voice small.

'Oh, yes, yes, she would. *I* want you to be happy, Joanna. More than anything in the world, I want you to be happy. You must believe me.'

I didn't know *what* to believe, regarding Alice. She was always so secretive.

'Please, stop crying! We are here to enjoy ourselves; forget what I said. I've never been good in company and I am nervous, that is all.'

It was true that Alice was awkward and riddled with nerves.

Alain stooped through the doorway to meet us. It was a compliment to be escorted by the lord of the estate and not just a maid, and I wondered if he already favoured me. I was pleased to see that he was wearing a decorative tunic with a woodland motif. Perhaps he had worn it especially for me.

'What a lovely tunic,' I remarked.

'Thank you.' His eyes crinkled warmly.

'Alice does wonderful needlework,' I said. 'She spends most days in the church, embroidering the vestments.' I wished his mother could hear, for it would appeal to her pious nature.

'My sister embroidered this,' he said, softly.

'Oh, then she must have a lot in common with Alice,' I said, brightly.

'Indeed.' His eyes crinkled at Alice, who (thankfully) returned the smile.

Alain's mother was waiting in the dining chamber, but Mathilde was absent today, so we all sat together at the board. We watched as Alain carved the venison and my eyes kept fixing on his shapely, sun-dyed hands. There was a stronger resemblance to John from afar, due to their height and build. Up close, Alain's hair and complexion was darker, his expression more soulful, his manner gentle and unassuming. John was the more confident, more arrogant brother.

Alice coughed and squirmed in her seat, and I realised I'd been staring.

'Your robe is a very unusual colour,' said Anne to me. 'Where did you come by it?'

'She dyed it herself. I told you she was extremely resourceful,' said John, smiling at me proudly.

As before, we ate our meal in silence and conversed only after the board was cleared.

My mind was on Alain all the time Anne was asking about my garden plot. I longed to speak with him. I tried to listen in to his conversation and I overheard John praising my courage and spirit. Alain glanced at me admiringly. I caught him looking at me a few times throughout the afternoon.

At one point, I bristled when Anne brought up the subject of his fiancée. To my delight, he showed little interest in discussing her and changed the subject quickly.

Anne took Alice and I on a tour of the smaller chambers and she pointed out the furniture that Alain had crafted, including the beds and foot stools. I ran my hands over them, as if I were touching the craftsman himself. The glassless windows were crude, but at least the shutters were hardy and kept out the midday sun. They could yet be fitted with glass. I loved all these funny-shaped chambers which gave the impression that the house was mushrooming.

I imagined filling the closets of the bedchamber with dresses and ordering a gilded glass from Paris I'd once seen, decorated with copper birds. I'd have a casket for my jewels just like the ones in the crypt at Fontevrault. I'd ask Alain to make a special, velvet-lined sweet chestnut box to display all my embroidered slippers in rows. I desired so many beautiful things, and I could picture how well they would furnish the house.

Alice woke me from my reverie. 'Joanna, it's getting late; we'd better return to the abbey.'

I could hardly bear the thought of going back.

Alain pressed his lips to my glove and looked deliberately into my eyes as I departed. 'A *great* pleasure, Lady Joanna,' he murmured.

'It was lovely to see you again,' I said.

'I hope you shall come again soon.'

I brushed my hand lightly along his arm. I couldn't help myself, even though I saw Alice's frown from the corner of my eye. I felt like a girl possessed by some powerful force. It was like the very air was pulling us together.

'You have to tell John,' Alice whispered.

'Yes, of course! Next time.'

'Before then.'

I was in such a blissful, almost drunk state the next day that Claudine — and even Cook — guessed I must be in love. Maddeningly, though, they thought I was in love with John.

Cook grumbled that I was throwing myself away on John 'lack-land', as she nicknamed him. Claudine said that she would not mind living in a cottage with a man as handsome as John.

I longed to tell them the truth about Alain.

In the past, little Arthur would have joined them in teasing me, or at least laughed along, but he stayed silent, serious. It made me feel so sad and ashamed that I wished I didn't have to see him anymore.

CHAPTER TWENTY-THREE

The summer's heat rose to such a frenzy that, by July, we were experiencing ferocious lightning storms. Often, we were caught out by the huge downpours and after such a soaking, Alice became so ill with chills and fever that she'd to keep to her bed for many days. I was vexed, for it meant that I couldn't visit Alain.

The bond between us had been growing with each visit, and even his mother and sister had taken a liking to me. I'd avoided addressing John directly, but Alice assured me that my behaviour towards Alain could leave no doubt about my feelings. I felt really badly over the tension which had developed between the brothers and I had resolved to speak to them both, but then Alice had fallen ill.

There was also the sickening factor that Alain was still engaged to the lady his father had chosen for him. I was convinced that he loved me, but worried that he might choose to do the honourable thing by marrying her and sparing his brother's pride.

I waited on Alice as faithfully as an old hound in the hopes that she'd recover quickly. The apartment was stifling, and the air was rather foul-smelling and humid. Alice's nightshift would stick to her and I held my nose in disgust whenever I had to change it. Luckily, Claudine was always by to lend a hand and willing to wash her down. I couldn't bear the idea of caring for Alice in such an intimate manner. Her body was so sunken and wasted, with rivers of blue veins all over her pasty skin. Her helplessness was both maddening and endearing, so that I wanted to hug her and shake her at the same time.

Alice would get blinder and more dependent, and I was worried about who would care for her in the years to come. Could I really expect Alain and his mother to take her in?

I was sitting under the window, staring out at the vivid, violet sky, when the abbess entered.

'La-dies,' she puffed, winded from the stairs.

'Holy Mother,' Marguerite said. 'Do please sit.'

'How is our patient?' She went straight to Alice and produced a small glass phial. 'Water from St Cuthbert's well.' She drew back Alice's covers, felt her forehead and frowned. 'Still feverish.'

'Yes, but we are doing all we can to bring it down,' I said.

'I came to speak with you, Marguerite,' she said. 'If you would come with me?'

My curiosity was sparked. Something must be afoot, if the abbess had come in person to seek her out. 'She'll not be gone long?' I asked, fishing for a nugget of intelligence.

'I'll have her back to you before dark.'

Alice was only fit to drink some watery soup before falling asleep again, so I waited impatiently for Marguerite's return.

The bell chimed for Vespers just as the sky split open and rain began pattering on the roof. Before long the lamps were lit and the sky had deepened to pitch, and yet there was no sign of Marguerite. Eventually, I climbed into her bed and lay there with my eyes open.

I must have fallen asleep, for the next thing I knew, I was being shaken awake.

Dawn light was filtering through the slit-window, and Marguerite stood above me with a peculiar expression on her face. Her eyes were gleaming, alert and feral. She looked so *alive*.

I sat up, confused. 'What, morning has come? What has happened? Is Alice all right?'

'Yes, she is all right. Nothing bad has happened.' She was smiling now, her face dazzling even in the pale light. 'Look,' she said. 'The storm clouds have cleared. It's going to be sunny again. Alba is here. She has come for me. She is not angry with me at all; she loves me as a mother loves her child. She has come *here* to the abbey.'

'Alba is here?'

'Yes! She came here with a party of ladies who were returning from Collioure. She got the letter you wrote and she came. The lady you gave the letter to passed it to my sister, and they went to find her in her village. She thought that I was married still and living with my husband, and that she would only cause trouble by seeking me out. She thought she'd die of a broken heart before she'd set eyes on me again. I said that I was slowly dying just the same. Now that we have found each other, there is a chance that we may live. We have some hope now.'

'Oh, Marguerite! I am so, so happy for you.' My heart flushed with deep joy.

Alice cried out from the bed, 'A miracle!'

'The abbess gave us her blessing to join the nuns for Lauds, so I must go,' said Marguerite. 'I'd love Alba to meet you both. Joanna, you could take a walk with us after breakfast? Alice, if you are not too weak, we'll come up here afterward.'

It was such heavenly news, I felt like crying and crying. Some tidings were almost too much for the heart to bear.

I helped Alice out of bed to make her presentable. She too had tears in her eyes, as she gripped my hands.

'It was your doing,' she said. 'You brought them together.'

'Anyone could have done it.'

'*You* did it.'

Was that a look of pride? I was amazed that Lady Sarah had kept her word.

Marguerite, Alba and I strolled together under the topaz morning sky. Petals and seeds were drifting through the air and the bees were humming as they flitted between flowers. With the sun on my face and with such sweet companions, I was content. We passed through the archway of brilliant sky and meandered through the fruit trees. They were so happy and grateful to be reunited that they spoke little, but smiled frequently — an old, familiar smile, with a touch of sadness. Their mutual loss had served to deepen their bond.

I felt the loss of my mama, but not keenly, more like the passing clouds. Like Marguerite, I would always search for her. Unlike Marguerite, I'd learned to live with the loss and was determined to flourish anyway.

I had Alice, and now there was Alain.

Alba's presence had altered Marguerite, who seemed to have shed years of worry overnight.

'I am going to return with Alba to her village,' she confided. 'I'll use my inheritance to build up the house so she'll have some comfort in her old age. We'll work the land together.'

'It's what you've always wanted,' I said. 'I'm so happy for you... I'll miss you.'

I'd miss her terribly. Why did we have to suffer so much loss?

Still, I too would be leaving soon, I hoped. Everything was changing for the better. The abbey was no place for young people like Marguerite and I to grow old...

'Some day we will meet again and reminisce about our time here,' I said.

After they'd gone to see Alice, I went to check my plot. I was enjoying the sun on my face and the drone of Ambrose's bees in the clover, when I heard my name called. It was Lady Sarah and Geraldine. My peace of mind was ruffled slightly, but I thanked her for bringing Alba here. It seemed she'd even gone to collect her from her village.

'I love a good ramble,' she said. 'I grow restless easily, so it was the perfect diversion. We took mules up the mountainside — dumb beasts and an uncomfortable ride — and there it was, perched on top like an eagle's nest. These peasants endure great hardships, but they're built for it, I believe. Still, I doubt the old woman would have survived there much longer on her own.' She was referring to Alba.

'She won't be on her own,' I said. 'Marguerite is going to live with her.' As soon as the words were out, I cursed myself.

'She is going to live in that peasant village?' Sarah sneered. 'The little fool. Good fortune to her! Her family's castle rests on the Collioure promontory, so perhaps she'll be able to view its turrets from up there.'

'Did you visit her family?' I was intensely curious.

'We were not asked! Her sister invited us to her estate nearby, though, and treated us most generously. Geraldine had a new brooch.'

The tansy-haired young woman looked adoringly at Sarah.
Ugh.

'We are on our way to picnic in the forest,' Sarah added. 'Why don't you come with us?'

'No! No … thank you.'

'Next time, perhaps?'

'I think not, Lady Sarah,' I said firmly.

She strode off, laughing heartily.

Another reason I hoped to leave the abbey soon was so I'd not have to encounter Sarah. I was convinced she'd always find a way to outsmart me.

Thankfully, Alice's health recovered and we arranged to visit with John on Sunday. In the meantime, I planned what I would say and what to wear. Alice strongly advised that I speak plainly to John about my feelings for his brother. I wished Alice was not so jittery, but at least Claudine managed to calm my nerves with her chatter and cheer, as she assisted us on Sunday morning.

As soon as we arrived at John's cottage, I asked to speak with him, alone.

'I shall step outside,' said Alice.

'What a lovely colour this is,' he began, touching my rose-coloured smock.

'John,' I said. 'Don't.'

He frowned and withdrew his hand.

'I don't know if you have guessed my feelings…'

'I hope your feelings are for me and not for my brother?' he said, sharply. He obviously suspected the latter. *So much the better.*

'I am so sorry.'

'So, Alain is to have *you*, as well as the estate.'

'I am no man's property, John. I never encouraged you or led you to believe that I cared more for you than I did…'

'No … I suppose not. Why do I not have better fortune with women?' he said, bitterly. 'Am I destined to be rejected again and again? First Therese and now you.'

His self-pitying tone made me impatient. 'Sister Therese is a *nun*,' I said, 'and as such she was unattainable, and *I* never encouraged you. You are a good and handsome man, John, and I believe that you will find a worthy wife, in time. It would be worse, would it not, if I pretended to be in love with you?'

'I did not invite you here so that you could fall in love with my brother.'

I was afraid he would tell me to leave and never return. '*Please*, John. Coming here has been the best ... the *only* good thing that has happened this past year. I don't think I could bear it, if you were to tell me not to return.'

'Have you spoken to my brother of your feelings?'

'Not yet. I wanted to speak with you first.'

'I suppose he is in love with you, too,' he said bitterly.

Oh, music to my ears! 'Has he said anything?'

'No, but just look at you — how could any man resist you? Besides, I know my brother... I suspected he had feelings for you when he broke off his engagement.'

'He has broken his engagement?'

'Yes.'

'I believe that Alain and I have a deep connection,' I said. 'I felt it from the first moment I met him, as if some force greater than ourselves was pulling us together.'

John was studying me. 'My brother has always been fortunate,' he said. 'He was fortunate to be the first-born. Perhaps his estate is also more attractive than my cottage?'

I flushed the same colour as my smock in anger. 'Believe what you will, if it makes you feel better,' I said, 'but my feelings for your brother run deep in my heart. I cannot explain why.'

'We should not leave Alice outside any longer,' he said. 'Let us call her back in.' As I went to call her, he added, 'Forgive me, Joanna, if my words offended you, but I am disappointed.'

'Oh, John, you are forgiven,' I said. 'You must believe me when I say that I esteem you highly.'

'But you do not love me,' he said with resignation. 'I suppose I must forgive you too.'

Now all I needed to do was speak with Alain.

CHAPTER TWENTY-FOUR

Alice and I walked alone in the beautiful wood, and I told her what had passed. Alain came to walk us to the house, but John would not join us. I couldn't bear to wait until after dinner, so I asked Alice to fall behind as I walked with Alain.

'I had a talk with John this morning,' I said.

Alain halted.

'I told him I did not have feelings for him. I told him that I ... had feelings for *you*.' I couldn't bear to look at him, so I walked on.

'Joanna, wait!'

We stopped under a leafy oak and he pulled me gently to face him.

'I have broken off my engagement because I am in love with you.'

'Is it true?' I was suddenly afraid. This thing between us seemed too precious, too fragile. I was used to losing things that were so precious. He pulled me towards him and kissed me. I began to cry.

I was sorry, but also glad, when Alice interrupted. She had seen the kiss and was smiling. Discreetly, she handed me a kerchief. She too had tears in her eyes.

The three of us went to dinner with his mother and sister. I noticed that they did not mention John's absence and were especially attentive to me, treating me like a sister. They knew. They approved!

Could it be true? I was so afraid that I would awaken from this dream. I looked at Alain's beautiful hands, gazed about at his sculptures, the beams and funny-shaped chambers that I would soon, with God's blessing, inhabit. I looked out at the wood, where I would hunt and go wandering at night… It was too wonderful to be true. Beneath these thoughts was the underlying sadness over all I'd left behind at Poitiers. *Eleanor.*

This place would help heal those wounds. I *needed* this.

It was Alain, not John, who brought us back to the abbey that evening. Before departing, he whispered in my ear, 'I'll call for you on Sunday.'

I confessed to Claudine that it was not John, but his brother Alain with whom I was in love. When I told her what had passed between us that afternoon, the little dear shed tears of joy. Even Cook grudgingly admitted I'd made a good match. I cautioned them that no proposal had been made and we must not be presumptuous.

Marguerite had already left for the South, so it was only Alice and I alone.

'I'm afraid that something will happen to spoil my happiness,' I confessed to her. 'I'll have to tell him that I am no maiden, I suppose.'

'I don't think anything bad will happen,' she said. 'You and Alain are well matched. He is a gentle man with an ample fortune and you are … a vivacious companion. He is fortunate to have found you, for you will liven up his home and fill it with beauty.'

'I wonder if he will propose next week?' I said, pacing about. 'Alice, I cannot wait to move there. Do you think we will like living there?'

'We?'

'Of course! You will come with me, Alice.'

'Oh, dear. No, Joanna. I shall end my days here at Fontevrault. I am too blind and too much of a nuisance to inflict on others. I'll not let anyone take me in out of pity. Besides, I am happy here at the abbey.'

I stared at her. *So this was it. This was the bad thing.* 'How can you say that, Alice, after all we've been through together? How can you say that you'll not come with me?'

'My dear, it is not even your home. They would take me in out of pity and they would tolerate my presence, but I would be useless there. At least here, at the abbey, I have some use. This is my home, Joanna, just as Alain's home will soon be yours. We are all fortunate that it is so close.'

I felt both bereft and angry with Alice for making so light of it. I could not contemplate living apart from her. 'We are being premature,' I said, frostily. 'Alain has not even made a proposal, and I'm sure you will change your mind.'

I tossed and turned in Marguerite's bed and thought how everything was changing. It seemed wrong that my life would move forward while Eleanor remained imprisoned. The idea of spending another year at the abbey was so intolerable to me, I was stunned that Alice could wish it. Was she simply being a martyr? It would not surprise me.

Over the next few days, I thought of nothing but Alain. If he proposed, I would accept and then we would be married at Christmas, so I could leave the abbey by the New Year and begin the rest of my life. I hoped that the five hundred days or so I had spent at the abbey would become a faint, fond memory, and I would enjoy returning there and visiting my friends as a lady of consequence — dressed in fashionable silks.

It was impossible for me to picture my new life without Alice by my side. We had *always* been together.

I could picture us in Alain's dining chamber, arguing, as we sipped hot drinks before a roaring fire. I'd cover the monastic furniture with rich, warm fabrics and we'd have knives with musical notations, so that after dinner we could sing. Alain could make a banqueting board to host all our friends and I'd invite everyone I knew to be loyal and kind. Ambrose would bring pots of his golden honey in exchange for seeds and saplings. Life at the abbey had taught me to value the good qualities of a lowly maid like Claudine over a powerful noblewoman like Lady Sarah. I'd see to it that Claudine shared in my good fortune.

It would be my ambition to cultivate the same refinement in fashion and especially music that I'd learnt at Poitiers, and I'd invite the most celebrated troubadours to perform and the most skilled hawkers to hunt in the wood. Silence would be frowned upon, and the house would resound with laughter and song.

Once the guests had left, Alain and I would go to bed and make love under the silk sheets. All my sorrows would grow fainter and fainter, like clouds burnt away by the sun. I'd never forget my loved ones, but I'd flourish despite their loss and I'd visit the abbey to offer prayers of thankfulness, of remembrance.

But what of Eleanor?

How could I possibly get on with my life without knowledge of her whereabouts, her safe-guarding against the evils of Henry? It was as unthinkable to me as trying to imagine my life without Alice.

On Friday, I woke at the call for Matins with a headache reminiscent of my first troubled days at the abbey. I lay there rubbing my temples. When I heard steps approaching, too heavy to be Claudine's, I sat up to listen. Moments later, the abbess was standing there, candle in hand, puffing after the stairs.

'Alice.' I shook my aunt, who groaned and rubbed her eyes.

'La-dies,' the abbess managed. 'Something urgent has arisen.'

My head was pounding now, and my stomach was nauseous. Alice sat up, confused.

'Please dress yourselves quickly and come to me,' said the abbess.

Still full of sleep, we pulled on our smocks and descended in the dark. In the kitchen, we lit our candles and watched the nuns' slow procession to the church, like white-clad angels floating to the heavens. We looked so rumpled, by comparison, our destination darker, more ambiguous. Alice's snail-like progress did not help my headache, nor my nauseous apprehension.

I was terrified of anything that might come between me and my future.

We followed the abbess into her bedchamber where, to our amazement and delight, Princess Marie was waiting.

Alice's face lit up with pure joy. It reminded me of Marguerite's altered aspect on being reunited with Alba.

She loved Marie. I'd not realised how much. I remembered her words to me: *Who are we to judge what is perverse...* That was her great secret. *Poor Alice!* Perhaps *I* was not her whole world, as I'd thought.

Marie looked troubled and I dreaded to learn why. I wondered why she'd come secretly — she must have still felt under threat from Henry, despite what we'd heard about him dropping arms to do penance for Becket.

We took the secret passageway to the crypt and I pressed my temples for relief.

The strange thing was that all the while we'd been at the abbey, I'd wished only for news of Eleanor. Now, when Marie said it, I almost couldn't bear to hear it.

'I've had intelligence of Eleanor.'

Some tidings are too much for the heart to bear. I stopped breathing and clutched the board.

'Henry set sail from Barfleur for England on the eighth of July on the *Esnecca*. My husband sent some of our men to assist, and they reported back to me. They said that my mother was on the ship. Henry has taken her back to England with him. Either to Winchester, or Salem. She gave the men a token to bring to me, so there can be no doubt.'

Marie slipped a gold ring from a little pouch. I recognised it instantly as Eleanor's.

'Oh!' I cried. I retched, like I was going to be sick. Alice and Marie came to my aid, soaking a cloth in holy water to cool my burning forehead. 'I am all right,' I said. 'Don't fuss.'

'At least now we know where she is,' said Alice, after.

'You *know* how much she hates England!' I said, tears streaming. 'She will be completely isolated there. At least here there was a chance that Richard would save her.'

'My mother is a survivor,' said Marie. 'She will find her way back to us.'

There would be no Christmas wedding with Eleanor in attendance.

'Come, let us return before it grows light,' said the abbess. 'You may spend a few hours with the ladies, Marie, before I call for you.'

'Thank you, Holy Mother, that would be wonderful.' Marie pressed Eleanor's gold ring into my palm. 'You were my mother's favourite,' she whispered. 'She would want you to have this, in remembrance of her.'

'Oh, Marie!'

We walked back to the tower kitchen, where little Claudine was sleeping in her crate. I envied her that innocent sleep.

Those violent soldiers pushing Eleanor's head down. Hurting her slender wrists. Captured on a ship destined for a hostile land. Daughter of the warm, fecund soil of Aquitaine.

'I advise you to get on with your lives now,' said Marie. 'Since Henry is gone, you may travel more freely, so long as you are discreet about your past. Soon, the same will apply to me and I should be able to travel here openly and much more often...' She smiled warmly at Alice. 'I hope my little daughter, Alice, will soon meet the lovely soul after whom she was named.'

'Marie,' I said, 'I hope we will not remain at the abbey for much longer.'

She was taken aback. 'Where would you go?'

'I have met someone. A baron with a grand estate not ten miles hence. He has not yet asked for my hand, but he has declared his love for me and I for him.'

She looked puzzled, probably thinking of Jean.

'I know what you must be thinking, about Jean, but I am in love,' I said. 'For the first time. His name is Alain.'

'Well, Joanna, I was not expecting such tidings. How exciting for you.' Despite her words, she seemed underwhelmed by the news and glanced at Alice, concerned.

'I am very happy for her,' said Alice, quickly. 'Lord Alain is a gentle man with a fine estate, and I believe they are well suited. I, however, am planning to end my days here, at Fontevrault. I have already discussed this with Joanna. I do not wish to go to a place where I will eventually become a burden. The baron's estate is so close that we shall be able to visit each other often.'

Marie smiled. She would be able to visit Alice frequently — and less conspicuously — at the abbey, I supposed.

'Let us go up,' suggested Alice. 'Cook will be rising soon, and we don't want to wake Claudine; the little thing works hard enough.'

'Please... Go on without me,' I said. 'I have a terrible headache. I'm going to get lavender and clover from the physic garden. I will see you at breakfast.'

They did not even notice me leave. Strange, I'd always assumed that Alice's ambition was bound up with mine, that all of her interests lay with me. Now I realised that I had been arrogant; my aunt had an interior world of her own of which I'd been ignorant. I felt peeved on my part, but impressed all the same that she had her own ambitions and ... *passions*.

The association of my stiff aunt, Alice, with passions made me smile.

My heart was pounding in my chest, but I knew what I must do. It was what Eleanor would have done.

I started off towards the physic garden, but then swerved off in the direction of the stables. I went straight to my smoky mare, who nuzzled me happily. I saddled her up in darkness and led her out stealthily, as far as the abbey gates, where I hid in the bushes and waited, anxiously, for the first delivery cart. Some monks were guarding the gates, and I knew I'd have to be fast. When the gates opened, I galloped off, ignoring their alarmed voices calling after me.

The abbess would be waiting for me on my return, but I didn't care.

Fortunately, I was confident of the route to Alain's estate and I galloped straight there in the faint dawn light. Incredibly, by the time I got there, my headache had disappeared. I trotted up the avenue to the big house, which looked so welcoming, with its sandy turrets. The dawn broke and the birds had just begun their chorus, when I knocked on the door. Fortunately, Alain answered himself, axe in hand for firewood.

'Oh, it is you.' His face lit up.

We gazed at one another in wonder. My hair was loose and wild and my colour high after riding, and I saw how lovingly he regarded me.

I showed him Eleanor's ring on my finger. 'It was hers.' I burst into tears. 'It was my duchess, Eleanor's.'

He hugged me tight and I kissed him then, with all the passion and pain that was in my heart.

We walked, hand in hand, into the wood.

CHAPTER TWENTY-FIVE

My eyes slit open onto the day. I grasped after a dream of Poitiers, but it had slipped away. The chamber was pitch, the air chilled. The bell's tolling for Lauds brought the abbey floating back to mind. My mind still foggy with sleep, I drew the sheepskin tighter. Alice stirred beside me.

'I thought this day would never come,' Alice whispered.

Oh heavens, today was my wedding day!

Wakefulness pumped through me, but I stayed frozen with apprehension under the rug. I imagined the nuns leaving a trail of footprints in the snow on their way to Lauds, grateful for the meagre warmth eked from the candles in their hands. Their cold breath would be rising as they chanted, purposeful in their destiny. I, too, was finally purposeful in my destiny — but also regretful that all was not as I had hoped it would be. *On my wedding day.*

I'd imagined that Eleanor would be presiding. I'd been certain that Alice would be accompanying me to my new home. I still hoped she would change her mind. We huddled together under the sheepskin, neither of us speaking. What was there to say? Yet, *not* speaking spoke loudly of our charged feelings.

'I shall visit every Sunday until you are settled,' she'd assured me over and over. We both knew it was not the same. We both knew that this was the best arrangement, for Alice to stay at Fontevrault, but still I was unable to comprehend it.

We moved to rise only when we heard Claudine's footsteps on the stairs. The little dear was bursting with all the excitement that I lacked. She brought candles, hot water and towels and soon we had risen and were preparing to dress. My dress and veil were laid out on Marguerite's old bed, and I felt my first tremor of excitement on sight of them.

The dress was created by Princess Marie's own dressmaker and was the most elaborate costume I'd ever owned. The fabric was coral and gold silk brocade, with a fitted bodice. At the waist was a filigree gold belt, finely crafted and studded with pearls in the shape of fleur-de-lis. The veil was a strawberry-coloured silk on the kind of light circlet of gold I preferred.

I stood in my chemise and knee-length stockings, and both Alice and Claudine came to attend my dressing. Claudine was so awed by the gown, she grew solemn, and concentrated as she tied all the ribbons on my trailing sleeves with her little hands. I was pleased at how moved they were when they stood back to survey me. They were both speechless, with tears in their eyes.

My absolute favourite was the wedding cloak, which was made of luxurious velvet in an oyster shade and decorated with gold falcons. There was no way the abbess would be getting her big hands on this!

I twisted Eleanor's ring on my finger, a constant reminder of her. I willed my prayers to reach her in that hostile land of England. I hoped that she would find her way back to us. Wretched guilt assailed me, for deigning to carry on with life without my duchess. Yet, for the first time in my life I had real clarity and purpose. There was no question of my love for Alain. If only Eleanor had not been taken. If only our court of love had not been dismantled. All that brightness, wasted. It was as though all of her ladies, including Marie, had been hurtled into darkness and loss. I longed for all we had lost and in my heart, I knew it was lost forever.

After she'd attended to her own dress, Alice presented me with a wedding gift. I took off the linen wrapping to reveal a cloth embroidered with scarlet, gold and emerald threads, bearing my own image in the wood at Alain's, surrounded by bright trees, a falcon on my sleeve.

'It's so beautiful.' Once again I felt a surge of loss, for Poitiers and Eleanor.

'Are you nervous?' asked Claudine, tentatively, softly. 'I would be nervous…'

I hadn't thought of it like that, but everything was about to change. *Alice and I were to be parted!* 'I suppose I am a little nervous. Maybe more than a little,' I admitted.

'It can be difficult to tell excitement apart from nerves,' said Alice.

'That is true. Alice, I have just one request of you for today.'

'Of course, dear Joanna, anything.'

'Would you stay at the estate with me this first night?'

She hesitated. I could tell she didn't want to, but after struggling for a moment she gave in. 'If you really wish it, I shall stay, but only for one night to see you well settled.'

'Oh, thank you, thank you, Alice!' I smiled with relief; that made me feel much better.

I remembered Marguerite's awful story of being bundled off alone at sixteen to live with a strange man in a bleak place with no friends to comfort her. And she had just suffered the most appalling heartbreak and grief. How unthinkable and horrible it must have been! Now, I hoped, she had some peace at last.

Marguerite's wild eyes with the warm, gold flecks full of compassion and love.

If we hadn't come to live at the abbey, we'd never have met her, and she may never have been reunited with Alba. So, *some* good had come of my sojourn here... Though Arthur would be happy to have me gone, I knew.

If we hadn't come to the abbey, I'd never have met Alain and *that* was the best thing that had ever happened to me.

The hearts in their jewelled caskets. Our hearts, encased as one. I would not want my heart to be buried alone, no matter how exquisite the casket.

The three of us went down to meet the abbess, for I was to receive her blessing. Claudine insisted on carrying our bags. The snow sparkled in the candlelight, like thousands of gleaming crystals. Icicles hanging from the black trees and archways had transformed the cloisters into a set of eerie, foreign shapes. I enjoyed feeling the freezing air on my face while remaining warm in my thick cloak.

We stood aside as the nuns began their procession back from Lauds, their chanting sweet as honey, their faces pale gold in the candlelight. One of them lingered behind, at a little distance, watching me. It was Heloise and she wanted to blow me a kiss, a tiny transgression from the rules. There was no sadness in her smile, nor envy, only sheer delight. I hoped that we would meet often, but we had already agreed to write.

Two nuns admitted us to the abbess's apartment, averting their eyes from my rich cloak and veil. The abbess's bulky figure appeared presently, moving languidly up the hallway. She regarded my fine clothes, I thought, with some amusement and invited us into her office for refreshments. She'd been so angry when I'd left the abbey that she'd almost refused to admit me when I'd returned, late that night. Alice had begged and I had acted contrite and, in the end, she'd yielded. I was sure she had only given in to avoid a scandal, and I sensed that she was glad I was leaving. My restlessness had upset her regime of silence and obedience, but I could not help my nature. Still, she was happy to bestow a blessing on me, and I was glad to receive it.

My head was bowed under her hand as she mumbled the Latin verse. I tried to focus fully on the moment, but I impulsively jerked away when she sprinkled me with holy water.

'You are staying with us,' she whispered to Alice when she'd finished.

'Yes, Holy Mother, with your blessing.'

'You have it, and welcome.'

'Alice will stay with me at the estate tonight,' I stated, firmly.

'Very well.'

We'd barely taken a sip of her brew when she left us for another appointment. I called in at the stables for Smokey and to say goodbye to the laywomen. They showered me with kisses far warmer than the holy water, and they presented me with a gift of a new saddle. I received it gratefully and told them I'd be back soon to distract them from their work. They said I'd not have any time for idle chat, once I was married and running a household. They were speaking from experience, for many of them had been married. Their advice made me feel grown up and important.

Alice's dappled mare didn't notice as I led Smokey away, but I wondered how she'd feel when Smokey failed to return, for they'd always been stabled together. At the painful reminder that Alice and I were parting, I felt panic rising.

'Perhaps we should take Dappled, too,' I suggested. 'Just in case.'

Alice shook her head. 'I hope I'll be able to ride over to you myself, once spring comes.'

'You'll stay overnight often, won't you?'

I didn't catch her reply, for then I spotted Alain coming through the trees. His eyes were crinkling with warmth and his smile was radiant. The rising, rosy dawn suddenly gave the snow a warmer cast, the naked trees a silken sheen. His face was so bright to me, it was like looking up at the stars. I felt myself growing calmer.

How fortunate I was.

'Joanna? Claudine must get back to work...' reminded Alice.

'Oh! My *dearest* darling,' I declared. 'This is not goodbye, for I'll arrange for you to visit almost at once. When we have our wedding feast, you'll be the most important person there — after the duchess, of course!'

She laughed, but then she cried and so did I, as we hugged each other.

I'd decided to delay the wedding feast until Eleanor returned and we could all be together again. It seemed the only decent thing to do, for she'd always said she would attend my wedding. Anything else would be like a betrayal. I needed to believe she would return.

Alain attached Smokey to the carriage, while we settled ourselves inside. It was much smarter and more comfortable than the cart we'd taken in the summer. The first delivery cart of the day just entered through the gates as we departed. I gave a little cry of delight, I was so glad to be leaving the abbey behind. In her crisp black frock and wimpled veil, Alice looked like a dignified elder and I was proud to have her by my side. I looked on her a little differently now that I knew of her inner life, her passions. She was a person of consequence, deserving of a respect that (I was ashamed to admit) I'd not paid her until now.

There was much more to Alice than met the eye. She had sacrificed her own needs to meet mine, and I hoped it was not too late to show her the gratitude she deserved.

Gazing out at the snow-covered landscape from the comfort of the carriage, I felt warmth surging in my chest. I thought of the intricate wedding trunk Alain had carved for me, filled with my beautiful things. I tingled with excitement when I thought of how later, he would undress me before the fire in our shared bedchamber. I was so grateful to be leaving our freezing apartment behind for the fairy-tale house in the wood, with its endlessly burning fires.

Nestled in the forest of crystalline trees, with candles burning in the windows and smoke billowing from its many chimneys, the house looked a cosy haven as we approached.

A maid rushed forth to brush the snow from our clothes and boots. The strings of shells usually hanging from the doorway had been replaced with bells, which tinkled prettily as we entered the warm hall and stepped across the jasmine petals mixed with the straw on the floor. All around the windows and arches had been decorated with winterberry and Christmas rose. We were led into a little chamber, where we were served ginger cake with slices of sugared apples by Alain's sister. We waited there and chatted by the fire awhile.

It was all so relaxed that I barely noticed the time arriving when they asked if I was ready, before they removed my cloak, fixed my hair and kissed my cheeks. Then, I was sent into the adjoining chamber where the priest was waiting. I knelt before him, while Alice went behind a panel to bear witness. The priest asked for the ring — Eleanor's ring — which I'd barely slipped off my finger when Alain entered, now wearing a silk brocade tunic over a linen shirt.

Our vows were spoken so softly, Eleanor's ring placed on my fourth finger so delicately, that it was like the most natural, intimate exchange of our love.

Deep winter was outside and the light was already failing by the time we had finished our wedding breakfast. I hoped it would not be long before Alain and I could slip off to bed.

With Eleanor's ring on my finger a constant reminder of my fealty to her and the snow gently falling on the woodland of my new home, I finally felt at peace. I knew that when she returned, she would come to Fontevrault.

A NOTE TO THE READER

Dear Reader,

Many, many thanks for taking the time to read this book.

In the summer of 2010, my family (parents and sisters) went on our second ever holiday together. Off we headed to a lovely old farmhouse in Brittany, stopping en route at the royal abbey of Fontevrault in the Loire, where Eleanor of Aquitaine, Henry II and Richard the Lionheart were originally buried. Having had some knowledge of the stormy relationship between these three, I was particularly struck by the image of their effigies, side by side, looking so peaceful in death. That's families for you, I thought, bound together for all eternity, whether they like it or not.

The abbey remained so firmly in my imagination — as powerful places can do — that I ended up setting this book there. The more I researched it, the more intrigued I became. To learn that, as early as the 12th century, there was a safe haven like Fontevrault dedicated to offering refuge to all women in need, no matter their class or background.

At the age of eighty, after a turbulent, adventurous life, Eleanor returned to her beloved abbey, to live out the rest of her days in (well-deserved) peace and quiet. It gives me great satisfaction to imagine her there, in that beautiful place of contemplation.

Thank you again for reading the book. I would be so grateful if you let us know what you think by leaving a review on **Amazon** or **Goodreads**. You can also contact me directly on my website: **www.coirlemooney.com**. Many, many thanks again.

Coirle

Sapere Books is an exciting new publisher of brilliant fiction and popular history.

To find out more about our latest releases and our monthly bargain books visit our website: **saperebooks.com**